DEATH AGENT
A Dr. Zack Winston Thriller, Book 3
Mike Krentz

Purple Papaya LLC

Contents

FREE BOOKS and OTHER PRIZES	VII
Dedication	VIII
Chapter One	1
Chapter Two	8
Chapter Three	14
Chapter Four	20
Chapter Five	23
Chapter Six	28
Chapter Seven	33
Chapter Eight	35
Chapter Nine	42
Chapter Ten	43
Chapter Eleven	47
Chapter Twelve	52
Chapter Thirteen	57
Chapter Fourteen	62
Chapter Fifteen	66
Chapter Sixteen	70
Chapter Seventeen	73
Chapter Eighteen	76
Chapter Nineteen	79

Chapter Twenty	87
Chapter Twenty-One	91
Chapter Twenty-Two	94
Chapter Twenty-Three	100
Chapter Twenty-Four	105
Chapter Twenty-Five	108
Chapter Twenty-Six	110
Chapter Twenty-Seven	119
Chapter Twenty-Eight	123
Chapter Twenty-Nine	127
Chapter Thirty	130
Chapter Thirty-One	132
Chapter Thirty-Two	136
Chapter Thirty-Three	140
Chapter Thirty-Four	142
Chapter Thirty-Five	145
Chapter Thirty-Six	150
Chapter Thirty-Seven	152
Chapter Thirty-Eight	154
Chapter Thirty-Nine	156
Chapter Forty	158
Chapter Forty-One	161
Chapter Forty-Two	163
Chapter Forty-Three	167
Chapter Forty-Four	169
Chapter Forty-Five	171
Chapter Forty-Six	173
Chapter Forty-Seven	176

Chapter Forty-Eight	178
Chapter Forty-Nine	182
Chapter Fifty	185
Chapter Fifty-One	187
Chapter Fifty-Two	189
Chapter Fifty-Three	191
Chapter Fifty-Four	196
Chapter Fifty-Five	198
Chapter Fifty-Six	201
Chapter Fifty-Seven	204
Chapter Fifty-Eight	208
Chapter Fifty-Nine	212
Chapter Sixty	215
Chapter Sixty-One	218
Chapter Sixty-Two	221
Chapter Sixty-Three	226
Chapter Sixty-Four	230
Chapter Sixty-Five	233
Chapter Sixty-Six	237
Chapter Sixty-Seven	240
Chapter Sixty-Eight	244
Chapter Sixty-Nine	248
Chapter Seventy	253
Chapter Seventy-One	256
Chapter Seventy-Two	259
FREE BOOKS and OTHER PRIZES	263
Also by Mike Krentz	264
About the Author	266

Acknowledgements 267

Copyrights 269

FREE BOOKS and OTHER PRIZES

Sign up to Receive Mike's regular newsletter that offers insights into military and emergency medicine, news about Mike's books, and a monthly contest for gift cards, novellas, free audiobook downloads, and signed paperback books. No spam ever.

Join Mike's newsletter mailing list here:
https://mikejkrentz.com/newsletter

Dedication

For JAK

Chapter One

*L*A MOSCA, "THE FLY," eased her sixty-two inch athletic body through the double doors from inside the terminal at Montgomery County Airpark, Maryland. She clung to the dusk shadows to avoid attracting attention from her quarry in the parking lot ahead.

Just a uniformed Montgomery County Police officer returning to her vehicle after a food stop in the terminal. No haste.

The Fly was not walking to the patrol car. And she was not police.

Her eyes fixed thirty yards ahead on a stout man striding from a parked car toward a chain-link fence with a gate to the tarmac. The mission briefing had described him as "Doctor Good," age in the fifties. He carried a shiny metal briefcase; the prize she and her colleagues sought.

A young woman shuffled a step behind the doctor, dressed only in blue surgical scrubs despite the frigid December air, her posture stooped, hands clutching her abdomen, pace languid in contrast to the doctor's determined stride.

On the tarmac beyond the fence, a Learjet idled with one engine turning and its boarding door deployed. The tail number started with *XA*, confirming its Mexican registration.

Los Hermanos de Guadalajara.

The woman in the parking lot dropped several yards behind her male companion.

From the Learjet, a lithe male figure in military camouflage advanced with arrogant authority toward the gate. *El Fuego,* "The Fire," youngest of the three Guadalajara cartel brothers. The Fly's onetime lover.

She'd found no *fuego* in that brief relationship. She had mocked his given name, Damáso, which she anglicized to "Damn asshole." He had retaliated by giving her the nickname *La Mosca,* a pesky fly.

The Fly put aside her personal animosity to concentrate on her assigned role: to back up *El Fuego* should either the "good doctor" or the woman not perform as planned.

Across the distance, she sensed tension between the couple. Her hand rested on the Glock 17 service weapon in the belt holster of the police uniform. Whenever the real police would find the uniform's dead owner in the patrol car trunk, The Fly would be long gone. She wiggled her leg to confirm her own pistol, a Beretta M9, in its ankle holster.

The doctor and his girlfriend would live only if they boarded the jet—with the precious metal case. Otherwise, *"Fuego!"*

The young woman stopped. The doctor slowed his pace. As he twisted to look back at the woman, a pistol in his other hand came into The Fly's view. She drew the Glock from the police belt.

The doctor kept walking. "Come, Emily."

"C'mon, c'mon, stupid woman," The Fly whispered.

"Can't." The woman backed away. All at once, she doubled at the waist and squatted.

She gonna take a shit? Now? Here?

The woman waddled backwards toward the couple's parked vehicle.

The doctor stopped and faced her. She retreated further.

"Good bye, Emily." The doctor raised his pistol and shot her. He turned toward the gate, clutching the metallic case like a heavy football.

At the sound of the shot, *El Fuego* scampered back to the jet. The Fly saw one chance to salvage the operation. She ran toward the doctor, raised the Glock. "Stop! Drop your weapon." She continued forward to give the crew in the jet's cockpit a full view of her actions.

For a second, she followed the doctor's gaze to the woman sprawled on the asphalt. A wide blotch of crimson stained the right side of her scrub top.

"Dr. Good" raised his pistol for a finishing shot. The Fly fired two bullets into his chest.

The Emily woman screamed.

The Fly ignored her, raced to where the doctor had fallen, seized the case, and rushed through the gate to the Learjet. No time to finish the doctor or his girlfriend. She waved her Glock at the pilot in the cockpit.

"Open the door, *cabrones!*"

The jet's boarding ladder lowered to the tarmac just as The Fly reached it. She climbed the steps two at a time, lunged into the cabin, and shouted toward the cockpit.

"Ándale! Ándale! Vámonos!"

The engines powered up, *El Fuego* raised and sealed the door, and the jet made a quick turn toward the takeoff runway.

No one in the cabin spoke as the Learjet soared away from the uncontrolled airfield and made a sharp turn to the southeast. It flew full throttle at low altitude until the aircrew announced it had cleared US airspace with no apparent detection.

The Fly clutched the doctor's metal case on her lap, sneered at *El Fuego* staring out the window from the seat facing hers, and cleared her throat.

He turned and sneered. "You got lucky."

She glowered. "You got lucky I was there. You know what *El Víbora* would do to you if you came back empty-handed."

El Fuego smirked. "Nothing." He spread his hands. "We are brothers." He squinted at her. "You, however, serve at my pleasure." He cast her a lascivious leer. "And I do mean pleasure."

The Fly glared at him, spoke in English. "Don't push me, Damnasso." She turned away and stared out the window.

El Víbora, "The Viper," the leader of the three brothers, would protect her.

***

The Learjet flew a straight course for an hour before it banked to the south. It continued through the total darkness over water for another two hours before it decelerated, descended, and landed on a lit runway. The plane taxied clear, then parked in front of a one-story terminal with illuminated letters across its facade.

JUAN G GOMEZ - Varadero

The Fly shot a troubled look at *El Fuego*.

"*Cuba?*"

He responded with an evil grin. "*Sí.*"

No one had mentioned Cuba in the brief. The Fly scowled.

"Relax," *El Fuego* said. "Just a fuel stop." He winked. "And picking up a passenger."

She folded her arms over her chest. "Why did no one tell me?"

El Fuego grunted. He reached into a bag at his feet and pulled out jeans and a blouse. He looked her body up and down and placed the clothing on the small table between their seats.

"Change your clothes."

The Fly didn't move.

"For your own good. Our new passenger will not take kindly to an American cop in his presence."

"I'm not American, and not a cop."

"He won't care. You look like American police." He pushed the clothing closer to her.

"Fine." She stood, picked up the clothing, grasped the metal case in the other hand, and started into the aisle to the bathroom.

El Fuego put out a foot to stop her.

"You change here." His malicious glare communicated dead seriousness.

The Fly stood in place and changed into the jeans and blouse, turning her back to Damáso's scrutiny. Resuming her seat, she set the case back on her lap and placed the gun next to her right thigh, where she could reach it with ease.

Damáso had seen the other weapon strapped to her ankle. More reason for him to stay clear of her. She hoped.

A black Lincoln SUV with dark-tinted windows drove up to the boarding side of the aircraft. Two men got out, each brandishing a semi-automatic weapon. One stood guard next to the SUV, while the other ascended the steps and entered the jet. He looked around the cabin, counted heads, then shouted through the open doorway.

"Clear."

The other armed man opened the rear door of the SUV. A portly figure dressed in khaki cargo pants and a long-sleeved white guayabera shirt emerged and climbed the stairs. When he entered the cabin, The Fly gasped at the vermilion scar crossing his face from left earlobe to the midline beneath his lower lip.

El Cubano!

The mission she thought had bought her favor with *Los Hermanos* had just taken a hard turn in the wrong direction.

The Cuban stopped in the aisle next to her, stared at *El Fuego,* and jerked his thumb over his shoulder. Damáso nodded in deference and surrendered his seat. *El Cubano* sat across from The Fly, then motioned for his bodyguard to take the seat across the aisle from her. The guard sat and pointed the weapon in his lap at her chest.

"Let's go," *El Cubano* said.

As soon as it left the ground, the jet banked westward into darkness. The Fly figured they had set a course for the cartel's headquarters in the hills outside Guadalajara, Mexico. Bone tired, she laid her head back, closed her eyes, and tried to sleep with her hand on the pistol beside her right thigh.

Three hours later, the Learjet broke through the clouds and descended.

Not Guadalajara.

That sprawling metropolis would fill the window with lights from the ground. Instead, the jet continued through darkness until it crossed over a populated area where clumps of city lights abruptly ended at a coastline.

The plane flew over a body of water, then made a 180-degree turn, descended, and landed on a wide lighted runway. As it slowed, The Fly spotted a sprawling terminal with an illuminated sign:

Aeropuerto Internacional de Puerto Vallarta

The Fly rubbed her eyes. Why land in one of the most popular resort areas in Mexico? Where heavy police and military presence struggled to protect Mexico's vital tourism industry from the likes of *Los Hermanos de Guadalajara*?

Dawn broke as the Learjet turned off the runway and taxied to an area distant from the major terminal. Two tan helicopters, without markings, perched with rotors turning on a pair of helipads.

The Cuban bodyguard yanked The Fly into the aisle. He clutched her arm until *El Cubano* left his seat and headed to the aircraft door, then he pushed her forward.

"Follow. No funny business or we leave your bloody corpse on the tarmac for the marines."

The Fly placed the gun in her waistband, held onto the case, and followed *El Cubano*. Behind her, the guard poked the muzzle of his weapon into her buttock. It took all her resolve to keep from wheeling and putting a bullet through his head.

Outside the jet, she followed directions to the first helicopter. *El Cubano* and his bodyguard strapped into the front seats behind the pilots. The other guard directed The Fly to sit in the second row next to him. *El Fuego* took the free seat on the other side. As soon as he strapped in, the aircraft revved its engines and lifted off in a dust storm of rotor wash.

***

Ten minutes of over-water flight later, the helicopter descended and touched down on the bow of a luxury yacht. The rotors slowed but continued turning. A deckhand opened the door and motioned for the passengers to disembark. *El Cubano* left first, accompanied by his bodyguard. The Fly followed, clutching the case. *El Fuego* walked next to her.

He sneered. "Screw this up and we're both dead."

The Fly and *El Fuego* followed *El Cubano* down a narrow passageway into a spacious lounge with banks of plush seating. *El Víbora* sat in the primary seat. A man with Asian features sat to his left. A man and woman, both of whom appeared to be American, sat to his right. The woman's freckled face and red hair stood out among the other attendees. *El Cubano* sat next to the Asian man.

A door opened. The Fly gasped at the unexpected arrival of a muscular man with a stylized skull tattooed on one arm, and a demonic face on the other. A cross-shaped smear in the middle of his forehead stood out like the typical smudge worn by Catholics on Ash Wednesday. Except Ash Wednesday was months away, and this cross was permanent; the product of a smoldering stick wielded upon him as a feisty child by a drunken, raging father.

El Vengador de la Sangre, "The Avenger of Blood," strode into the room and took a menacing stance behind *El Víbora*. Half-brother to *El Víbora* and *El Fuego*, he had a reputation for killing with gusto. He preferred his own hands and arms as weapons, which allowed him to get close enough to smell his victims' fear as they tasted death. No one knew how many men, or women, had died by *El Vengado*r's powerful hands. His unexpected and rare attendance at a 'civilized' meeting such as this amped up The Fly's anxiety.

A guard directed Damáso and The Fly to the remaining two seats.

Servants entered bearing crystal glassware and carafes containing a clear liquid with a slight auburn tinge. As they distributed and filled the glasses, *El Víbora* beamed and spread his arms in a magnanimous gesture.

"*Bienvenidos, amigos y compañeros.* Welcome, friends and partners." He stood and raised his glass. "*Salud!*"

The attendees rose, returned the toast, and quaffed the liquid. The Fly recognized the aroma and taste of the finest tequila. An unusual measure from her otherwise pecuniary boss. Servants immediately refilled the glasses.

El Vengador did not imbibe. He kept a watchful eye on all the room's occupants.

El Víbora sat, and the others followed suit. He nodded in The Fly's direction. "Thanks to the quick action of *La Mosca*, our operation can proceed. She not only eliminated an unreliable middleman, but also retrieved and delivered the critical component for our initial mission." He gestured in her direction.

"*Dámelo, hermana.*"

As directed, The Fly left her seat and brought him the case she'd guarded all the way from the USA.

El Víbora raised the prize over his head. "These contents will enable the most audacious revenge the world will ever know." He glanced at The Fly and *El Vengador*. "After we tie up a few loose ends."

He smiled. "*Salud!*"

"*Salud,*" all replied.

El Fuego's intense gaze scorched The Fly's back while the steely eyes of *El Vengador* seared into her chest.

Chapter Two

Sixteen-year-old Annie Winston relished her first proper breakfast since her admission to the Bethesda Metro Hospital after a near-drowning two weeks ago. Five days out of the intensive care unit, she'd finally progressed to a regular diet. She stuffed a forkful of scrambled eggs into her mouth and stared at the early January light coming through the window of her room.

I should be dead. Except for Dad. And Bridget...

As if on cue, her dad, Dr. Zack Winston, entered the room. He wore dark blue surgical scrubs, his uniform when on duty in the Bethesda Metro ER. He approached her bed and hugged her.

When they released the hug, he cast a hungry look at her breakfast tray. "Hmm. That looks wonderful." He snatched a slice of bacon from her plate.

"Dad!"

Her dad recoiled. His bacon-snatching hand stopped midway from plate to mouth.

Had Annie's voice sounded as harsh to him as it did to her? She hadn't meant it that way. "Sorry, Dad."

Dad returned the bacon to her plate. "No, I'm sorry. You need the nourishment for recovery."

"Says 'The Doctor.'"

Annie and her dad both turned toward the voice from the doorway. Her mother entered the room and planted a kiss on Annie's forehead.

"Word of advice," the mom said. "Never trust an ER doc around food. They will steal meat from a starving hyena if given a chance."

She gave Annie's dad a searing stare. Then she smiled. "Kidding, of course."

"Sure you are," the dad said with a knowing smile. He pecked Annie's mom on the cheek. "You okay?"

Mom scoffed. "Of course."

I almost died so my divorced parents could fake being nice to each other?

Dad turned serious. "Annie, are you really okay with talking to the detectives this morning? You don't have to do it yet."

Annie shrugged. "I'm fine, Dad. If I can help them bring those...whoever...to justice..."

She startled and her voice trailed off when the door opened. A middle-aged, hefty man and a younger woman entered. The woman looked like she'd come straight from the gym—except for her tailored suit that made a sharp contrast to the man's ill-fitting khaki pants and rumpled shirt without a tie.

"We can wait until you finish your breakfast," the woman said.

"I'm done." Annie would have liked to eat more, but worried that would be weird under the circumstances.

Her mother took the tray from the table and set it outside the door.

"Annie," her dad said, "this is Agent Mason from the FBI, and Detective Martinez from Montgomery County Police Department."

"Pleased to meet you, Miss Winston," the stuffy agent said.

"Call me Tina," the detective said.

Annie's dad introduced her mother. "This is Dr. Natalie Lewis, Annie's mother. She's a psychiatrist who practices in California."

After everyone exchanged pleasantries, Annie's dad positioned two chairs near her bed. "Please sit," he said to the visitors. "Dr. Lewis and I will stand back."

"Call me Natalie, please." Mom gave Dad a withering look.

"Right," the FBI agent said. He and the detective took their seats.

Detective Martinez looked at Annie with a pleasant expression. "You know you're not in trouble here, right?"

Annie felt unsure, but nodded.

"Also, you're free to talk to us as much or as little as you like. If you get tired or uncomfortable, just say so and we'll end the interview. We're grateful you agreed to meet with us so soon after your, uh, trauma."

"I'm okay." Annie forced her voice to sound firm.

The detective turned to the FBI agent. "Why don't you start?"

"Sure," the man said. "Annie, can you tell us what you remember? In your own words. We're most interested in what happened at The Good House, and, if you're willing, at the river."

A door in Annie's brain slammed shut. She flinched. "The Good House? I don't..." She looked to her dad for help.

Dad glanced at mom, his face wary, then back to Annie. "How about you start with whatever you remember from that day? The day after Christmas."

Another door closed in Annie's brain. "I... Sarah. I met Sarah at a Starbucks, and..."

Detective Martinez spoke. "Would that be Sarah O'Brien?"

Annie grimaced. "I think so. I mean, that could be her last name. I... I don't remember." She scrunched her face and glanced at her mom, then back at the detective. "Sarah was Dad's girlfriend." She blinked. "I think she was."

Her mind went numb.

The detective spoke in a kind voice. "Do you remember why you met Sarah O'Brien at that Starbucks on the day after Christmas?"

Annie winced, gave a pained look to her mother, and fought off a sudden urge to cry. "I... I'm so sorry, Mom."

Her mom moved forward and touched her hand. "It's okay, love. I know about it."

Annie wanted to be anywhere but in that room with her mom and dad and these law enforcement people. She pictured herself floating over them, watching the scene below as if another girl occupied her bed.

"Do you need a break?" asked Tina.

Annie's mind crashed back down to the bed. She closed her eyes, calmed herself, then looked at the detective. "I'm okay."

"Go on then," the FBI man said, his voice impatient. Tina shot him a scolding look.

Annie looked between her parents, then back at Tina. She pretended she was acting in a play. "I was... pregnant. Sarah promised to take me for an abortion." Annie wiped a tear from the corner of her eye.

"Did she? Take you for an abortion?" Tina asked.

Annie searched her brain. Found no answer. "I... I don't know."

The detective glanced at Annie's parents, then spoke to Annie in a soft voice. "Can you tell us what you do remember? Anything at all?"

Annie's mind became a blank sheet. She strained to find the slightest memory.

"I remember meeting Sarah at Starbucks. Then..." She tried hard, but her memory had become a dense fog. "Dad was talking to me in the ICU here at the hospital." She looked at her dad. "You said you love me more than your own life." A tear erupted from the corner of one eye.

Dad wiped a similar tear from his own eye. "I did say that. I meant it."

Annie's mom stepped forward. "Maybe this is a good time for a break."

The FBI man tried to protest, but Tina stopped him. "That's fine." She looked at Annie. "Would you like us to come back in a little while, or should we wait until another day?"

Annie felt like her brain would explode. "Please, can you all just leave me now?" She pleaded with her parents. "You too." Then she turned away and faced the window.

To Annie Winston, her entire world had just ripped apart.

***

Outside the room, Zack alerted the nursing staff to look after Annie. He placed a call to Dr. Jerry Hartman, his friend and Annie's attending physician, and described his daughter's sudden memory lapse and apparent anxiety attack. Then he joined Natalie and the law enforcement people in the small conference room at the end of the hall.

He looked at Natalie. "Thoughts?"

She shook her head and spoke in a terse voice. "Rather not say yet."

Detective Martinez winced. "So sorry that we upset her."

Zack waved a reassuring hand. "You didn't." He glanced at Natalie. She remained stoic. He looked back at Martinez. "Something else went on in there. Maybe clinical."

The detective nodded. "We should leave. Come back when she's, uh, better?"

"Yeah," Zack said. "Sorry, not sure when that might be."

"You know how to reach us," Agent Mason said.

Zack tilted his head. "I do."

The agents stood.

Zack held up a hand. "For the record, because I know how critical this is for your case, she remembered more after she first woke up in the ICU."

"Such as?" The FBI man said.

Natalie sat with arms folded across her chest. Her eyes pierced Zack.

He took a breath. "She said that Sarah O'Brien and Fiona Delaney were both present at the river before she escaped and ran into the water. Those two women are sisters, but Annie didn't know that, or their real names. They identified as 'Flossie' and 'Nan,' the so-called Bobbsey Twins, among The Good House conspirators."

"Did your daughter tell you anything else?" Mason asked.

"She said that the youth we know as Tyler Rhodes, and an unknown man called 'Spider' were also at the river. She heard Spider say that 'Nan,' aka Fiona Delaney, had botched the attempted murder of Bridget Larsen's husband, Marshall Hilliard."

"Fiona Delaney, our confidential informant?" Mason asked.

"The same. I got her to flip by threatening retaliation for what happened to Annie."

Mason's eyes narrowed. "The same Tyler who later confessed to Annie's abduction and attempted drowning?"

"Yes. The Good House conspirators called him 'Roach.'"

Mason scoffed. "Well, Doc, coming from you, that's all hearsay and inadmissible in court. Even if your daughter could remember and tell us herself, still hearsay." He scowled. "Meanwhile, that Tyler guy is in the wind, and Ms. Fiona Delaney ain't saying much." He rubbed his forehead. "We still have no clue who's actually behind the larger conspiracy. For sure not that Dr. Good guy. He was a stooge. Maybe this Spider character, but we think he reports to someone else. If Delaney can't or won't give us substance, we're up shit's creek."

He turned to Natalie. "Sorry, ma'am."

She looked up and smiled. "Seriously? I hear worse every day before my first coffee break."

Before Agent Mason could respond, the door opened to admit Dr. Jerry Hartman. He looked at the visitors, then at Zack and Natalie. "I just saw Annie. We need to talk."

Detective Martinez rose. "We'll take our leave now. She shook hands with Zack and with Natalie. Call us for anything, anything you need, for you or your daughter. Otherwise, we're out of your hair until you say we can return."

"We appreciate that," Natalie said.

Zack saw the visitors out, then returned to sit with Natalie and Jerry Hartman.

"Well?" he asked.

Jerry looked at Natalie. "As a psychiatrist, you probably know what…"

Natalie cut him off. "Please. Stop. Here, I'm the mom, not the shrink. Zack's the dad, not the ER doc. Talk to us like parents. Please." She gave him an icy stare. "What do you think is going on with Annie?"

Jerry reeled from the frontal attack but recovered. "I did only a brief exam, but clearly she's suffering intense anxiety and has lost some memory of the events surrounding her ordeal. She remembers none of the things she told us when she woke up in the ICU."

"Go on," Natalie said.

Jerry spread his arms. "We'll have to do some tests before we know anything. Plus, get neuro and psych consults."

"Okay," Zack said. He glanced at Natalie. "Concur?"

"Of course, Zack."

Jerry spoke. "I've requested consults from Bogart for neuro and Wiggins for psych. We'll get a repeat CT scan. Also, an MRI and a PET scan. I don't see that taking more than a couple of days."

"Until then..." Zack said.

Natalie's response was quick. "Until then, everything we've discussed is on hold. Including her living with you after she's discharged from the hospital." She folded her arms. "And no more law enforcement interviews."

Chapter Three

Two days later, Zack and Natalie left their daughter asleep in her hospital room and went downstairs for their meeting with the team of medical specialists responsible for Annie's final diagnosis and care plan once discharged from the hospital.

Dr. Jerry Hartman introduced Natalie to Dr. Ray Bogart, Chief of Neurology, and Dr. Samantha Wiggins, Chief of Psychiatry. After exchanging pleasantries, all sat.

Jerry Hartman began the discussion. "Given the trauma that Annie sustained, she's doing remarkably well. If anyone met her in a non-clinical setting, they would consider her a typical teenage girl with a tendency to mood swings and histrionics."

Zack looked at Natalie. "She's strong, like her mother."

Natalie rolled her eyes.

Jerry turned to the neurologist. "Ray will lead us through a discussion of her neuro status."

Dr. Bogart shrugged. "In a word, no permanent neurological effects from her near-drowning, or the antecedent trauma."

Zack interrupted. "You all know Natalie is a psychiatrist."

Bogart cast him a condescending smile. "We do, Zack."

Zack sat back in his chair.

Bogart continued. "The differential diagnosis, from a neurological perspective, includes drug effects, traumatic brain injury, hypoxic brain injury, or a combination thereof. We would also consider seizure disorder, but that seems unlikely with no prior events. Her initial toxicology screen showed traces of Rohypnol, which we would expect based on the history of being drugged and abducted. Also, residual evidence of general anesthesia, consistent with the, uh, surgical procedure performed on her."

Zack exploded. "They invaded her body and stole her embryo. Call it what it was, Ray. Flagrant sexual assault."

The neurologist looked at Zack. "I'm sorry if my unemotional clinical approach offends you, Zack. It's what we need right now."

Natalie put a hand on Zack's shoulder and spoke to Bogart. "We're good."

Zack calmed himself. "Right."

The neurologist continued. "Annie's CT scan and MRI were normal. An FDG-PET scan showed some impairment of glucose metabolism in the posterior middle temporal gyrus. Some articles in the literature correlate this finding with psychogenic amnesia."

Zack and Natalie both gave him blank stares.

"That's primarily of academic interest," the neurologist said. "In short, we've found no direct organic cause for her symptoms."

"Which brings us to the psychiatric elements in the differential." Dr. Bogart turned to the psychiatrist. "Sam?"

Dr. Wiggins spoke directly to Natalie. "I feel odd telling you what you probably already know."

Natalie gave her a reassuring smile. "Don't. In this room, I'm the mom. You're the shrink."

"Thank you," Dr. Wiggins said. "As you know, not much to consider. Acute stress disorder comes to mind, as does PTSD. It's a bit early for that, but within the window." She redirected her gaze at Zack. "You mentioned sexual assault, Dr. Winston. We all agree with you there. I recommend further psychological evaluation for a definitive diagnosis. We need that to decide the best treatment."

"Will you do the testing and treatment?" Natalie asked.

The psychiatrist drew a breath. "Zack and I are too close. As professional colleagues, I mean. We see each other socially at hospital and medical staff functions. Annie needs an independent practitioner. Someone in whom she can confide with guaranteed confidentiality and no hint of conflict of interest."

"Did you have someone in mind?" Zack asked.

"I believe I've found the perfect match."

Zack knew most of the physicians on the medical staff, some better than others. "Anyone I know?"

"I doubt it. She's not on our full-time clinical staff. Has an adjunct appointment as a clinical psychologist."

"Name?"

"Dr. Maria Santos. Her office is in Rockville."

"You're right. I don't know her," Zack said.

Dr. Wiggins looked between Zack and Natalie. "Maria would be a perfect fit. She has both professional and, uh, personal experience with PTSD and dissociative disorders."

"Sounds perfect," Zack said. He looked at Natalie. "I trust Sam's judgment."

Natalie remained silent for an interval. When she spoke, her voice broke. "Can I meet Dr. Santos before I give my okay?"

Zack jerked. "So much for being just the mom."

Natalie shot him a hostile stare.

Jerry Hartman eyed Zack and spoke. "That seems reasonable."

Samantha Wiggins said, "Anticipating as much, I've determined she has an opening in her schedule this afternoon." She looked at Zack and Natalie. "Would that work for both of you?"

Feeling steamrolled, Zack looked at Natalie. "Up to you." She nodded.

"All good," Jerry said. "If you can let us know by the end of the day, we'll plan on discharging Annie to her new home tomorrow."

Natalie cringed at Jerry's term, "new home."

***

That evening, Zack and Natalie met in the hospital dining room. Zack attacked a cheeseburger while Natalie picked at a chicken salad.

"Well?" Zack said after waiting for what seemed to be the right interval for pleasantries before getting down to the subject at hand.

"Dr. Santos has solid credentials and experience. Doctorate in Psychology from the University of Texas. Maintains an active clinical practice, plus she's also certified as a forensic psychologist. She sometimes consults with law enforcement."

That last tidbit surprised Zack. "Really?"

Natalie scoffed. "No, Zack, I made it up. Yes, really."

Zack looked away. "That could be a plus."

Natalie raised her eyebrows. "How so?"

Zack couldn't come up with a straightforward answer. "I don't know. Seems like someone with experience about criminal minds might have…"

"Better insight into Annie's trauma?"

"I suppose."

Natalie thought for a few seconds. "Maybe. Maybe not."

"Okay," Zack said. "Just a first impression."

"Those are often wrong, you know."

"Yeah." He forced a smile. "What else about her?"

Natalie pursed her lips. "She shared some personal stuff that I'm not at liberty to disclose."

Zack huffed. "Why the hell not? We're talking about Annie here. Our daughter."

Natalie raised a conciliatory hand. "I know, Zack. Chill." She waited for Zack to calm himself before she continued. "Maria, Dr. Santos, shared some personal medical history with me. I can't disclose that without her permission, even to you."

"Did you ask for her permission?"

"She declined."

"What? That's..."

Natalie again raised a hand. "It's not about you, Zack."

"What, then?"

His ex-wife looked him in the eye. "If, and I do mean *if*, Annie were to stay here and begin therapy with Dr. Santos, the two of them will establish a relationship. A therapeutic relationship, but a relationship in every sense of the word."

"Psychotherapy 101. The point?"

"Maria can't let her personal history into that relationship."

Zack suddenly understood. His anger flared. "So, you two women shrinks decided not to tell me because I might tell Annie?"

"Bingo."

"That's BS, Nat."

Natalie spoke in a flat voice. "Doesn't matter."

Zack knew what would come next. "Out with it."

"It doesn't matter because Annie won't be seeing Dr. Santos. She's coming home with me. I'll set her up with an outstanding psychotherapist in La Jolla."

Although he'd expected it, the words stunned Zack. He struggled to respond.

"But you already said..."

Her face softened as her eyes communicated empathy. "I'm sorry, Zack. That was before we recognized her new symptoms." She sucked on her lip. "And before I realized she may be in danger here. From whatever elements or people caused her trauma."

Zack glared at her.

"I can monitor her progress in therapy, and she'll be safer in California."

At last, Zack found his voice. "No."

"No, what?"

"First, you also would have to keep a distance from her therapeutic relationship with whatever super-shrink you set her up with." He scowled. "You just preached that principle to me."

"Well…"

"I'm not done. Don't for one second think she'll be safer in your La Jolla manse than she'll be living with me. If those people want to come after her, they can do it anywhere. I'm dead serious. Your touchy-feelie world, not to mention your robust social life, is not conducive to her protection."

Taken aback by his frontal attack, Natalie flushed. She spoke in a trembling voice. "Annie's my daughter."

"She's my daughter too, and she wants to live with me. I'll do whatever I must to support her therapy and keep her safe." Zack folded his arms and glowered. "You don't get to decide. Annie does. It's her life. End of discussion."

Natalie looked away and pondered what seemed like forever. She turned back to him. "Okay, Zack. We'll put it to her. All of it. Pros and cons, safety issues. We lay it all out. Once she's fully informed, she can decide."

"You'll abide by her decision?"

"As will you, Zack."

Zack stood. "Okay. Let's go talk to her."

***

Forty-five minutes later, Zack pulled his Lexus into the driveway at the Bethesda Marriott Hotel. He got out and walked around to open the passenger side door for Natalie, but she opened it herself and stepped out. They faced each other several feet apart in the artificial light of the driveway.

"Thanks for the ride," Natalie said.

"I can pick you up tomorrow and we can go to the hospital together."

She nodded. "Sure. What time will they discharge her?"

"By ten, maybe earlier."

"Pick me up at nine?"

"Sure."

She turned away, then turned back. "Better idea. Meet me here for breakfast at eight-ish. We can talk before we go pick her up."

Talk about what?

He spoke in a non-committal voice. "Okay."

Natalie made no move to walk away. "I'll, uh, make my plane reservation for the day after tomorrow, if that works for you." She paused. "That way, I can help her get settled at your place."

"Good idea," Zack said. "She'll see us both supporting her decision." His turn to pause. "You can stay the night there. You and Annie could share the spare room. Then we can drive you to the airport the next morning."

"We'll see," Natalie said. "Might depend on flight time." Her voice turned bitter. "Plus, you need to get her enrolled in school and such. You know, obligations the custodial parent must meet."

Zack let it roll by. "Whatever works for you, Nat."

She took a deep breath. "Sorry for the rude comment."

"It's okay," Zack said. "You'd hoped for a different decision. I don't blame you for..."

"Stop. We made a deal. Annie wants to live with you. It's done."

"Thanks," Zack said. "We'll make it work. You'll for sure be in the loop."

Natalie smirked. "Yeah." She walked away a few steps, then turned back. "One last thing, Zack."

Her sharp tone alarmed him. "What?"

"If anything happens to her, I will fucking kill you."

Natalie spun on her heel and strode into the hotel.

Chapter Four

LESS THAN A MONTH had passed since the poisoning murder of Bridget Larsen's philandering husband, Marshall Hilliard, of which Bridget was an early suspect but later cleared.

Bridget's personal and professional lives had turned tumultuous since those events. Used to always being in control, she now struggled to meet her conflicting responsibilities as a single mother and successful malpractice defense attorney. Much less maintaining any sort of social life or relationship with Dr. Zack Winston, the details or import of which she could not define.

Per her new routine, Bridget left her law office in mid-afternoon to be present when her son, Dustin, got home from high school. In the last semester of his senior year, Dustin had earned admission to Harvard Law School to follow in his parents' and stepbrother's footsteps. But since his father's death and the drama surrounding it, he'd shown little interest in the typical pre-graduation activities.

Through two decades as a lawyer, Bridget had learned to read people. She harbored no doubts about her son's depression. More than expected in the grief process. She had made being Dustin's sensitive, helpful mom her primary goal in life. She pushed aside a wave of guilt that it had not always been so in the past.

Bridget eased her dark-green Range Rover into the two-car garage next to her late husband's Mercedes 450 SL. She looked at her watch. Dustin would already be home. She felt a pang of guilt that she had delayed her departure, "just this once," to prepare for an interview with a new emergency physician client the next day. Her hope of Dustin hanging out with friends to play video games after school had been a weak excuse.

I must do better. Be more consistent.

Her phone buzzed just as she turned off the ignition.

Zack Winston.

Bridget considered letting it roll to voicemail, then thought better. Zack and she had been through too much together. No matter that his timing sucked, as usual.

"Hey, Zack."

"Where are you?"

"Just got home. Dustin beat me here. Again."

A pause. "Oh."

"What's up, Zack?" Bridget activated the garage door closure and got out of the car. The noise from the garage door blocked Zack's response.

"Sorry," she said. "Garage door." She opened the interior door and entered the house.

"No problem," Zack said. "I have news about Annie."

Bridget entered the kitchen, where Dustin snacked on chips and dip while playing a game on his phone. She pecked his cheek and pointed to her own phone. "Dr. Winston," she whispered.

Dustin rolled his eyes.

To Zack, she said, "What did you find out about her?"

He sounded annoyed. Had he heard her greet Dustin? Why should it matter?

"Well, her neuro workup is clear. In short, she's suffering from psychological trauma, PTSD or something like it."

Bridget held the phone to her ear while she took a leftover meat loaf from the refrigerator. "Most often from sexual assault, as I recall."

"Right. I consider what Annie went through as severe sexual assault."

"Agreed."

Instead of the elective abortion Annie had planned, the "Good House" conspirators had drugged her, stolen her embryo in an illicit surgical procedure, then abandoned her in the icy Potomac River. Zack Winston had saved his daughter's life, with a major assist from Bridget. Zack would later say Bridget saved both lives, his and his daughters.

Bridget turned on the oven and thrust the leftover meat loaf inside. "What's the plan now, Zack?"

Another pause. "Referral to a clinical psychologist for further testing and treatment. Natalie met with her today and gave the 'go ahead.' She specializes in the effects of severe emotional trauma."

Bridget pulled a loaf of store-bought garlic bread from the refrigerator. "And?"

"I just dropped Nat at her hotel. I thought you and I could get together for dinner and talk about it."

Saw that coming a mile away. Talk about what?

"I'm sorry, Zack. That's not possible. I'm about to make dinner for Dustin and me, then we plan to spend the evening doing mom/son stuff."

Whatever that is.

A longer pause from Zack. "Of course. I should have thought about that."

"It's okay, Zack." She made her own pause, then spoke. "We need to adjust, you and I. Our lives have changed since last month. Makes it hard to…"

He spoke over her. "I know, Bridge. Sorry. I should have been more sensitive."

Now Bridget rolled her eyes. "Enough apologies, Zack. Maybe we can talk later on the phone."

"Sure. Just call me when you can."

"I will. Now I really have to go make dinner."

"Right."

She was about to click off when Zack spoke again. "Oh, real quick, one other thing. You're interviewing Paula Cho tomorrow, right?"

Dr. Paula Cho, an emergency physician colleague of Zack's, faced a malpractice suit over a missed ectopic pregnancy. Zack knew the details because he'd been the physician who followed her on duty. An irate obstetrician had challenged Zack about the case. That same obstetrician, Dr. Sebastian Barth, had later turned out to be the infamous "Dr. Good" who stole Annie's embryo.

Bridget blew out an annoyed breath. "Zack, you know I am. You should also respect Paula's and my client-attorney privilege. I can't, and won't, talk to you about it."

Zack's breath quickened over the phone. His voice became detached. "Yeah. Sure. Sorry. Again."

"I'll call you later, Zack. We can talk about Annie."

"Sure. Thanks."

He disconnected before Bridget could reply. She clicked off her phone and went about fixing dinner.

Dustin looked up from his phone. "What's with that guy?"

"He almost lost his daughter is what's with him."

Dustin thrust out his lower lip. "Yeah, well, I did lose my dad."

Chapter Five

ANNIE WINSTON SAT IN uncomfortable silence between her parents on the sofa in the waiting room of the psychologist's office. Her mom and dad had not spoken to each other beyond superficial greetings when Annie and her dad picked up her mom at her hotel. Annie's impression that her recent tragedy had caused her parents to be more civil to each other teetered on the edge of oblivion.

The door to the inner office opened and an attractive cinnamon-skinned woman with jet black hair stepped into the waiting room. She smiled at the three occupants of the sofa, then smiled at Annie.

"You must be Annie Winston," she said. "I am Dr. Maria Santos, but you can call me Maria."

She greeted each of Annie's parents, starting with her mother. "Good to see you again, Dr. Lewis." then she turned to Annie's dad. "Pleased to meet you, Dr. Winston. I have heard some good things about you."

Annie's mom snorted, which earned a surprised glance from Dr. Santos. The psychologist turned to Annie. "Please come into the inner sanctum." She stepped back to allow Annie to precede her into the office.

"We'll be about an hour," she said to the parents. "So, if you two have anything you need to do, you have time."

"We'll be fine here," Annie's mother said.

Maria followed Annie into the office, closed the door, and directed her toward the couch and two side chairs. "You can sit wherever you want, Annie. Wherever you're comfortable."

Annie had read stories and seen TV shows about psychiatrist's couches, so she made a beeline to one chair.

Dr. Santos sat on the end of the couch closest to Annie's chair. This allowed her to regard Annie at an angle rather than face-to-face.

Annie noticed a scar line across the psychologist's neck, just below her left jaw. Similar to the scar she'd seen on Bridget Larsen's neck.

Knife wound? How weird is that?

After about a minute of silence, Maria spoke. "So, Annie, tell me why you are here."

Annie hesitated. "I thought you knew."

"Okay. Here's our first 'rule' for these sessions. What I know isn't on the table. I need to hear what you know, or don't know. Or want me to know." She waited a few seconds, then smiled. "So, I wonder what you're willing to share with me."

Annie shook her head. "I... I'm not sure." She looked at the ceiling and then back at Maria. "I'm not sure." She pursed her lips. "PTSD maybe."

Maria nodded, but remained silent for several seconds before speaking. "That's interesting."

Annie felt anxious in the ensuing silence. "I... I've forgotten some things that happened to me." She looked away. "I guess it's important for me to remember those things."

"Important," Maria said.

Annie thought she might cry. She held it back. "I think... There was a crime and I know who did it."

Maria's voice turned softer. "Did that crime involve you?"

Annie shook her head. "No, no. I didn't do anything. I... I.... I did nothing wrong. I..." Her face flushed.

Maria raised a hand. "No one is accusing you of doing anything wrong, Annie." She paused, then leaned forward. "Let's talk about something else."

Annie felt instant relief. "Oh, yes. Thank you."

Maria thought for a few seconds. "Tell me anything that's not uncomfortable."

Annie stared into the distance. "I... got pregnant in California before I came to visit my dad in Bethesda for Christmas. My older sister, Jennifer, came with me."

"I'm going to guess that your pregnancy was unplanned, that you didn't wish to have a baby," Maria said.

"That's right."

"That must have been scary for you."

Annie's breathing became more rapid. She sniffed. "It... It was terrifying..." She could not continue.

Maria paused for several seconds, then spoke. "I take it you're not pregnant now."

Annie shook her head. "I'm not."

"I wonder how that came about."

A blurry image arose in Annie's peripheral vision. A man. A woman. Something... Her mind went blank. She looked at Maria with a blank expression. "I don't remember."

"Let's shift gears again," Maria said. "Let's talk about happy memories. Any happy memories that you have from any time in your life. Include any happy thoughts that you have today."

For the next twenty minutes, Annie and Maria discussed her childhood, growing up in San Diego, her friends, her relationship with Conner, the boy who got her pregnant. As she talked, Annie became bored. As if she was talking about someone else, someone she used to know from a different time and place. Not Annie Winston, the girl talking to the charming woman with a knife scar on her neck.

Annie liked this Maria Santos, the doctor who seemed open to anything Annie wanted to say yet accepted that there were things Annie wouldn't say—or couldn't.

When Annie stopped talking, Maria sat beside her in silence. Such a pleasant change from her mom and dad, both of whom seemed driven to fill silent space with their own monologues. Even her mother, a psychiatrist who was supposed to know how to listen, wasn't so good at it with her own daughters.

After what seemed like five minutes, Maria looked at her watch and broke the silence. "We have some time left, Annie." She leaned forward and looked into Annie's eyes. "Tell me the first thing, or the last thing, that you recall before whatever you don't remember."

Annie nodded. "I met a woman, actually my sister Jennifer and I both met her while we were shopping with my dad. Her name is Sarah. I thought she was my dad's girlfriend. She... She figured out I was pregnant. Offered to help."

"So she helped you."

Annie looked away. "I think so."

"I wonder how Sarah helped you?"

"I think she got me an abortion."

Maria's spoke in a gentle, non-accusatory voice. "You don't seem certain about that."

"I... I don't remember."

A fleeting memory crossed Annie's consciousness. When she spoke, Annie pronounced each word slowly and distinctly as she remembered each detail.

"I was supposed to meet Sarah at a Starbucks in Bethesda, where I was staying with my dad. He and Jennifer had gone to the hospital to see a patient, but I said I didn't want to go to the hospital. I faked sleeping in. As soon as they left, I got up and got dressed and went to meet Sarah at that Starbucks."

"So you got coffee with Sarah at a Starbucks?"

"Sarah had already ordered for me." Annie's voice trailed off as she struggled to remember beyond drinking the soy latte that Sarah had offered her.

Maria spoke in a gentle voice. "Go on, if you can."

A fuzzy vision crossed Annie's mind. She gasped. "Someone else. A boy…" She shook her head. "I'm… I don't know." All at once, her body trembled and her breathing became rapid.

"Try taking slow, deep breaths, Annie. One breath at a time. Just concentrate on the breath."

To Annie's amazement, the trembling stopped, and her breathing normalized. Surprised, she looked at Maria.

"Okay now?" Maria asked.

"Yes. Thanks."

Maria looked at her watch. "We have only a few minutes left, so let's leave it there for now. We might pick it up there the next time we meet." She looked at Annie. "That is, if you want to meet again. It's up to you, Annie."

Annie blinked. "Up to me? I thought I had to come."

Maria smiled. "Nope. You can choose to come back, or you can choose not to come back. No one can or will force you to meet with me against your will."

"I want to come back." Annie said that with gusto.

"Good. Because I would like very much to continue talking to you, Annie."

Maria closed the notebook in which she had been writing. "Here's what you can expect. To the extent that you choose, or that you can do, we will explore memories, or feelings, or thoughts that are comfortable for you. If we find that some of those memories trigger an adverse reaction, we won't go there. Instead, we'll try to find a way or ways for you to become comfortable with scary memories. As a psychologist, I have professional training and I know techniques to help you through this. At no time will I leave you hung out to dry or in any terrible position. Am I making any sense?"

Annie really liked this woman. "Yes, ma'am. I get it."

Maria stood. "Okay, then, I will need to talk to your parents in private. I promise I will not give away any secrets. What you and I say in this room remains between you and me. I just need to discuss with them about process and logistics and that boring stuff. Then we will decide when you can come back. I hope it can be soon. I know you'll be starting a new school and adjusting to living at your dad's place, but I would like to see you three times a week. If we can make that work."

Annie stood. "I would like that, ma'am." Without thinking about it, she reached out to give Maria a hug.

Maria returned the hug and stood back. "While I talk to your parents, I wonder if you'd mind filling out a brief questionnaire for me. It will help me decide how to approach our next session."

Annie wasn't sure, but she agreed. "Yes, ma'am."

Maria handed her a clipboard with a sheet of paper on it, like a survey. "You can do this in the waiting room while I talk to your parents."

Annie nodded and started toward the door.

"One other thing," Maria said. "You don't call me 'ma'am.' I am Maria."

Annie smiled. "Thank you, Maria. I feel better already."

Chapter Six

When Zack and Natalie entered Maria Santos' office, they went to opposite ends of the couch. Maria sat on the side chair to Zack's right.

Zack did a double take when he noticed a linear scar along the left side of Maria's neck below the angle of her jaw. It crossed the anatomical location of carotid and jugular blood vessels, a common assault target. Similar to the wound Bridget had suffered at the hands of a medical assassin, Zack's former colleague and friend, whom he had later killed in self-defense.

A knife wound? Zack stifled the urge to wonder about such a bizarre coincidence.

Random chance. He did not convince himself.

Maria leaned forward in her chair. "I rarely converse with medical professionals such as you two. I want to be clear and detailed, but I will also try to respect your expertise."

Zack spoke up right away. "You don't…"

Natalie interrupted. "Talk to us however you'd like, Maria. In this room, we are parents first. Physicians, by coincidence."

Zack shot Natalie a withering stare. She returned it in kind.

Maria blinked, then offered a conciliatory smile. "Okay. Let's move on."

She sat back. "Without doubt, your daughter suffered significant physical and emotional trauma. My working diagnosis is post-traumatic stress disorder, with an element of avoidance expressed as amnesia. She's repressed the most painful memories of what happened to her, but those memories live in her subconscious. With no coping mechanisms, it's too excruciating for her to allow it into her consciousness. Hence, the memory loss—especially for the most terrible recollections. She doesn't know how to deal with them, so she suppresses them."

Zack became impatient. "So, PTSD or dissociative amnesia?"

Natalie shook her head. "Appreciate the summary, Maria." She gave Zack a dismissive look. "Annie suffers from PTSD. Pure dissociative amnesia is rare."

Zack sat back, crossed his legs, and folded his arms. He turned to Maria Santos. "Proceed, please."

Maria took a breath. "While we talk in here, she's completing the CPSS test." She noted Zack's furrowed eyebrows. "That's the Child PTSD Symptom Scale. It gives us a measure of the intensity of her PTSD. Part one measures the frequency of typical symptoms of PTSD. She'll do Part two in two weeks. That measures the extent to which those symptoms interfere in her life."

"Got it," Zack said. In his mind, he pictured the calamities that would occur with emergency room patients if the treating physician wasted time having the patient fill out a questionnaire.

Maria gave him a knowing look. "Let's talk about goals of therapy. Then we can discuss the modalities."

She looked between Zack and Natalie, neither of whom showed any reaction. "The goal of therapy is to get the patient to become comfortable with the triggers. So she can accept the memories, rather than subjugate them. That will require significant time while I build a relationship with her, and she can trust me as a nonthreatening confidante. We will establish this office as her safe place. She will understand that here she cannot suffer harm." She looked at Zack. "Clear so far?"

Annoyed that Maria looked at him and not Natalie, Zack said, "Crystal. Please continue."

Maria nodded. "I consider Trauma Focused CBT as our best option."

Zack had some familiarity with PTSD treatment from his Navy medicine days, treating patients, especially Marines, affected by combat. "What about EMDR?" he asked.

Natalie gave him a condescending look. "You mean Eye Movement Desensitization and Reprocessing used in the treatment of PTSD of soldiers and victims of natural disasters and such?" She turned to Maria. "Maybe you should explain it to the ER doc here."

Maria spoke to Zack in a collegial voice. "Not as effective in teenagers as in adults. Hence my recommendation for TF-CBT."

Zack fumed at Natalie's jibes, but forced himself to settle down. "I'm familiar with CBT, but not the trauma-focused variant."

"The description I like best for CBT," Maria said, "is teaching the patient to become her own therapist."

"I like that one too," Natalie said. Zack shot her a dismissive look.

Maria filled the resulting void. "We teach the patient to recognize unhelpful ways of thinking, and to develop better ways of assessing and coping with traumatic memories." She leaned forward, hands on her lap. "I briefly described that with Annie, and she seemed quite intrigued. She will be an excellent candidate for CBT."

"And the trauma-focused part?" Zack asked.

Maria drew a breath and looked straight at him. "Requires parental involvement."

Zack felt like she'd slugged him between the eyes. "What, uh, kind of parental involvement?"

Maria glanced at Natalie, who remained silent, distant. "The parent participates in the therapy, at first parallel and eventually joint."

Zack sensed Natalie fuming at the opposite end of the couch. "How does that work, exactly?"

Maria pursed her lips. "I would like to see Annie three times a week. Also see you, as the custodial parent. We will do separate sessions until you and Annie are comfortable coming together."

Natalie cast Zack a look that screamed, "Told you so."

Zack drew a breath. "Annie starts a new high school on Monday, a week late. Three visits per week will be difficult for her, not to mention my ER work schedule for me." Despite his reluctance, he looked at Natalie for help.

Natalie turned on him. "Would have been easier to do in California." She smirked. "But I'm sure you can work it out here."

Maria looked from Natalie to Zack and back. "Do I sense some parental discord here?"

Zack spoke in a matter-of-fact voice. "We let Annie decide where she wants to live. She chose here."

Maria nodded. "Got it."

Natalie said, "I concur that TF-CBT, a minimum of three times per week, will be most important if Annie is going to get through this." She looked at Zack. "If that's too difficult for you, we can revisit our prior agreement about where she lives."

Zack fumed. "We'll do the treatment schedule."

The ensuing silence became uncomfortable for Zack. He opened his mouth to speak, but Maria stayed him with a raised hand.

"I understand the differences you both have about Annie's decision. May I suggest that her decision not become a wedge between any of you, and I mean all three of you? I assume you both want to give her the best chance of recovery."

Natalie closed her eyes and took a few deep breaths. "Understood. It won't come up again."

Damn right it won't, Zack thought.

Maria looked at Natalie. "I understand you have to go back to California soon."

Natalie frowned. "Tomorrow."

"All the more reason to get along and start offering her support while you are all together."

Discomfort overcame Zack's brief sense of victory over Natalie. "What kind of support are you talking about?"

"Empathy. Understanding. Acceptance. Emotional support."

"Yeah, I get that," Zack said. "But what else?"

Maria raised an eyebrow. "Else?"

"What else do we do?" he said, with emphasis on *do*.

Maria squinted. "I don't understand."

Natalie broke in, a knowing smile on her face. "He means take action, attack, intervene, words like that."

Maria offered a quizzical look at both of them.

"Like a typical ER doc," Natalie said. "Shoot, ready, aim."

"She's right," Zack said. "Emergency physicians rarely take a supportive role. I don't ask a patient with a gunshot wound how he feels about being attacked before I dive in to save his life." He looked at Natalie. "I prefer 'Straight in, no waiting' as a better description of action."

Maria nodded. "I get it." She tented her fingers. "Here, in your daughter's case, maybe you do need to be the father, not the ER doc."

Zack's pulse quickened. "Look," he said. "I get what you're saying. But the fact remains, these vile creatures violated my daughter in the worst possible way, then left her in the river like trash." He huffed. "You want me to hold her hand and help her through therapy? I can do that." He moved to the edge of the couch. "But whoever did this...this 'thing' to my daughter, is still out there. They may return. Sure, I'll give her emotional support. But I will also defend her. I must. And I'll teach her to defend herself. These vermin won't get away a second time."

The room fell silent in the wake of Zack's outburst. He thought he saw Natalie and Maria cast meaningful glances at each other.

At last, Maria spoke. "Dr. Winston, may I call you 'Zack'?"

Zack nodded. He sensed Natalie steaming at the other end of the couch.

"Zack, I get it. I might feel the same if she were my daughter." She touched the scar on her neck. "I've had some, uh, personal experience with traumatic assault." Her eyes softened. "I can help you both."

Zack scrunched his eyebrows. "How?"

Natalie stirred. "She already told you, Zack."

A light went on inside Zack's mind. "Oh. The TF-CBT. It's as much for me as for Annie."

"Bingo," Natalie said.

Maria glanced at Natalie, then looked back at Zack. "TF-CBT is an effective intervention for PTSD in many cases, not just you and Annie."

"How?"

"You talk. About your well-founded desire to protect your daughter, and how that might affect her recovery. How you can collaborate with each other on the road to..." She half-smiled. "Acceptance."

To Zack, it sounded like psychobabble. But if it would help Annie...

"Okay," he said. "I'll do it."

After they had scheduled the next sessions with Maria, Zack and Natalie stood.

"Just a second before you leave," Maria said. She went to her desk, rummaged through a drawer, and pulled out a business card. "You mentioned Annie defending herself. I'm not just about behavioral therapy. I also believe a woman must know how to defend herself." She handed the business card to Zack. "You might enroll Annie in this Krav Maga class." She touched the scar on her neck. "It saved my life."

Chapter Seven

AFTER A WEEK OF treating their foreign guests to a plethora of delights aboard the yacht and within the seaside resorts of Puerto Vallarta, the cartel members bid them adieu and returned to their headquarters in the hills outside Guadalajara, Mexico.

The Fly had long since tired of the debauchery and self-indulgence of her bosses and *El Cubano*. She grew restless, not only from the inactivity, but also from her lack of critical information. What was this "revenge" of which *El Víbora* had spoken the first night on the yacht? Why had *El Cubano* come? Who were the Americans? Why the Asian? Was he Chinese or North Korean? What did *El Víbora* mean by loose ends?

More disturbing, why had *El Vengador* stayed on board? The man never cared about partying and frivolity. He had his own evil pursuits for pleasure.

El Vengador terrified *La Mosca*.

A few times, she happened on hushed conversations among the three brothers. Each time, *El Fuego* would make them hush. *El Vengador* would glare at her until she retreated in both fright and anger.

What are they not telling me?

Desperate to find out, she'd sucked it up and given in to *El Fuego's* clumsy sexual advances. She got him stoned and drunk, then took him to her bed. Once he'd had his fill of weed, booze, and her, she popped the question.

"What's going on, *querido*? Why do *Los Hermanos* huddle and speak in whispers? Why is *El Vengador* here? Why the foreigners? Who are the Americans?"

He had sneered at her. "Wouldn't you like to know, pesky fly?"

"After everything I do for *Los Hermanos*, I have a right to know."

Damáso gave her a wicked laugh. "You are no *Hermano*. You are a stupid *puta*."

She slapped him hard across the face. "I am no whore, and you do not talk to me like that."

He raised a fist to strike her, but stopped and rubbed his cheek instead. "Then I do not talk to you at all." He rolled over and put his back to her. Within seconds, he snored.

The next day, *El Víbora* summoned The Fly to his private quarters. She halted just inside the doorway when she saw *El Fuego*. What had he told *El Víbora* about last night?

Just then, the two Americans appeared.

They came here instead of going home from Puerto Vallarta?

The Fly pursed her lips. What else had the brothers hidden from her?

El Víbora beckoned the Americans and her to sit on his sofa.

He addressed The Fly. "We need you to return to *Estados Unidos* to wrap up loose ends. That idiot Doctor Good left too much trash behind. We didn't care because he left no trail to us. That has changed in the last two days." He gestured toward the Americans. "These people will give you the information."

Uncertain, The Fly turned toward the Americans.

The redheaded woman showed several photographs, taken in secret when the subjects were unaware. A girl of about sixteen, a young woman, a middle-aged man, and a blond woman of about the same age as the man.

"These people know too much," *El Víbora* said. He nodded to the American woman. "There is more."

The woman showed The Fly a new photograph, posed, official. It showed another red-haired woman, freckle-faced, perhaps a few years older. "My sister," the woman said.

El Víbora planted an index finger on the face in the photograph. "This traitor must die, at any cost." He stood. "Damáso will take charge. You depart tomorrow by separate pathways. *El Vengador* will meet you there."

El Vengador? They never sent him to the USA. Something big happening, to which The Fly had no clue.

El Fuego smirked at her. "*Pues, vámonos.* We have much to cover before tomorrow." He led the Americans out of the room.

Flummoxed and frightened, The Fly followed at a distance.

Chapter Eight

AFTER THEIR PSYCHOLOGY APPOINTMENT, Annie, her dad, and mom went to lunch at a nearby bistro. Her parents' phony efforts to seem reconciled caused her more discomfort than when they openly sniped at each other. She checked out of their small talk conversation and rehashed her meeting with Maria Santos. What had Maria said to her parents that motivated them to act so phony?

"You'll want an iPhone," her mother said. It took a second for Annie to realize she was talking to her. "So we can Facetime."

"I have an Android," her dad said. "Galaxy Ultra."

"Of course you do," her mother said in a sarcastic tone. "But teenagers all have iPhones. You don't want your daughter to be the class geek, do you?"

Dad twitched. "Of course I don't." His face changed from irritated to resolved. "An iPhone is fine. I can get either with my Verizon account."

Her mother wrote on her iPad. "Okay. We can do that after we get her enrolled in school."

Annie glanced at the list. It looked long.

Mom is in manager mode. Avoids stuff that makes her uncomfortable.

What would be her dad's equivalent?

BAFERD, for "bad ass freaking ER doc." It was one of her dad's favorite sayings.

Mom looked at her watch. "We'd better get going. Lots to do, and it's Friday afternoon. Lord knows how traffic will be in this...place."

Dad winked at Annie. "It will be fine. But, you're right. We need to get going. Might get in some shopping for the high school girl before we call it done."

They spent an hour at the Stone Ridge School of the Sacred Heart in Bethesda getting Annie enrolled, buying her schoolbooks, and meeting the principal.

Just as Annie thought the meeting had ended, the principal asked her secretary to find a student named Raquel Duran. Minutes later, an attractive girl entered, her face flushed with friendly enthusiasm.

"Raquel," the principal said. "This is Annie Winston from California. She's just moved to Bethesda, and she'll enter tenth grade next week. I'd like you to be her 'sponsor,' so to speak. You know, make her feel at home, introduce her around, show her how to get from one class to another." She smiled. "And the informal system you all hide from the faculty."

The girl smiled. To Annie, it seemed genuine. "Sure." She greeted Annie. "Hi, Annie. My name is Raquel, but my friends call me 'Rocky.' You can too."

Annie forced a smile. "Sure, Racq—Rocky. Thanks."

Rocky looked at the principal.

"Yes, Raquel, you can go now."

"One minute," Annie's dad said. He spoke to Rocky. "Your last name is 'Duran'? Are you related to Dr. Olivia Duran?"

"My mom," Raquel said.

"I know her," Dad said. "A recent addition to our medical staff. Anesthesiologist. You all just moved here, too."

"Last semester," Rocky said.

Dad smiled. "So you know how hard it can be to integrate into a new high school?"

The principal smiled. "That's why I thought she'd be a good fit for Annie."

From the school, they went to a Verizon store in Bethesda to buy Annie's new iPhone, to replace the one dad said she'd lost in the Potomac River. She shivered at a memory that flitted across her consciousness. Her dad calling her name just before she sank below the surface of the frigid water. The memory disappeared before Annie stopped shivering.

Neither parent seemed to notice.

Although Annie's mom offered to add the phone to Annie's existing number on her Verizon account, her dad insisted on putting it on his own account.

"That tracking function saved Annie's life last month," he said. "But if we hadn't been able to contact you when we did, it might have been too late. Not taking that chance again."

To seal the deal, he promised to share the tracking link with Annie's mom.

Annie cringed. Now both parents could track her phone's movements.

What joy.

Once Annie had her new phone in her jeans pocket, they went shopping in downtown Bethesda. Her dad seemed shocked at the prices for the clothing and accessories Annie needed/wanted, but the mom didn't blink.

"You should try shopping in La Jolla," Mom said to Dad.

"No thanks," he said. "I'm all about Amazon, Lands' End, and LL Bean."

"You always hated going to shopping malls," Mom said.

Annie recalled how her dad had taken her and her sister, Jennifer, on a shopping excursion when they first came to visit just before Christmas. He hadn't let on that he hated going to malls.

She did a brief gasp when she remembered meeting Sarah at the mall on that shopping trip.

"Are you alright?" her mom asked.

"Yeah, just an uncomfortable memory." She glanced at her dad. The look he gave her suggested he'd felt it, too.

Mom stopped walking. "Do you want to talk about it?"

Annie shook her head. "It's nothing, Mom."

Mom gave Dad a quick icy stare. "Are you sure, Annie?"

"Of course. C'mon, I want to do more shopping."

Dad squirmed. "Sure."

Evening had fallen by the time they finished their shopping and errands, still in downtown Bethesda.

"Let's get some dinner around here," Annie's dad said. "The traffic should thin out by the time we're done."

"Suits me," Mom said. She turned to Annie. "Any preferences? It's on me."

Annie shrugged. "Not really."

They walked for about a block before Mom stopped in front of a restaurant. "This place looks nice."

Annie recognized it at once as the restaurant where Dad, Jenn, and she had dined with Sarah on Christmas Eve. The night...

Dad sucked air through his teeth. "Uh, no. Been here. Not that good. Expensive." He gave Annie a quick glance.

Mom put her hands on her hips. "What?"

Annie shook her head, quizzical. "I don't know what you mean, Mom."

Mom looked at Dad, then back at Annie. "You two are acting strange. What's going on?"

Dad let out a long breath. "Okay." He paused. "We came here with Jenn on Christmas Eve. Sarah O'Brien was with us."

Mom's eyes narrowed. "*The* Sarah O'Brien? The one who...?"

"Yeah," Dad said.

Mom shook her head. "Fine. Where do you suggest we go, then? I wouldn't want to conjure any other uncomfortable associations."

Dad shrugged. "Any place but here will work. Really." He paused. "There's a great Mediterranean bistro around the corner. Less of a hit on your wallet, too. If you're still buying."

Mom glared at him. "Lead the way, Zack."

After a glass of wine each, the parents relaxed and became civil again. Much to Annie's relief, because the whole restaurant thing had caused such a knot in her stomach, she wasn't sure she could eat. Not only the interaction between her parents but also the memory of that night when Sarah had later challenged Annie about her pregnancy, then offered to help her "take care of it."

By dessert, the three had all put the recent unpleasantness behind them and enjoyed being together. They mostly talked about Annie's school and her new friend, Rocky. Also, Mom and Dad both shared information about their professional lives. Annie thought how much more pleasant her life would be if her parents could at least be friends again.

When Mom paid the check, Dad looked at his watch, glanced at Annie, and spoke to Mom.

"Do you want to come by the apartment for a nightcap and 'inspection,' Nat?" He hesitated. "I can either drive you back to your hotel later, or you can stay over with us. We have room."

Mom chuckled. "You are not driving me anywhere in your condition, Dr. Winston. I'm not about to become a trauma patient in your hospital." She took a last sip of wine. "And you sure as hell aren't driving my daughter anywhere."

"Our daughter," Dad said.

Mom smiled. "Indeed. Our daughter, who somehow inherited each of our better qualities."

"For sure," Dad said.

"Okay," Mom said. "Can we get an Uber to your place, even with all this stuff we've bought for said wonderful daughter?"

"We can," Dad said.

"Okay," Mom said. "We can do that. Get her settled and all, then I'll Uber back to my hotel."

Dad spread his arms. "Your choice."

***

Zack awoke to a sharp pain across his forehead. He reached across the bed to...the back of the sofa. Not his bed. He opened his eyes and looked around. Early morning sunlight streamed through the windows of the living room in his apartment. As slow as the sun rising, memories of the prior evening drifted into his consciousness.

As planned, Annie, Natalie, and Zack had taken an Uber the short distance from downtown Bethesda to Zack's upscale apartment. While Natalie helped Annie get settled into her new bedroom, converted from Zack's single-man office/guest room, he had made hot toddies with cognac, one of which he'd handed to Natalie when she came out of Annie's room while Annie changed into sweats.

Natalie had always attracted Zack from when they were both rookie staff members in the San Diego hospital, where both had ended up after their respective residencies in psychiatry for Natalie and emergency medicine for Zack. They'd enjoyed a torrid romance and brief engagement, getting married seven months before the birth of their first daughter, Jennifer.

Three years later, they'd had Annie.

The marriage fell apart as precipitously as it had begun, with Natalie accusing Zack of not being in touch with his feelings, not engaged in being a father, blah, blah, blah.

He and Natalie may have drifted far apart on emotional and intellectual levels, but he had never lost his attraction to her. Now, as he admired what had become her mature beauty, he reflected she was twice divorced, and he once divorced, once widowed. They were both free to...

He dismissed the idea as soon as it germinated in his mind.

They spent another hour engaging in discussion with Annie, split between memories of her childhood—especially when her parents had been together, much of which she didn't remember—and her anticipation of her new life in Bethesda living with her father.

All three avoided any discussion of Annie's current psychological issues.

As the hour approached eleven, Annie yawned, stood, and hugged both her parents. "This little girl is going to bed." At her bedroom door, she shot them a wicked smile. "Whatever happens after I close this door... That's up to you two." She winked at her dad, turned, walked into her room, and closed the door.

"Should I call an Uber," Zack said, "or do you want to stay the night?"

Natalie's eyes narrowed. "Under what specific circumstances, Zack?"

He moved closer, into her personal space. She did not flinch or draw back. "Well," he said, "I can imagine several scenarios. Three, to be exact. One, you take my bed and I take the couch. Two, you take the couch and I take the bed." He moved in closer. "Or..."

"We share the bed," she said, her voice titillated.

Zack put his arm around her, drew her into himself, and kissed her with ardor. She returned it.

He broke the embrace and turned toward his bedroom, guiding Natalie in that direction.

She stomped on the brakes.

"What?" he said.

Natalie smiled and cocked her head. "Terrible idea, Zack."

"Not so much," he said. "One night..."

"With you, it's never just one night."

He couldn't disagree. Then he thought about Bridget and his unresolved feelings about her. He stepped away from Natalie. "Yeah," he said. "Bad idea. Sorry."

"I'll take the couch," she said.

"You take the bed," he said. "It's the least I can do."

She laughed. "You got that right." She turned and walked to the bedroom, paused at the door. "Good night, Zack." She blew him a kiss. "And, thanks."

"No," he said. "Thank you."

Zack got off the couch and used the restroom in the hallway. With Natalie asleep in his bedroom, he dared not enter to retrieve fresh clothes. He made coffee, which brought Natalie out.

"Sleep okay?" Zack said.

Natalie smirked. "Big bed for a single guy."

Zack shrugged. "Room to spread out."

She winked. "Sure, Zack."

Annie came out of her room, looked between her parents, then at the couch where Zack had left a sheet, blanket, and pillowcase rumpled. She shrugged but said nothing.

After a brief breakfast, Natalie and Zack took separate Uber rides. She to her hotel, he to pick up his car they had left parked in downtown Bethesda the night before.

***

Later, Zack and Annie drove Natalie to the airport for her flight to San Diego. They waited until Natalie boarded, then stopped for dinner on the way back to the apartment building. At Annie's request, it was the same restaurant where he'd taken her and Jennifer when they first arrived three days before Christmas. Before Sarah and Dr. Good changed their lives.

"A lifetime ago," Annie said.

"You're not even close to a lifetime on earth yet," Zack said.

She sniffed. "I almost died, Dad."

He reached out and touched her hand. "Thank God you didn't."

"God, and Bridget." She paused, then looked him in the eye. "Now that mom's gone..."

"We'll have Bridget over, eventually. Maybe after we get into our new place." They planned to move into a three-bedroom apartment after Zack's lease on his current bachelor pad expired in two months.

Annie gave him a knowing smile and a wink. "Yeah. More privacy for you and Bridget there."

For one of the few times in his life, Zack Winston was speechless.

Should I worry my daughter thinks about me having sex, with her mother, and with Bridget?

After dinner, they returned to the apartment and watched a movie together. Then Annie went to bed. Zack went into his bedroom and pulled out his journal.

He hadn't written to Noelle since Christmas night, a lifetime ago.

Chapter Nine

Dearest Noelle,

I write with a full heart. My daughter is asleep in <u>her</u> bedroom in <u>our</u> apartment. <u>Our</u> home. Never did I imagine such a gift would come into my life. More wonderful because it was her idea. She wants to live with me, to know me, to build something together that we never had as father and daughter.

I am ecstatic.

Someday soon, I will tell her all about you. How you were and still are the true love of my life, my soulmate, even now in separate worlds. I hope to teach her what it means to love and be loved without guile, with complete vulnerability, and absolute trust. She and I both will become better persons for it. I will do my best to model you for her.

I realize it's possible to have more than one love of my life. You. Annie. And . . . But you know that.

There's still that dark side of me that wants to tear Sarah to pieces for what she did. If I ever find her again. Maybe by the time that happens, Annie and Bridget will have helped me close that compartment in my life. I know you would.

Thank you for loving me, Noelle, for showing me true love, and for helping me become capable of giving that gift to another.

I am nearly at peace tonight. You alive would make it perfect, but I am reconciled to your death. Mostly.

I love you.

Always.

Zack

Chapter Ten

THE FLY PRESSED HER head against the window of the basic economy seat she occupied on the flight from Guadalajara to Houston's George Bush International airport. She wrinkled her nose in response to the foul body odor and fetid snores of the obese man seated next to her. Why had *El Víbora* not allowed her to fly first class, or at least in economy plus? Even with her shorter stature, she struggled for space and air crammed into the seat next to this sweaty jerk.

She could survive this flight for just over two hours. A better seat would reward her on the flight from Houston to Washington, DC. Maybe catch a nap before the start of the mission. She looked around to assure no one was watching her, then reached a finger under the blond wig to scratch a pesky itch.

Can't wait to ditch this lid.

An hour and a half later, The Fly waited for the fat man to disembark ahead of her at the arrival gate. After sidling across the remaining two seats, she had to push her way into the aisle in front of two young American women wearing the sombreros sold by hawkers at the tourist traps. Did they realize they had paid four times what the cheap hats were worth?

The Fly whispered in Spanish under her breath. "Thanks for stimulating the Mexican economy, American trash." She smiled at the ladies, retrieved her carry-on, and walked down the aisle ahead of them.

The line at Customs and Immigration was shorter than she had expected. She paused before entering, taking a moment to compose herself. Who knew what the idiot US Customs agents would try this time?

At the front of the line, an agent directed her to the next available window. She stood behind the same obnoxious seat mate from the plane. Maybe he would so annoy the agent to motivate him to expedite the next passenger's entry.

The agent dispatched the jerk in record time, then beckoned The Fly forward. He spent what seemed like several minutes inspecting her fake USA passport, glancing back and forth between the document and her face. He typed on a computer keyboard, then watched the screen for what seemed like another full minute. Just as she was considering her options if discovered, he stamped the passport and handed it back to her.

"Welcome back to the US, Ms. Marietti."

The Fly nodded, walked at a nonchalant pace into the main terminal area, and found her way to the most remote ladies' room. She sat on the commode in the locked accessible stall, removed the blond wig and fake eyebrows, flushed the toilet, and peeked out the stall door. No one was there. She undressed to her underwear, then crept out of the stall, opened her carry-on, and donned a full-length loose dress. The Fly stuffed the wig and her old clothes into the carry-on, then went to the sink, brushed out her long dark hair, put it up in a bun, freshened her face, then donned a hijab to cover her hair and the lower part of her face.

Satisfied with her appearance, she extracted a fresh ticket from the side pocket of the carry-on, a one-way flight from Houston to Washington's Reagan International Airport for one Fatima Aziz. She got to the gate just as the plane started boarding. The Fly greeted the flight attendant with a downward gaze, then proceeded to her assigned seat in the first-class cabin. The young man in the adjoining seat tried to engage her in conversation. She pretended not to speak English, opened a book in Arabic, and feigned reading for the rest of the journey.

Three hours later, The Fly trod the meandering walkways through the maze at Washington's Reagan International Airport into the passenger greeting area. She scrutinized the crowd until she saw a young man with a full beard and dark ponytail holding a sign that read, "Aziz." She approached him and displayed her photo ID. He compared it to a similar photo he held in his hand.

Satisfied, he took the carry-on from her. "Do you have checked luggage?"

"Never," The Fly said.

The young man raised his eyebrows. "Please come with me."

She followed him to the parking area. He opened the door to a blue Cadillac SUV and stood aside for her to enter. In the opposite seat, a man in his mid-forties greeted her.

"Welcome back to the US. Good to see you again."

"Likewise, Mr. Snyder."

The young man who had greeted her took the driver's seat and guided the SUV out of the airport area. As soon as they left the area, she removed the hijab and stuffed it into her purse. She freed her hair from the bun and shook it out.

The man named Snyder lifted a briefcase from the floor in front of him and passed it to her. "You will find the most important items in there. In the vehicle's rear, we have some luggage with sufficient clothing for the mission, plus the other items you requested."

The Fly tilted her head toward the driver.

"One of us," Snyder said. "Goes by 'Roach.' Like *la cucaracha*." He chuckled as if he'd made a joke.

She cracked open the briefcase and peered inside. Documents in the lid flap. A suitable Smith and Wesson M&P automatic pistol in the well.

Snyder turned to her. "You will stay at the Bethesda Marriott Hotel under the name Mirasol Velasquez with an Argentinian passport. The others are staying on the same floor, the concierge level. No one outside our group will have access to that floor."

The Fly nodded.

"Once we arrive at the hotel, you'll have about a half-hour to prepare before the mission brief in the private lounge."

***

The youth who had greeted The Fly at the airport opened the concierge-level lounge door for her. The other attendees had preceded her. She hated to be the last to arrive anywhere. She paused for a few seconds in the alcove to sweep her gaze over the other players.

Douglas Snyder sat in a plush lounge chair spaced in the middle of a semi-circle of smaller chairs. To his right, the same red-haired woman she'd met on the yacht surveyed The Fly's appearance and nodded approval. On Snyder's left side, an American man in a dark blue business suit stared at The Fly with intense eyes. Fermin Esperanza, *El Cubano*'s first lieutenant, sat to the red-haired woman's left.

The young, bearded man directed The Fly to a seat next to the Cuban.

Snyder stood at his place. "Okay. You all know we had planned a multi-pronged series of staged and coordinated events in which each of you, and your various associates, will play a role. I can summarize the outcome in one word: vengeance."

The attendees shifted in their seats.

"But first," Snyder said. "We must eliminate certain, uh, undesirable elements."

Three hours later, The Fly returned to her hotel room. Exhausted as she was from the long day and intense meeting, she had one more task before she could crash into bed.

El Víbora answered on the first ring.

"All is in motion," she said. "Stand by."

"Good job, *hermana*." He hung up.

Damn right. And I am not your sister. You will pay a heavy price for what I do.

Chapter Eleven

For her second visit to the psychologist, Annie reclined on the couch while Maria sat in the side chair, taking notes as usual.

"Tell me about your first day at school," Maria said.

Annie shook her head. "A blur."

"Must have been a challenge, being the new girl."

"Weird."

"New experience for you?"

"Yeah, most of those girls have known each other for years. Like me and my friends in La Jolla. We mostly all grew up together." Annie paused. "I should have been kinder to new girls at my old school."

Maria nodded. "That seems a worthy insight." She paused. "I'm interested in how you coped with being the new girl today."

Annie drew a breath. "I mostly hung out with my new friend, Rocky. She's pretty cool, and she was the new girl last semester."

"So she understood what you were going through."

"Yeah."

Maria didn't respond.

After a few seconds, Annie spoke. "Still weird, though."

"I hear it gets better with time," Maria said.

"That's what my dad said."

As if either of you two grown-ups know what it's like today.

Another silence, which made Annie uncomfortable enough to speak. "Weird not having any boys in the school."

"How so?" Maria asked.

"In my old school, I got along better with the boys than the girls."

"How so?"

Annie shrugged. "Easier to talk to. You know, they don't hide behind phony shi— uh, pleasantness."

Maria smiled, but did not speak.

Annie smirked. "Guess I got too familiar with being around boys. Especially Conner."

"Conner was the boy who..."

"Got me pregnant. Right."

"Do you keep in touch with him now?"

Annie scoffed. "Nah. He's too...immature for me." She thought about her earlier life in California, how far away it seemed now. How different she had been. How naïve. "I'll never go back there."

"I'm curious why you say that."

Annie shook her head. "It's not me anymore."

Maria paused for a few seconds. "Tell me what is."

"Huh?"

"What are you now?"

Annie frowned. "You know. I'm here. With my dad. I'm grown up. Well, almost. Dad lets me be me. Mom wasn't like that."

"Moms can be different."

Annie sighed. "She can be so controlling, you know. Worried about me and... Boys for one thing."

"I wonder if that had anything to do with your getting pregnant."

"Huh?"

"Rebelling, or making your own way. Something like that."

Annie scrunched her forehead. "She didn't even know Conner existed."

Maria remained silent.

Annie's breathing picked up. "Mom was easy to fool. She was gone so much, especially during the day, from when I got out of school until she came home from work." She scoffed. "Conner would come over after school and we would fool around. He would always be gone before my mom got home. Except for one time, when... I think that's when I got pregnant. We, uh, lost track of time." She blinked hard. "I heard the garage door open when her car pulled into it." She snickered. "Didn't know I could get dressed so fast. Conner, not so much. Clumsy dweeb. I made him hide in the closet while I went downstairs and headed Mom off. Told her there was something wrong with the swimming pool, so we went outside to check on it. Conner ran out the front door."

"Interesting ploy."

"Well, there really was something wrong with the pool, so..."

Annie turned serious. "She knew. She knew I just had sex with Conner. I don't know how she knew, but..."

"A mother can tell."

"Mom never talked about it. Just went on like everything was normal."

"I wonder how that made you feel."

"I thought we'd gotten away with it. Now..."

"I sense second thoughts."

Annie frowned and shook her head. "She either couldn't handle it, or didn't give a shit."

"Maybe she was waiting for the right time and place to bring it up."

"Yeah, that would be mom. Put off the unpleasant stuff till later."

Maria didn't respond, but waited before speaking.

Annie was getting more comfortable with the silence. It felt like her head was clearing.

Maria leaned forward a bit. "Our time is almost up, Annie. I'm wondering if you've had any memories since we last met. Anything at all that seems new."

Annie stared off into space. A brief vision flitted across her mind.

"I think I just had one, but it's gone."

"Remember, Annie, we've made this your safe place. Whatever you bring up, whatever you say or remember, it stays here. Between us. No one else ever has to know."

"But aren't you supposed to...?"

"Tell the law enforcement folks?"

"Yeah."

Maria shook her head. "Nope. I don't talk to them. That will be your choice whether to tell them, if you remember anything and if you feel comfortable sharing it. Otherwise, it's just us girls."

"I like that," Annie said.

"So..."

"I remember a woman. I can't see her, but I hear her voice. She's kind, caring. Promises to help me."

"Do you know where you are when you hear this kind woman talking to you?"

Annie closed her eyes, tried to remember. A fuzzy picture developed in her mind.

"I... Somewhere I don't recognize. A room. It's cold. I mean, cold temperature, but cold in other ways. The walls are all white. The light is white."

She struggled to pull the memory into consciousness.

"I'm on my back. On my back on a hard bed. My arms are spread out." She extended her arms on both sides. "I think they're tied down."

The picture focused a little more.

"The woman, the kind woman, she's holding my hand, talking into my ear. Then..."

Maria said nothing. Waited.

"I fall asleep." She squeezed her eyes hard, striving to remember. "I wake up, and..." She hyperventilated.

"Go on, if you can."

Annie rocked back and forth in her seat. "My knees are bent, my legs spread apart, and..." She grimaces. "I feel pressure..." She pointed to her crotch. "Down there." She looked away.

"Take your time, Annie. We can stop anytime you want."

Annie breathes hard and deep. "I look up. There's...a man. Between my legs." The rocking intensifies. "He's wearing a mask."

The picture sharpens and Annie gasps. "Oh my God, he's inside me!" She sobs. "Wait. No. He's not inside me. He puts something inside me. I scream."

Annie rocks hard twice, then stops. "He looks past me and says something. To someone behind me. Then...I'm asleep."

Maria hands Annie a packet of tissues. "Take a few minutes, Annie. Try that breathing exercise we learned."

Annie dabs her eyes. Her breathing slows. She feels safe.

She and Maria sit together in silence for a few minutes, then Annie speaks. "So, that was a memory, right?"

"Right. And you're still safe in here, Annie."

Annie took a deep breath. "It's about what happened to me in that place, right? I've heard people call it 'The Good House.'"

Maria nodded. "I think so. I believe that whatever happened to you there triggered your memory loss. One terrible memory just broke into consciousness."

Annie thought for a minute. "Do I have to do this? Do I have to bring back those memories?"

Maria offered a gentle smile. "No, Annie. You don't. No one can make you. It's your choice and yours alone."

Annie pondered what had happened and what Maria had said. "I think I want to continue."

"Okay," Maria said. She looked Annie in the eye. "Are you okay now? Feel okay to move on with your day?"

A new sense of resolve washed over Annie. "Yes, I am."

Chapter Twelve

ZACK HAD TAKEN OFF the first three days of the week following Natalie's departure so that he could be present for Annie as she adjusted to her new school and their new life together. He'd also kept his promise for parallel meetings with Annie and Dr. Maria Santos. The first session, he'd reluctantly admitted to himself, had been a positive experience for him. Besides sharing his past with Natalie, and the tragic loss of Noelle, he'd found the courage to admit he had no idea how to parent a teenager.

"Few parents do," Maria had said. "Sometimes, like when facing a difficult clinical challenge, you just go with your judgment and hope it works out."

Now halfway through his day shift in the Bethesda Metro Hospital Emergency Department, he walked into the physician workstation from the treatment area, set down the Samsung tablet he'd used to make notes on the four patients he'd just seen, completed lab and x-ray orders on each, then eyed the large screen display on the counter showing new patients waiting to be seen.

People occupied each of the department's twenty-four treatment beds—as they had since Zack's arrival at 7:00 AM. He had discharged some and admitted others to the hospital, but new patients took their places as soon as the staff put fresh sheets on the beds and entered their clinical information into the electronic record system that sent the data to Zack's tablet.

He rubbed his eyes and spoke to the charge nurse in a weary tone. "ED overcrowding is one thing. We are friggin' overstuffed here."

The nurse returned Zack's frayed expression. "Yet we do not burst."

"Yet." He glanced around. Other staff members showed the same overworked, tired expressions or body language.

Soldier on, BAFERD.

That well-worn acronym for "Bad Ass Fucking ER Doc" had become his mantra over the past three years of personal and professional challenges and tragedies.

"You can help most by clearing out the suture room," the charge nurse said. "We have other lacerations waiting in triage."

Zack rendered a half-salute. "Aye, aye, ma'am." He started toward the suture room. "Hopefully, we'll get some actual lab reports back so we can discharge a few more patients."

Two patients occupied the narrow surgical beds in the suture room. Zack examined the first one, a sixty-year-old disheveled man with what most people would call a "busted lip." The patient described how the left side of his upper lip had sustained an unplanned collision with a younger man's accelerating ring-wearing fist.

Zack feigned a smile. "I should see the other guy, right?"

The patient winced.

"How long ago?" Zack asked.

"Walking home from the bar, around three."

The odor of stale alcohol on the man's breath validated the timeline. Zack looked at the clock. At 1:00 PM, they were within the safe window to close the facial laceration without increasing the risk of infection.

Zack inspected the wound, an irregular gash that crossed the line where lip meets skin, the vermilion border. The bruised edges of the cut looked swollen and dusky. This repair would take meticulous technique and considerable time. Zack considered asking a plastic surgeon to take over the case, but a quick look at the patient's tablet record showed he had no health insurance. No plastic surgeon on this hospital's staff would accept this patient. They would argue liability, but they really meant no chance of getting paid for their inflated fees.

Zack sighed. "Okay, Mister, uh…" He looked at the top of the chart. "…Martin. We'll get you all fixed up. Let me look at this other fellow first."

He turned toward the other suture bed, closer to the door than the first bed. When he had entered the room, Zack had just nodded to this patient, then proceeded to the man furthest from the door.

Now he did a sharp double-take at this patient's appearance, his attention drawn to a ruddy cross-shaped scar on his mid-forehead. Next, he noticed two grotesque tattoos, one a depiction of a skull, the other a garish demon.

Zack tried to hide his reaction as he greeted the patient, a swarthy, mustachioed man who appeared in his mid-forties. According to the record, he sustained an accidental slice across his left forearm while "cutting meat." The chart also noted that he spoke little English.

The man offered no verbal response to Zack's greeting, just a slight nod. Zack examined the wound. *Slice indeed.* It ran about four inches across the back of the patient's arm, mid-way between the wrist and elbow. Clean and straight, as if made by a sharp knife. Not deep. An easy repair.

He turned to the technician who staffed the suture room. "Set up a full tray for Mr. Martin, including a #10 scalpel for debridement. I'll take care of, uh... He looked at the tablet. ...Mr. Gonzales here first, so we can clear the bed for the next victim."

Zack turned back to the patient. "I will numb and clean your wound, then stitch it up. We'll have you out of here in less than twenty minutes."

The man cast him a curious look, shook his head. "*No hablo inglés.*"

Zack smiled. "No problem. I speak a little Spanish." He repeated his direction in imperfect but passable Spanish, along with pantomiming his treatment plan.

The man shrugged.

The door to the suture room opened. A nurse Zack didn't recognize poked her head into the room. "I need to borrow your tech to move an obese patient in the main treatment area."

"Sure." Zack watched as the tech followed the nurse out of the room. He didn't recall seeing that nurse earlier in the shift. Probably sent from another floor to help in the overcrowded ED.

His phone buzzed just as he turned back to his patient.

Caller ID showed "Dr. Maria Santos."

About Annie?

"I'm sorry," he said in Spanish to the patient. His limited vocabulary failed him, so he pointed to his phone and mouthed. "I have to take this."

The man shrugged. Again.

Zack looked at the other patient. Snoring.

"Be right back."

He stepped into the hallway. "Dr. Santos, what's up?"

"Nothing serious. And to you and Annie I'm Maria."

Zack frowned. "Right. Sorry. What's up, Maria?"

"I'm really sorry to do this, but I need to reschedule our appointments this afternoon. An emergency has come up."

"Nothing serious, I hope."

"I have another patient I need to see as soon as possible. Can I see Annie and you tomorrow instead?"

"I think so." Zack's awareness returned to the ED. "Sorry, Maria, but I have a department full of patients. Let's pencil that in until I can confirm with Annie. Can I call you later today?"

"Sure. If I don't answer, I'm with a patient. Just leave a message."

"Will do."

Zack punched off the call and returned to the suture room. He paused in the doorway. The tech had not returned. The patient with the lip laceration snored away. Zack turned toward the other patient.

The empty bed startled him, just as powerful hands encircled his neck from behind and squeezed. Zack's airway collapsed under the pressure, causing immediate air hunger and a sense of imminent fainting. Blood from the man's forearm laceration dripped onto Zack's neck. With a resolve and reserve he didn't know he had, Zack grabbed his attacker's left arm over the open wound and squeezed hard. The man growled in pain, and his grip on Zack's neck loosened just enough for Zack to inhale fresh air. He delivered a sharp elbow blow to the man's gut and twisted out of his grasp. Zack lurched to the suture tray next to the other patient's bed, grabbed the scalpel, and wheeled to face his attacker. He swept the blade in slicing motions at chest level.

"I'm a surgeon," Zack said. "I make my living cutting people, and I know just where to cut you."

The man glared at him and spoke in English. "Next time I don't miss." He bolted out the door.

Zack went after him. "Help! Security!" He chased the man down the hallway toward the waiting room. "That man attacked me."

A nurse tried to block the assailant, but the man knocked him away with a swipe of his arm.

An obese, puffing security guard joined Zack and several others chasing the man through the waiting room. No one sitting there got up to assist, as if terrified of a crazed, psychotic patient. The assailant charged out the front door and jumped into the passenger side of a vehicle in the driveway. It sped away while he closed the door.

Zack stared at the others. "That car was waiting for him."

Chapter Thirteen

Bridget Larsen made notes in the margin of the legal document in front of her. Her empathic eyes regarded the woman sitting diagonally across the conference table.

Dr. Paula Cho's downcast gaze and slumped shoulders seemed nothing like the person Zack Winston had described as the most competent and caring emergency physician he'd ever known. Bridget had witnessed similar dejection many times in defending physicians against malpractice claims. The competent and caring ones always suffered the most. They reacted to lawsuits, even frivolous ones, as if they pronounced divine judgment against the physicians' professional and personal integrity. Less compassionate doctors often just got angry and belligerent. They were easier to defend.

Bridget nodded to Ange Moretti, her associate attorney.

Ange spoke in a quiet tone. "As you probably know, Dr. Cho, Ms. Larsen lost full use of her voice two years ago from a vicious attack."

Dr. Cho looked up. "Yes. My colleague, Dr. Zack Winston, intervened."

Bridget cocked her head and spoke in her chronic hoarse voice. "Not just intervened. Saved my life."

The doctor cast an admiring look at Bridget. "Zack speaks highly of you."

Bridget nodded, then gestured for Ange to continue.

"Bridget is arguably the best malpractice defense attorney in the National Capital Region. She will represent you against this lawsuit. I will function not only as her associate, but as her voice in conferences, depositions, and trial. If it gets to trial."

Dr. Cho stared at the table. "Can we just settle it? No depositions? No trial?"

Bridget smiled. "That's a liability insurance company's dream, Doc. First thing they want is to settle. They already know how much they can spend on you. They don't want to risk losing more in a trial." She scrunched her eyebrows. "But why not defend yourself?"

The doctor's eyes moistened. "I messed up. That girl should not have died."

Bridget and her associate exchanged glances. Ange leaned toward the doctor. "How about we get all the facts on the table and talk about it before you jump to that conclusion?"

Dr. Cho cast a defeated look between the attorneys. "Won't make a difference."

"Okay, Doc," Bridget said, her voice now stern over the hoarseness. "Here's the deal. I promise I won't walk into your ED and tell you how to practice medicine, okay? Can you show us the same respect? At least let's have the full discussion. After that, it's your call alone on whether to proceed or settle. We'll do whatever you decide, as long as you weigh all the facts and options. Fair?"

Dr. Cho sighed. "Okay."

Bridget cleared her throat, took a swig from the water bottle she always had with her, and nodded to her associate.

Ange tapped the open folder in front of her. "We have the plaintiff's complaint and the medical records in front of us, which you have seen." She closed the folder. "We prefer to hear the story from you, in your own words. However feels most comfortable for you." She leaned toward the doctor. "Take your time, Doc."

Dr. Cho dried her eyes and folded her hands in front of her. "I evaluated Abigail Watson, a fourteen-year-old girl, for a complaint of lower abdominal pain. I discharged her with a diagnosis of constipation. She returned to the ED later that day with a ruptured ectopic pregnancy. The obstetrician on call took her to the OR and removed the ectopic. She died the next day in the ICU from a complication, disseminated intravascular coagulopathy or DIC."

The doctor took a deep breath and shook her head. "I didn't do a pregnancy test or ultrasound in the ED because I thought there was no chance she could be pregnant. I was wrong." A sob. "So she died."

Bridget had heard from Zack Winston about this case soon after it happened. It was one of several obstetrical cases that piqued their suspicion of a shared, sinister cause. She tried not to lead Dr. Cho, but needed her to clarify her thinking when she saw the young girl.

"Why didn't you think she could be pregnant?"

"I thought of it. I mean, you must think of pregnancy in any woman of childbearing age with lower abdominal pain. Her physical exam threw me off. She was virginal. I couldn't imagine her ever having intercourse." Her voice trailed off.

Bridget prodded. "Anything else?"

Dr. Cho rubbed her eyes. "I know Zack discussed this case with you when it happened."

Ange interrupted. "We need your version now, so we can decide how to advise you regarding this malpractice suit."

The doctor nodded. "I understand." She collected herself. "The girl seemed mentally and/or emotionally deficient."

Like many victims of the so-called "Dr. Good," Bridget thought.

She addressed the doctor. "A caretaker brought Ms. Watson to the ED, right? No parents?"

"Right. In retrospect, this was a straightforward case of abuse. The girl was a runaway, controlled and manipulated by evil people. She might have been a victim of that Good House thing." She paused. "Doesn't excuse my negligence in not performing a pregnancy test or ultrasound."

Ange spoke. "You know that Dr. Sebastian Barth, the obstetrician who accused you of negligence, was that same Dr. Good?"

Dr. Cho scowled. "The late Dr. Barth. May he rest in peace, despite his evilness." She cast a worried look at Bridget. "I don't know if my patient, Abigail Watson, was one of his victims."

A light flipped on inside Bridget's head. "We might know someone who can tell us."

Cho raised her eyebrows. "What difference would it make? I messed up. The girl is dead. The rest is…irrelevant."

A knock on the door interrupted. Bridget frowned when her secretary entered the room. She had a strict protocol that no one should disturb her in conference except for a genuine emergency.

"I'm sorry, Bridget," the woman said. "Dr. Winston is on your office line. He's tried your cell phone several times."

Bridget never took her personal phone into a client conference. "What?"

"He needs to talk to you at once. Emergency."

Bridget excused herself and hurried to her office. She worried Zack had bad news about his daughter. She stood beside her desk and picked up the phone. "Zack?"

"Sorry to pull you out of your meeting."

"What, Zack?"

"A guy, a patient, attacked me in the ED."

Bridget felt sudden relief that it was about Zack and not Annie. "What? Are you okay?"

"Sure. Just shaken up."

Relief morphed to annoyance. "Well, I'm glad to hear that."

She paused for him to continue. When he didn't, she spoke up. "Why are you calling, Zack? I wouldn't think you need my sympathy. At least not as an emergency."

His voice cracked. "You may be a target, too."

"What? How?" She rubbed her forehead. "Here? In my office?"

Zack cleared his throat, spoke in a serious but subdued voice. "The guy planned the attack."

Bridget squeezed her eyes. Zack had been uptight for over a month, ever since Dr. Good's co-conspirators almost killed his daughter, then disappeared. He saw villains everywhere.

"How do you know he planned it?"

Zack described how a patient had tried to choke him, but Zack got away and held him off with a scalpel. "We chased the guy out the front door. He got into a waiting car and drove off."

Bridget sat in her desk chair, took a deep breath, and cleared her throat. "That's it? A waiting car?"

A pause. "Uh, yeah."

Bridget wished she had brought her water bottle from the conference room. "Zack, I'm in conference with Ange and Dr. Cho about the malpractice suit against her. I doubt anyone in that room is out to get me. How about I get back to my meeting and we discuss this later?"

Zack huffed through the phone. "Have you forgotten the attack on you in your office parking garage two years ago?"

Bridget bristled. "You damned well know I'll never forget it. You saved my life."

"It could happen again. I might not be there to help you."

Ange appeared on the other side of the glass from Bridget's office. She twirled her finger, then shrugged.

Bridget mouthed, "I'll be right there."

To Zack, she said, "I need to get back to my conference. I promise I won't go to the garage alone, not without talking to you first." She raised an eyebrow. "But please consider whether the Good House conspirators would be so stupid as to attempt an attack on you in the ED in front of your staff and patients. They are too sinister for that." She swallowed.

"Violence in emergency departments has become a national problem. That attack makes more sense as a random act, not a poorly designed and worse executed plot to kill you."

Zack's voice became petulant. "That car was waiting for the assailant."

"Maybe it was his wife, an attorney who needed to get back to her legal practice."

"Ouch."

"Hanging up now, Zack." She clicked off before he could respond.

Bridget returned to the conference room. Dr. Cho sat more erect, less subdued.

Ange nodded toward their client. "She's agreed to consider all her options before giving in to a settlement."

"Great. Let's get to it."

Bridget shivered at the sudden memory of a powerful arm grabbing her from behind as a sharp scalpel blade slid across her neck.

Chapter Fourteen

Near the end of her fourth day at Stone Ridge School of the Sacred Heart in Bethesda, MD, Annie felt scattered, as if the two sides of her personal coin had no relationship with each other. Hard enough trying to get used to a new school. But the flip side, the jagged, disconnected memories of her recent life, made it almost impossible to feel whole. If that was ever possible.

In California, Annie hadn't cared about being a social misfit, but here she craved relationships with kids her own age. Most of the other tenth graders had attended Stone Ridge together at least through middle school, if not from first grade. They had established a solid social hierarchy. Annie had no clue how to break into it. Sometimes when she joined a group of girls chatting, she felt like she was outside the circle watching herself try to fit in. Not a pleasant sight.

At least she had Rocky Duran's friendship, but she was also a relative newbie. They both found the unofficial social codes difficult to ascertain, much less navigate. Rocky seemed better at breaking into those circles, so sometimes Annie just went along as if in tow.

Annie had always attended private schools, a perk for the child of divorced physician parents. But those Southern California schools had all been co-ed, not exclusive for girls like Stone Ridge. Annie had always preferred boys, with the undesired effect she'd confessed to Maria Santos. At least Conner was out of her life forever now.

She smirked at the misconception that Stone Ridge girls, for all their snootiness, had never done it with a boy. Annie had watched them hook up after school. Sometimes one or another would even talk about it, but not in explicit terms. That annoyed Annie.

If she had a choice, she would attend a public high school for a totally different scene. Her mom and dad had joined forces to nix that idea. No chance of persuading them, given the recent complication of her attachment to Conner. A pregnancy that seemed so ancient history now, an absent memory. Almost.

Annie heaved a sigh. So much she didn't remember. What did Sarah even look like? Red hair was all Annie could remember.

"What up, Annie?"

Raquel Duran's voice broke through Annie's reverie. Her friend waved to her from ten feet away.

"What up yourself?" Annie waited for Rocky to join her.

"Wanna hit the JV basketball game?"

Annie squinted. "I, uh, I'm not into sports."

Raquel shrugged. "Me neither, but it's a chance to hang, and the snacks are good. Plus, guys in the crowd."

"I'm supposed to go straight home after school." Annie rolled her eyes and spoke in a sarcastic tone. "Dad's rules. Plus, I have an appointment."

"Doctor Dad a bit of a control freak?"

"Not really. He's just…anxious."

Raquel touched Annie's arm. "After what you and he went through in the Potomac, can you blame him?"

Annie pulled away, put a finger to her lips. "Don't talk about that."

Raquel winced. "I'm sorry. I didn't think it was a secret." She sounded genuine.

"Well, duh. Of course, it is." Annie looked around to make sure no one eavesdropped, then turned to face the other girl. "I don't want the girls here to know about it, okay? I don't need that kind of attention."

"Look, Annie, I'm sorry. I only brought it up because we're friends."

Annie straightened her back. "If you want to be my friend, that stuff has to be between us, no one else."

Raquel smiled. "I'd prefer that."

Annie thought about it. "I'll go with you to the game, but I have to be home by the time Dad's shift ends so he can take me to my appointment." That would be better than walking home alone and being by herself in the apartment until he got home.

"Deal," Rocky said.

"Just make sure I get home on time," Annie said.

She and Rocky stopped by their respective lockers before going to the school gym. They stored their Spanish books and retrieved their cell phones, which were prohibited in the classrooms. When Annie looked at her phone, a voicemail from her dad surprised her. She pointed at the phone, nodded to Raquel, and put the phone to her ear.

"Annie, it's dad. Call me as soon as you get this. Do not go home until you talk to me."

His ominous tone of voice alarmed Annie. She frowned at Raquel. "My dad wants me to call him. I'll be right with you." She stepped away and pressed the speed dial to her dad.

"Annie, are you still at school?"

"Hi yourself, Dad. I'm fine. How are you? And, yes, still at school. Why?"

A brief pause. "Maria had to cancel our appointments today. We'll go tomorrow instead."

Annie's breath quickened. She could stay for the entire game, and maybe do something with Rocky and whoever afterwards.

"You need to stay at school until I can come get you," her dad said.

"What?"

"You heard me."

"Why?"

"Because I said so." A brief pause, and his voice softened. "For good reason."

"You don't get off duty for hours. I can't hang around school that long."

"Dr. Ritchie is relieving me early. I have some things to do before I can leave. I'll let you know when I can be there, but it won't be late." His voice sounded more hopeful than sure. If anything, a note of worry.

"Dad, what's going on?"

"Maybe nothing. Just a precaution. We'll discuss it in person. For right now, I just need you not to walk home alone."

Annie glanced at Raquel, who watched with intense interest. "There's a JV basketball game in the gym. I could go there."

Dad heaved a sigh. "Great idea. Better if someone can go with you."

That seemed odd. "I'm going with Rocky Duran."

"Good."

Annie thought more. "Maybe Raquel can walk home with me after the game."

"No. You don't leave the school until I come get you."

Annie's mind whirred. "Can I go home with her? Then I won't have to hang around here for hours." She emphasized the next word, "Alone."

A long pause from her dad. "Tell you what. You go on to your game with Raquel. I'll call Dr. Duran to see what we can work out."

A sense of actual freedom washed over Annie. "Cool. Thanks, Dad."

"No problem. But let me reiterate. You may not be or go anywhere alone, including home, until I can come get you. Got that?"

Annie thought about her mother's frequent lament, that one of her dad's more annoying traits was how he would beat a topic to death. She smiled. "Got it, dad."

Chapter Fifteen

Dr. Louise Ritchie, the emergency department director and head of their contract group of emergency physicians that staffed the Metro Hospital ED, came from her office to take over Zack's patients.

After his calls to Bridget and Annie, Zack approached his boss as she completed the record on a patient she'd just seen.

"I owe you, ma'am."

"Ditch the 'ma'am' crap, Zack. I'm not your mother, nor your commander. You know I'd rather see patients than shuffle paperwork any day."

"I owe you a future shift, ma'—Louise."

"Yeah, sure. Now let me go sew up that busted lip before it's too late and we need to leave it open for a secondary repair by a plastic surgeon. At no enormous cost to the patient, just an arm and a leg. After that, I'll get to the patients who are waiting."

"I can do the lip lac."

She scoffed. "Can but won't. Talk to the police, then get out of here. Spend time with your daughter, or whoever else you need."

Zack nodded. "Okay. I'll still cover my next shift tomorrow."

Louise smiled. "I'll be the judge of that, Dr. Winston." Without waiting for a reply, she turned and headed to the suture room.

The triage nurse approached Zack. "Dr. Winston, the police are waiting for you in the conference room."

When Zack entered the ED conference room just off the waiting room, he smiled to see Detective Tina Martinez among the three Montgomery County Police personnel sitting at the table. The detective rose, approached Zack, and held out a hand.

"We meet again, Dr. Winston."

Zack shook the woman's hand. "Sorry about the circumstances. It's good to see you, Detective."

Martinez introduced the other two officers. "Dr. Winston has an unfortunate habit of attracting ruffians. Not our first rodeo together." She directed Zack and the others to sit. "I'm told you think the attack was planned?"

He wondered who had informed her. Detectives rarely responded to a simple ED assault—even one involving medical staff. Had Bridget contacted her? He focused on the question. "Yeah. I think it was a set-up."

"Explain."

"First, the guy's laceration didn't match the history. He said it happened while he was cutting meat. I can't feature how you slice the back of your forearm doing that."

The detective and the two officers stared at him. None spoke.

Zack took a breath. "Second, the vehicle waiting for him in the driveway. A getaway car."

"That's it?" Martinez said, skeptical.

"Yeah. After a few decades in this business, I've developed good instincts."

"I can't make an arrest on instinct, Doctor. You know that."

Exasperated, Zack looked at his watch. "I need to get over to Sacred Heart to pick up my daughter."

"Of course," Martinez said. "But can you give us more here? Did anyone see the 'getaway' car's license plate, get a make and model?"

"I don't think so." Zack hung his head. "I didn't think to look at the plates. It was a dark blue SUV."

"That's why you're the doctor and I'm the detective. I assume you have CCTV at your ED entrance?"

Zack let the dig pass, knowing she offered it in jest. "We do. I can call security."

"Never mind. We'll do that." The detective tented her fingers in front of her. "Any other ideas?"

Zack hesitated. "We have the guy's bloodstains on the suture drapes. You could test for DNA, right?"

"We'll collect anything in the room that might be evidence. But we'll need probable cause to run a DNA test. They don't give those out like free candy." She gave him a patronizing smile. "Your opinion about a getaway car does not probable cause make."

Zack let out a heavy breath. "Seriously? Zack pointed to the bruises on his neck. The guy attacked me. Damn near choked me to death. How much more cause do you need?"

Detective Martinez paused for a few seconds. "I don't see those bruises defining premeditation."

Zack glowered.

The detective shrugged. "I hear that spontaneous violence in emergency departments is a growing problem these days."

Et tu, Martinez?

Zack scoffed. "Yeah. I did a presentation on the topic for the local medical society. I know the stats. Two-thirds of emergency physicians reported being assaulted in the last year. One-third of those suffered some injury. Many, like me, missed part of or all their duty shifts."

"Any reason to believe this wasn't a random assault?"

Dammit, Bridget, you did talk to her.

"You're the second person to suggest that since it happened. So, here's an important stat for you. The vast majority of those ED assaults are random. They include verbal abuse, spitting, slaps, kicks, punches. Not a vice-like choking. Not a getaway vehicle."

Martinez backed away. "Sorry. I had to mention it."

Alarmed at his own tone, Zack forced himself to settle down. "Yeah. Of course. Sorry." He glanced at his watch. "Anything else?"

"No. We'll take it from here, interview your staff, collect evidence, and such. We'll let you know if we find anything that might support your impression or justify a DNA analysis."

Zack forced a smile. "Sure."

"Get your daughter, go home, rest."

"Thanks, Detective."

Two minutes later, Louise Ritchie spoke the same words to Zack about daughter, home, and rest. He retired to The Bunker, a room at the back of the ED that functioned as a combined sleep room, office, and refuge for the emergency physicians on shift. Feeling alone and abandoned, he changed from hospital scrubs into jeans, a pullover shirt, and a light tan jacket. He called Dr. Olivia Duran and caught her between surgical cases.

"Of course," she said. "I have a short conscious sedation to do, then I'll pick up the girls at Stone Ridge." She paused. "Annie is welcome to spend the night with us. I can take them both to school tomorrow on my way to the hospital."

Albeit tempted for reasons he didn't want to admit, Zack declined. "Maybe another time. I'll need Annie home tonight. I shouldn't be too late picking her up."

"No problem," the anesthesiologist said. "We'll pick up pizza on the way home. Save you some."

"That sounds good. Thanks, Olivia."

She gave him her address in a high-value neighborhood in north Bethesda.

In the parking lot, Zack started his Lexus, then called Annie.

"Dr. Duran will pick up you and your friend at school. You can hang at their house until I can come get you. I have one other thing I need to do first."

"Cool. Thanks, Dad." Her voice sounded lighter than it had since he'd brought her home from the hospital a little over three weeks ago.

We all crave human contact beyond immediate family.

As Zack backed his car out of its spot, he called Bridget.

"We need to talk. In person. Can we meet some place?"

Chapter Sixteen

BRIDGET FELT BOTH EMBARRASSED and prudent when she asked Ange Moretti to walk with her to the parking garage. She could have asked a male associate, but Bridget refused to play the "fair damsel in danger" game.

"What's going on?" Ange asked as they rode the elevator down to the private executive level of the garage.

Bridget shrugged, tilted her head sideways. "Zack called to warn me that I could be in danger. A patient attacked him the ED today."

Ange huffed. "Well, that's a bit of a leap."

"Yeah. Consistent with his emotional state these days." Bridget paused. "I think. Haven't been around him that much."

As they left the elevator, Ange gave Bridget a sly look. "Why haven't you? Been around him? Seems like now..."

"Nothing."

Duly chastised, Ange did not pursue the subject.

Bridget had lost her husband to murder only a month ago. Of course, she wouldn't rush into Zack's arms, even if she wanted. Did the excuse of a short time interval enable her not to think about what she wanted? Or how she felt about Zack? Or what she didn't want to feel?

As if hitting an invisible wall, both women stopped when they came into view of Bridget's Lexus parked in its usual spot.

Ange spoke first. "We haven't been here together since..."

Bridget turned to her. "I have no memory of you here that night. Just a blurry picture of Zack leaning over me." She stopped and touched Ange's shoulder. "Have I ever thanked you?"

"You thank me every day with your trust and mentorship, and by letting me be your voice. I'm no hero. All I did was call 911, then hold a flashlight for Zack while he saved your life."

Despite two years of counseling, Bridget had only spotty memories of what had happened after a murderous physician named Dennis King seized her from behind when she opened her car door. She touched the scar over her neck where Dr. King had sliced a scalpel across her throat—a sensation she remembered in gross detail.

Bridget would have died on that concrete floor had not Zack and Ange come looking for her. The scar and her permanent hoarseness served as reminders of that trauma, and the daily price she paid for survival—long after Zack killed his former colleague and mentor. Not in revenge, he always said, but in self-defense. Believable enough for the authorities not to charge him with any wrongdoing.

Had Zack killed Dennis King in self-defense, or had it been revenge? Did Bridget now avoid contact with Zack because of his brimming desire for vengeance against the medical conspirators who had almost taken his daughter's life?

"Hello?" Ange's voice brought Bridget back to the now.

"Sorry. Terrible memories here."

"Move your danged parking spot, Bridge. You're a name partner in the firm. You can do that."

Bridget smiled. Typical Ange, pragmatic and direct. "Thank you, counselor. I'll do that first thing tomorrow."

"Never mind. I'll do it for you," Ange said.

Bridget looked around the space, then opened the door to her Lexus. "Hop in. I'll drive you down to your car."

"Unnecessary."

"Yeah, it is. Zack would disown me if anything happened to you, given you all's romantic history."

"That's beyond ancient history, with which I am fine." Ange shrugged, went around to the passenger side, and got into Bridget's vehicle. As she fastened her seatbelt, she gave Bridget a knowing look. "One could do much worse than partner with Zack Winston."

"If one were the right woman, perhaps." Bridget started the vehicle, backed out, and drove two levels down to where Ange had parked her new Hyundai Sonata.

Bridget waited for Ange to get in and start her car, then drove behind her to the garage exit. She stopped there and called Zack. "On my way."

Seemingly from nowhere, a dark blue Cadillac SUV pulled up so close behind her that Bridget thought it might hit her Mercedes. She dumped the phone on the passenger seat, put the car in gear, and drove forward to the street. She stopped, looked, and turned right.

The SUV turned right behind her without stopping. It trailed her to 14th street following too close for any other vehicle to get between them.

Although not a direct route to her meeting with Zack, Bridget made a left on H Street. The SUV turned behind her, still following close. Bridget sped up.

The SUV dropped back, then made a right turn onto Connecticut Avenue.

Bridget let off the accelerator. "Damn it, Zack," she said aloud. "Now you've got me paranoid."

Chapter Seventeen

Zack and Bridget met at a coffee shop midway between the Bethesda Metro Hospital and Bridget's office in Northwest DC. He arrived first and ordered lattes for both of them, then found an isolated booth where he could watch the front door for Bridget's arrival.

Five minutes later, she rushed in, looking harried and tense. She scanned the shop, spotted Zack, and joined him. A forced smile crossed her face as she sat across from him.

"I got you a latte." Zack pushed the coffee toward her.

She pushed it back. "Thanks, but I can't. I haven't been sleeping well, so I'm refraining from caffeine after noon." She tossed her head. "Not that it helps."

"Sorry," Zack said. "Can I get you a decaf or something else?"

She waved him off. "No, thanks. I can't stay long. Dustin stayed out too late last night, so I've grounded him for a while. I need to pick him up from his basketball practice, drop him at home, then get to my hair appointment." She brushed strands of long blond hair out of her eyes.

Zack raised his eyebrows. "A hair appointment at night?"

Bridget grimaced. "My new life as a working single mom. You do your personal stuff when you can." She gazed into the middle distance. "I didn't realize how much Marshall did until after he died."

Zack scoffed. "Yet he found time for an extramarital affair that enabled his murder."

Bridget glowered at him. "Don't be an ass or I'm leaving." She folded her arms and looked away.

"Huh?" Zack said. "It was true." A sudden pang of guilt arose within him. He shook his head, sighed. "You're right. I'm sorry." He reached across the table to touch her hand.

She withdrew the hand, looked him in the eye. "What did you want to talk about, Zack?"

Zack swallowed. "Did you talk to Annie?"

"What? When, or why, would I do that?"

"After the attack on me in the ER, I called her for the same reason I called you. She had almost the same response you did. Almost the same words."

"Smart girl."

Zack looked away, pondering. He took a deep breath, then turned back. "How is it that the two most important women in my life, both of whom nearly died at the hands of criminals, can minimize an ongoing threat that might target all of us?"

"Because we need to get on with life, Zack. Annie made a big jump, moving in with you, thousands of miles away from her mom and older sister, going to a new school, dealing with all that normal teenage angst stuff. Plus, whatever's going on with the after-effects of almost drowning." She gave him a patronizing smile. "And the other emotional trauma."

Bridget's eyes narrowed. "Meanwhile, I'm adjusting to being a widow and single mom to a teenage son who's grieving the loss of his dad." She paused. "Back to Annie. How's the therapy going?"

Zack huffed. "Fine."

"That means…"

"We'll deal with it. Right now, I'm more worried about the immediate threat."

Bridget shook her head. "If we all look for devils around every corner or under every table, it will drive us effing nuts."

"What if the devils are real?"

"We deal with them when we must." She gave him a patronizing smile. "Like you need to deal with Annie's psychological issues."

Zack shook his head. He didn't know what to say, but her silence and penetrating eyes forced a response.

"She sees Dr. Santos three days a week." He paused. "And I have to see her too, in 'parallel' sessions."

Bridget snorted.

"Now who's being an ass, Bridge?"

"Sorry." She reached across and touched his hand, looked him in the eye. "Annie and I aren't the only ones dealing with stuff, you know."

Zack stiffened. He didn't like where the conversation headed. He narrowed his eyes. "What?"

She shook her head, smiled. "You, Zack Winston. You've had your own life threatened, your career, your loved ones." She leaned back. "Not two months ago, you had this grand plan to reunite with your daughters over Christmas, then it all turned to hell. You almost lost Annie."

Bridget leaned forward, gave him a penetrating look. "And you're still not over losing Noelle. How many years ago was it?"

Zack's breathing got heavy. He couldn't talk to Bridget about his dead wife. "What's your point, Bridge?"

"How do you deal with your own issues? Besides projecting onto Annie and me?"

Zack fumed. "You sound like my ex-wife, Natalie the shrink."

Bridget sighed. "I merely suggest that Dr. Santos could be good for you, as well as helping Annie."

Zack glared at her. "When I want medical advice from you, I'll ask for it."

Bridget shook her head. "Look, Zack. I say this because I care. Annie and I both love you, always will. Talking Santos one on one will help you deal with..." She waved her hand. "Your own shit."

Zack looked at his watch. "I have to go get Annie." He stood.

Bridget stood as well, looking at her phone as she did so. "Dustin's wondering where I am."

Zack started toward the exit, but Bridget moved in front of him. She touched his arm. "Let's take a rain check on this discussion. Revisit when we're both less rushed and, uh, tense."

He gave her a blank stare. "Yeah, sure. Thanks."

Bridget turned to leave. Zack followed her out. Before she headed to her car parked on the street, she looked back at him. "You're still my favorite BAFERD, Dr. Winston."

He scoffed. "Yeah. The only one."

She shrugged. "Favorite nonetheless."

Zack watched as Bridget walked the short distance to her Mercedes. He smiled and waved when she got in, then watched as she drove away. In his peripheral vision, he saw a dark blue Cadillac SUV pull out of its space. It seemed to speed up and follow her.

He took a deep breath. His assailant's getaway car?

Lots of dark blue SUVs in this area.

Maybe she was right about him looking for devils everywhere.

Chapter Eighteen

Annie took an immediate shine to Dr. Olivia Duran. Where her dad was often uptight and unsure around Annie, Raquel's mother seemed comfortable and open. Annie trusted her at once.

She had bonded with Raquel in the time they had spent together at the basketball game. They took turns making up funny nicknames for the girls on the team, such as "Ball Hog," "Clueless," and "Never Pass." They also tried to guess which of the few young men in the crowd might be related to or involved with the team members, and which boys might be available. Annie enjoyed the repartee, but had no intention of hooking up with a boy soon.

The game had entered the fourth quarter when Raquel got a text from her mom. She turned to Annie. "Mom's here. Let's go."

"Fine by me," Annie said. "I've seen enough sweat for one night."

Their team was losing by twenty points. "Not enough sweat to do any good," Rocky said. They both laughed.

Raquel sat with Annie in the back seat of the Lincoln Navigator while her mother drove. Annie felt like a chauffeured princess, or a rock star diva. All the while, Mrs. Duran (Annie no longer thought of her as a doctor) talked to her as if she were a new friend. Mrs. Duran learned more about Annie during the short drive to the pizza place than her dad had learned last December. He had taken Annie and her older sister, Jennifer, to dinner after meeting them at the airport two days before Christmas—five years since they'd last seen him. Four days before her world turned black.

They drove south from the school, past the Walter Reed Military Medical Center and the National Institutes of Health, to a strip mall with a storefront restaurant called Cheesy Pizzi.

"It's out of our way," Mrs. Duran said. "But worth it." She opened her door. "Come on. You girls can choose what you want."

A fantastic savory aroma struck them when they entered the restaurant. Thrilled to be there, with her new friend and a mom who enchanted her, Annie Winston decided on the spot that she was no longer vegan.

They ordered three different varieties, a Quatro Formaggio, Meatzza, and Mediterranean. Annie learned that Mrs. Duran was a vegetarian. They also got appetizers of fried calamari, chicken nuggets, and "Borek," phyllo dough wrapped with mixed cheese. It all looked and smelled wonderful.

Eager with anticipation for a meal so unlike any she'd had with her dad, Annie took the bag of appetizers from the counter and followed Rocky and her mother to the front door.

All at once, she froze in place.

A group of three boisterous young men had just entered the restaurant. One guy, who sported dark shoulder-length hair and a full beard, stopped and gazed at her with penetrating eyes.

Annie broke into a sweat, even as an icy shiver ran up her spine and her heart froze. Her lips and fingers went numb. A wave of dizziness converted the restaurant's delightful aroma into a nauseating stench. Annie quivered all over and almost dropped the bag of appetizers onto the floor. In the next instant, she wanted to flee. Her feet would not move. As if she no longer had control of her body.

The guy approached her. Annie hyperventilated.

He looked at her face and tilted his head. "Do I know you?"

Rocky and her mother had stopped at the door and now flanked Annie on either side.

Annie struggled to find her voice. "I don't... I don't think so." The boy looked somewhat familiar, but who could he be? She swallowed hard, forced herself to speak. "Sorry. You must be thinking of someone else." She moved away from him.

Mrs. Duran touched Annie's arm. "Are you okay, Annie?"

The boy looked at Mrs. Duran, then back at Annie. Then he turned away and joined his friends at the takeout counter.

Annie took several deep breaths. "I'm okay." She slowed her breathing. "That guy thought he knew me."

Mrs. Duran pressed. "You seemed upset."

Annie shook her head. "I'm..." She couldn't finish.

Mrs. Duran took Annie's arm and guided her to the door. "We need to get home before the pizza gets cold, or your dad gets there ahead of us."

"What a jerk," Raquel said when Annie got into the car.

Annie hoped the darkness in the car hid her florid blush. "Yeah."

Mrs. Duran huffed, put the car in reverse, and backed away from the pizza place.

Annie spotted the boy watching them through the window. Another shiver ran up her spine.

Chapter Nineteen

During the short drive from Cheesy Pizzi to the Durans' house, Annie clutched the bag of appetizers on her lap while Raquel chatted with her mother about the latest gossip from Stone Ridge. Annie couldn't get the thought of that boy out of her mind. Why did he scare her? Where, and when, did she know him? For sure not in California. Had to be since she came to visit her dad just before Christmas. But where?

Mrs. Duran turned the car into the driveway of an upscale sprawling home on a cul-de-sac with similar manses on either side. As soon as the car stopped, Rocky opened the door and got out, pizza boxes in hand.

"C'mon, Annie," she said. "Get a move on. I'm dying for some of that calamari."

"Manners, Raquel," Mrs. Duran said to her daughter.

Annie clutched the bag of appetizers and followed her new friend into the house. She left the strange boy dilemma back in the vehicle.

While they dove into appetizers and pizza, Annie learned more about the Duran family. Rocky was the oldest of three siblings. Her younger brothers, ages twelve and thirteen, attended St. Jane de Chantal middle school where, unlike Raquel, they excelled in athletics. Dr. Duran was a single mother whose husband had died in combat in Iraq.

Annie's dad arrived just as the girls finished their meals. He looked distraught and rushed. Mrs. Duran greeted him and offered the one remaining slice of pizza. He took one bite and chewed it, seemingly without tasting it, as he thanked Mrs. Duran for keeping Annie until he could get there.

He turned to Annie. "Time to go, Annie."

"Dad, we were going to watch a movie."

"You'll have to catch it later. We need to get home."

Annie scowled. "Why? What are we going to do at home?"

Before he could respond, Mrs. Duran touched his arm. "Can I talk to you? In the kitchen?"

Looking puzzled, he followed her.

They were gone only a short time. When they returned, Dad spoke to Annie in a bearish voice. "Okay, Annie. Get your things and let's go."

Annie huffed. She stood, thanked Rocky and her mom, ignored the two boys, and followed her dad toward the door. Raquel whispered something to her mom, after which Mrs. Duran came up to Annie and her dad.

"Rocky would like to invite Annie for a sleepover tomorrow night. Some of the other girls from school will join. A chance for Annie to meet other kids."

Dad pursed his lips. "I don't know…"

"Please, Dad. Don't you work in the ER this weekend?"

Dad rubbed his eyes. "Yeah. Night shifts." He looked off into the distance, seeming to ponder what Annie felt was a no-brainer.

He spoke to Mrs. Duran. "What would they do?"

Mrs. Duran chuckled. "Same things teenage girls have done at sleepovers for centuries. Talk a lot. Mostly about boys. Giggle a lot, about boys. Eat a lot. Figure out which boys they like."

Dad took a deep breath. "I don't know…"

Annie pouted. "Seriously, Dad?"

Mrs. Duran gave him a conspiratorial smile. "Don't worry. I'll be here the whole time. No one's getting into any trouble."

Another deep breath before Dad gave in. "Okay. Just let me know when to bring her."

"Anytime will be fine. If you're working nights and need to bring her early so you can get some sleep before you go on shift, that would be okay."

Dad nodded. "Thanks. We'll do that."

"We can nail down the details tomorrow," Mrs. Duran said.

Dad still looked troubled. "Okay." He turned to Annie. "We really must go, Annie. I need to talk to you."

Mrs. Duran gave him a puzzled look.

Dad smiled. "Tomorrow night it is. And thanks."

"It's what parents do. It takes a village, especially with teens. You can return the favor some future day."

"No doubt," Dad said. He hustled Annie out the door.

Annie confronted her dad as soon as they drove away from the Duran home. "What's going on, Dad?"

"It can wait till we get home."

"No, it can't. You acted strange in there. You've acted strange since you called me. Is it about me?"

"Not entirely."

"Is it about Bridget? Is she okay?"

Dad gave her a puzzled look. "It's not about her. She's fine."

"What, then?"

He drove in silence for a long block. "A patient assaulted me in the ED today." He glanced at her. "I'm okay. It was just such a surprise."

"What do you mean, 'assaulted'?"

Dad blew out a breath. He'd done that a lot since he arrived at the Durans. "Tried to choke me."

"Choke?"

"Yeah. A pair of powerful hands around my neck."

"Are you okay?"

He turned down the collar of his shirt. The purple bruises startled Annie.

"Why would a patient do that?"

"It seemed deliberate. Like he'd planned it." He pulled the car into the parking garage under their apartment building. "We can continue this in the apartment." He parked the car in its usual place. "Don't get out yet."

Annie gave him a puzzled look. "What?"

"Just stay where you are." He got out of the car, stood, and gazed all around the garage. He waited a few seconds, then came around the car and opened the door for Annie.

"Dad, you're scaring me."

He looked all around again. "Let's get inside."

***

Zack and Annie got off the elevator on the floor to their apartment. He followed her down the hall. What to do? How much to tell her? Wait for Maria Santos to draw out those details from her? Followed by how many months, or years, of psychotherapy to deal with her memories? At what personal cost to her?

They had not talked about what happened since he had brought Annie home from the hospital to his apartment, both choosing avoidance over frankness. How much could she bear to know now? How much did she deserve to know?

If it were me? Everything.

Now settled into the safe environment of their apartment, Zack and Annie sat together on the couch, each with a mug of chai. He had never drunk chai until Annie came to live with him. One of many ways his life had changed; for the better. He glanced at her, his mind a jumble of mixed thoughts and emotions. Maybe now was not the right time for this conversation.

Was there ever a "right" time?

Straight in, no waiting.

"Annie, how much do you remember about what happened to you in December?"

Her face flushed, and she leaned away from him. "Is that why you wanted to talk to me?"

Zack shrugged. "Not directly, but it's related."

She scrunched her forehead. "That tells me nothing."

He took a deep breath. "Okay. Maybe talking about what happened will help you understand why I'm doing the things now that I need to do to keep you safe." He paused. "To keep us all safe."

Annie stared straight ahead, her breathing quickened and heavy, lips pursed. Then she turned to him.

"Maria said…"

Zack blinked. He recalled Maria's admonition to be supportive, to help Annie feel safe with her memories. If her office could be Annie's safe place, couldn't this apartment that she shared with her father be another one?

"Annie, I'm not asking you to divulge anything you've told Maria Santos."

Her breathing quickened. She hugged herself, elbows pressing into her sides. As if trying to make herself small.

"I don't want to do this right now, Dad."

Zack pulled himself back from the cliff that he'd almost forced both of them over.

"Okay," he said. He placed his hand on hers. "Just know that I'm always here to talk. About anything. Whenever you're comfortable."

Another thought caused him to wince. He swallowed hard. "Your mother is also there for you. Call her, or Facetime her whenever you want." A difficult pause. "I'll give you all the privacy you need for that."

Annie squeezed his hand, then turned and hugged him with palpable relief. "Thanks, Dad." She looked at him. "I love you."

"I love you too, Annie. More than anything."

They sat together in silence for a few minutes before Annie, now relaxed, spoke. "What did you and Mrs. Duran talk about in the kitchen?"

Zack weighed how much to tell her about his own fears. He turned to face her. "Mrs. Duran told me you saw a boy at the pizza place that set off a panic attack."

Annie shivered. "He looked at me like he knew me."

"Did you recognize him?"

She shook her head. "It was weird, Dad. Like I should have known him, but..." She shrugged. "I had no clue who he was."

Zack had a pretty good idea who it might have been, but he couldn't tell her. If correct, all the more reason to consider them in danger. He had to warn her.

"People involved in The Good House conspiracy may have had a hand in the attack on me today. I worried someone might come after you or Bridget. That's why I called you."

"Did you call Bridget too?"

"I did. She's not convinced."

"Smart lady."

***

Annie thought her dad had overreacted to what happened to him in the ER today. Apparently, Bridget thought so too. Annie would trust Bridget's judgment on that one.

Exhausted from their talk, Annie told her dad she needed to get to bed. She was excited about spending the next day and night with Raquel. Dad's anxiety was his problem, not hers, although she promised to comply, within reason, with his need to protect her.

In the privacy of her bedroom, she called her mom and reported on the day's events. She ended by describing what had happened to her dad, and his worry about it. She didn't mention Bridget.

"I understand," Mom said. "But I wouldn't totally dismiss your dad's concerns." She paused, as if pondering what to say next. "You underwent serious emotional trauma,

Annie. Not to mention the physical component. The people who did that may still be around." Annie could almost picture Mom biting her tongue. "One reason I thought you might be safer back here."

"Geez, Mom. Can you just let that go?"

"Okay," Mom said. "But promise you won't totally dismiss your dad's concerns. He can be short-fused and kind of knee-jerk at times, but he's a good man, a competent emergency physician, and he loves you. He's only looking out for you, which is what I would do."

"Got it, Mom."

"Do you mind if I call him and get the scoop straight from him?"

Annie furrowed her brow. "Of course. You can call him anytime. You don't need my permission."

"Okay," Mom said. "One other thing. May I suggest you mention this to Maria next time you see her?"

Annie scoffed. "You can suggest all you want, Mom. What Maria and I talk about is between us. You know that."

"Yeah, sorry. Can't help being a mom sometimes."

They exchanged statements of love, then hung up. A minute later, Annie heard her dad's phone ring.

She had changed into her nightwear and gotten into bed, scrolling Snapchat and TikTok hoping to settle down for sleep. She'd had enough drama for one night.

The sudden buzz on her phone startled her.

No caller ID.

She hesitated, then answered. "Hello?"

"Hello, Annie Winston from California." The male voice sounded familiar, but she couldn't place it.

"Who is this?"

"You don't remember?"

"I don't play games. Tell me who you are and how you know who I am in the next ten seconds or I'll hang up."

A dark laugh. "Wow. You really don't remember." A pause. "It's Tyler."

An electric shock ran up Annie's spine. Her breathing quickened and her skin felt clammy as the memory crashed into her consciousness. Tyler, the boy she'd met in December. The boy she'd liked. The boy who... Did what?

Despite the beard and long hair, she had known him in the pizza place. Had recognized his voice, just as she did now over the phone. What was happening? She recalled her dad's admonition about "The Good House conspiracy," and her mom's subtle agreement.

She played along. "Uh, yeah. Of course I remember."

A pause before he spoke again. "Guess you're not vegan anymore, based on what you carried out of Cheesy Pizzi."

Definitely the Tyler she'd known in December.

Annie feigned a gasp. "Wait. That was you?" She rubbed her forehead, labored to control her breathing. "You looked, uh, different. Long hair, scraggly beard, and all. You going for the homeless look?"

"Says you. What happened to all your Goth shit? That's why I didn't totally recognize you. You've changed your style."

How much to tell him? She felt uneasy. "Had to. School rules."

"School?"

"Yeah. I, uh, live here with my dad. I go to Stone Ridge."

"Wow. You never went back to California?"

"So, uh, yeah. I was in the hospital. For a while, I guess. When I got out, I wanted to stay here and live with my dad." Was she revealing too much? "I never really knew him as a kid."

"Oh, yeah. I remember we talked once about being children of broken marriages."

Annie remembered talking about that at the Georgetown pizzeria where she first met Tyler. She had gone there before Christmas with her sister and Bridget's stepson. Tyler had showed up and sat next to her. Cast himself as a fellow sufferer among a gathering of "preppy" older kids.

A shadowy memory emerged. "So, uh, did we meet up another time? A Starbucks?"

"We did. In Bethesda. You played hooky from your dad and sister. We kinda fooled around a little, but you almost got caught. I saved your ass getting you back to your dad's place just in time."

Annie pursed her lips. "Yeah, I remember that now."

Had there been another time? Another Starbucks? "Was that the only time?"

Tyler paused. "Uh, yeah. Never saw you again. Figured you ditched me."

Annie ran her fingers through her hair. "I don't remember. There was some sort of accident, and I ended up in the hospital. It's all a blur."

"Probably better you don't remember. Trauma and all."

An uncomfortable silence descended.

Tyler broke it. "Look, I gotta go catch up with some friends."

"Okay."

"Nice talking to you again, Annie from California. Maybe we can meet up sometime. Pick up where we left off, you know."

Annie sighed. "I don't know. There's a lot of stuff going on in my life. I wouldn't be good company. Besides, my dad . . ."

"Overprotective?"

"Yeah."

"Typical doctor."

He knows dad's a doctor? Did it come up in a conversation I don't remember?

"Tell you what," Tyler said. "You have my number now. Just call or text me if you want to hook up sometime. Your choice."

"Yeah. Okay."

"Good. I hope you do that. Gotta go. Nice talking to you again, Annie."

A new memory shot through her mind. "Wait. Do you, uh, know a guy goes by the name of Roach?"

He took in a breath. "No. Don't know anyone by that name. Sorry."

"Okay. It was just a weird, uh, memory. We'll see about hooking up."

"I'd like that. Gotta go now. Bye."

"Bye."

Annie set the phone on her bed. An unwelcome shiver coursed through her body.

Chapter Twenty

ZACK HAD HUNG UP from Natalie's phone call with a sense of semi-vindication. At least she had not dismissed his concerns like Bridget and Annie had. He could have done without her not-so-veiled threat of retaliation if anything happened to Annie. She had made that clear earlier, and Zack didn't need the added anxiety.

He tried to go to bed, but the events of the day buzzed around his mind like pesky flies, never contiguous like a well-plotted story, but random like the meanderings of a disheveled mind.

The genuine nature of Zack Winston's mind?

The vise-like hands of the assailant around his neck, the altercation with Bridget, Annie's situation, the unexpected phone call from Natalie, Zack's assailant running through the ED waiting room, Annie's planned sleepover at the Durans, Bridget's skepticism, Annie's memory loss and apparent panic attack, Louise Ritchie's empathy, the attacker getting away in a waiting car, Bridget telling Zack he needed to get therapy...all in one cacophonous swarm in Zack's brain.

He thought about taking an Ambien, which he sometimes did to aid transitions from night shift to day shift and back again. A glance at the clock stopped him. Almost midnight. Had he tossed and turned that long? Probably he'd dozed in brief spurts. Too late now to medicate. It would leave him groggy when he had to be sharp during the day. He needed to be up in time to get Annie to school—after getting her packed up for the overnighter at the Duran's. He could rest later, before going into the ED for his night shift.

The sound of Annie's bedroom door opening surprised him. Still up? A few minutes later, it closed again. Maybe she had just needed a drink or the bathroom.

Zack went to his own bathroom, then ambled out to the kitchen. He thought he heard Annie talking on the phone. She'd already talked to her mother. Maybe she'd called her sister, a medical student at Stanford. He poured himself a small glass of milk, downed it in a single swig, then returned to his bedroom.

The light under Annie's door flicked off.

Must have been a quick conversation with whomever.

Zack awakened to his phone buzzing. The milk had worked better than the drug would have because it took a minute to orient himself to place and time.

Six AM.

Who would call that early? Caller ID showed "Restricted."

"Damn telemarketer." He hit the "End" button and rolled onto his side, pulling the covers over himself.

The phone buzzed again. "Restricted" caller ID.

Zack rejected the call.

Before he could resume his position in bed, it buzzed again. "Restricted."

Damn!

He hit the *Answer* button. "Who the hell?"

He recognized her voice at once. "Why, Zack, such a terrible thing to say to me. After everything we had together."

"What the hell, Sarah?" He sat up in bed and shook his head to clear the remaining fog from his mind.

Her voice cooed. "Did you think I'd gone for good?"

Zack flipped on his bedside lamp and glared at the phone. There must be a way to trace the call.

As if she'd seen him do it, Sarah chided. "You can't trace a restricted number, Zack."

Zack's anger exploded. "Why the hell are you calling me? I have nothing to say to you. Except I hope you rot in hell for what you did to my daughter."

"Tsk, tsk, tsk. I see your anger management hasn't improved. So sad."

"This is bullshit. Why did you call me, Sarah?"

She blew a raspy breath into the phone. "Just to hear your voice again, sweetheart. I miss you."

Zack could only manage shallow, irregular breaths.

"Ooh, are you stroking yourself, Zack? That so turns me on."

A brief flash of red-headed, freckled Sarah naked on his bed invaded Zack's memory. He squashed it like an intruding spider. "Shut up, whore!"

She moaned. "Oh, my God, Zack, keep it up. You are so hot when you talk dirty. You're making me come."

"Go to hell."

Zack hit the "End" button and threw the phone onto the bed.

A soft knock on his door. Annie's voice. "Dad? Are you okay?"

He got up and spoke through the door. "Yes, I'm, uh, fine. I just had a nightmare." He cracked open the door.

She looked at him, eyes soft. "I'm sorry. Can I do anything for you?"

The irony struck Zack between the eyes. The daughter assuaging the father's angst. He settled himself.

"Give me a second," he said. He put on a robe, then let Annie into the room. They sat on the edge of the bed, a few feet apart.

"I won't lie to you, Annie. That was Sarah."

"Sarah?"

"Yes. She taunted me. I don't know why she called. Or from where."

"Sick woman. Scary woman."

Zack put an arm around his daughter. "I'm sorry I woke you. Sorry to worry you."

Annie rested her head on his shoulder. "I, uh, got a phone call too."

Zack startled. "From?"

"Tyler."

Zack jerked away, regarded her at arm's length. "Tyler Rhodes?"

A look of recognition crossed her face. "I'd forgotten his last name. Yes, that Tyler."

Annie told him about the unexpected call, and that she had seen Tyler in the pizza place but didn't realize it was him until after he called her.

Tyler? And Sarah? What the hell?

He affected a casual attitude, hoping she did not sense his alarm.

She did sense it. "What's going on, Dad?"

"I don't know."

Zack wondered how safe Annie would be at the Durans.

Safer than alone in this apartment.

Maybe she should stay with Bridget instead. No, Bridget had made the fullness of her current life clear. She didn't need extra responsibility.

Zack needed to minimize his concerns, for Annie's sake.

"We should just ignore them." Zack made a mental note to change his phone number and Annie's. "I'll make some coffee and start breakfast. You can get ready for school and your big sleepover with Raquel and...whoever."

She hugged him. "Thanks, Dad. I was worried you wouldn't let me go after..."

Zack took a deep breath. "We need to live our lives, Annie."

As soon as Annie left his room, Zack got a text message from a "Restricted" number.

You should have been nicer to my amigo in the ER yesterday.

Chapter Twenty-One

Zack and Annie talked little during breakfast, both preoccupied with their own thoughts. While they cleared the dishes, she stopped and looked at him. "Dad, it seems too coincidental that you and I heard from Tyler and Sarah like that."

Zack had thought of little else. "It does seem odd."

A vision of crab-like pincers encircling them both caused Zack to shudder.

"Dad, you okay?"

"Yeah." He looked her in the eye. "I am a little freaked out about it all, especially after that guy attacked me in the ED yesterday." He didn't tell Annie about Sarah's text message that mention her *amigo* in the ER the previous day.

"Are you telling me everything, Dad?"

"What do you mean?"

"Would you keep something from me, you know, so as not to 'worry' me?"

Zack touched her shoulder. "No. Annie. I promise, I will always be honest with you. I was just getting to know you, then I almost lost you. I'll never betray your trust. You are too precious to me."

She hugged him. "Thanks. I needed that."

"Okay," he said. "Now go ramp up to be a teenager for the weekend."

She pecked him on the cheek and hurried to her room.

He finished loading the dishwasher. When he heard Annie's shower running, he dialed the number for the Montgomery County Police Department.

A man's burly voice answered. "MCPD, Officer Ralston."

"Detective Tina Martinez, please. This is Dr. Zack Winston."

"Detective Martinez is off today. If it's urgent, I can direct you to another detective."

Zack paused. "Uh, won't be necessary. Just ask her to call me when she's back on duty."

"Okay. Is this regarding a particular case?"

Zack didn't know how to answer.

"Still there, Doctor?"

"Uh, yeah. Sorry. I got a strange phone call earlier that may relate to The Good House case, but I'm not sure."

"I'll punch you through to the detective on duty and you two can sort it out."

Seconds later, Zack spoke to a Lieutenant Kvaska, who recognized Zack's name and seemed familiar with The Good House case. Zack told him about Sarah's call and Tyler's interaction with Annie. He also mentioned the attack on him in the ED.

"Glad you called, Doc. We have ways to trace those restricted numbers. Tina will want to know about it. I'll get in touch with her and see if she can contact you direct. Meanwhile, can you bring your phone to the headquarters? We can start on that trace."

There goes my nap.

"Sure. I have to take my daughter to school, then I'll head over to your shop."

"Good. I'll see if can get in touch with Detective Martinez."

In the car, Zack told Annie about the second text from Sarah, his conversation with the MCPD, and his intention to follow up as requested.

"That's everything," he said. "Nothing left out."

"Thanks, Dad. I'm glad you contacted the police."

"You don't think I'm overreacting?"

She huffed. "Are you kidding? Especially after I talked to Mom. We can't be too careful."

Zack let his annoyance at her mention of Natalie roll past. He gave her a serious look. "Let me know if you run into Tyler again."

"Way ahead of you, Dad. Will do."

"I mean immediately."

"I know."

They pulled into the driveway. Rocky Duran stood on the curb, waiting for Annie. "Now go have fun. Be a teenager," Zack said. He leaned over and pecked her cheek.

She made an immediate ugly face and wiped her cheek. "Ew. Not in public, Dad. Please."

He blushed. "Got it. Sorry. Have fun. Call me if you need anything."

"Sure."

Then she was out of the car and ran up to where Raquel waited for her.

Zack waved and drove away.

He felt all at once very much alone.

Chapter Twenty-Two

Now a month after her unfaithful husband's death by poisoning, Bridget cherished sleeping alone in the king-size bed. She awakened sprawled naked diagonally across the mattress; the covers tossed aside during the night. She looked at her watch. 9:30 AM.

Finally, a more restful night.

Perhaps foregoing her nightly single-malt scotch nightcap had helped.

She remembered Dustin had a rare Friday off from school. He would still be in bed. Bridget sat up, yawned, and stretched. A long shower would prepare her for the last workday before what promised to be a restful weekend. A rarity in her life, as much after as before Marshall's untimely demise.

An unusual noise, like someone sneaking around on the first floor, alarmed her. An intruder?

She thought about Marshall's pistol in the bedside drawer next to her head. "Home protection," he had called it.

Bridget loathed the thing. It had been a serious bone of contention in their marriage. She opposed the need for "home protection" in their upscale Alexandria neighborhood. Any neighborhood. Any time.

Early in their marriage, she had given in to Marshall's insistence that she get firearms training. One time. Her accuracy in hitting a human-shaped target had surprised her husband and disgusted Bridget. She refused to go back.

But what if there was an intruder downstairs?

I'd rather hide in the closet than pick up that murder piece.

She lay still and listened for more sounds. Nothing.

Then Dustin's voice calling up the stairs. "You up yet, Mom. I'm fixing breakfast."

That had been the sound she'd heard.

The chance of a frightened mother mistaking her son for an intruder and killing him did not seem far-fetched. She promised herself to get rid of Marshall's weapon first chance she got.

Bridget took advantage of a moderation in the January weather to go for a long run, a cherished and missed ritual. Her triathlon training had fallen by the wayside since her family life exploded over Christmas.

An hour later, Bridget entered her kitchen after the run and drained the last quaff from her water bottle. She lifted the half-full carafe of French Roast and poured it into her souvenir Harvard Law School mug, complete with logo showing the Latin word for truth, *veritas*, on the crest.

Truth had been her quest ever since she flipped the tassel on her graduation cap now many years ago.

Bridget intended to savor the coffee while cooling down from the run. Then she would shower and relish the rest of her free day.

Her phone buzzed. Caller ID showed "Zack Winston."

Bridget reached for the phone, then stopped. Why risk his current chaotic emotional state upsetting her pleasant mood?

Because Zack.

"Hey, Zack."

"Hi, Bridge. First, I'm sorry about yesterday. I was a jerk. It's just that…"

She interrupted. "Apology accepted. Justification neither needed nor wanted. What's up?"

In the silence that followed, she wondered if her words had sounded as dismissive to him as they had to her.

He gulped. "You're right. Sorry."

"One more 'sorry' and I'm hanging up."

"Uh, yeah, sor— I mean, how are you?"

"I'm pretty damned great this morning. Just got back from a long run. Cooling down before I shower and head into the office."

"Good for you. Wish I could say the same."

Bridget raised her eyebrows. She should have expected this. "What's wrong, Zack?"

"Some things I must share with you, because you need to know."

"Not another ER attack, I hope."

"No." He chuckled. "Not yet. I'm working nights this weekend, so anything could happen."

Bridget wondered how alternating day and night shifts affected an emergency physician's circadian rhythm, or mental health. "Shouldn't you be sleeping?"

"Yeah, but I had to drop Annie off for a sleepover, and now I'm on my way to Montgomery County PD."

"Why are you going there?"

"Some weird events since our talk yesterday." He described how his daughter, Annie, had run into Tyler Rhodes the evening before; and a disturbing phone call he'd received from Sarah O'Brien that morning.

Bridget sat down at the table and took a sip of coffee to keep her response under control. "Sarah called you? You sure it was her?"

"No doubt. Her voice, and some of the personal things she said... Had to be her."

Bridget wondered what "personal" things Zack's wicked ex-girlfriend had shared, but chose not to ask.

"What do you make of it, Zack?"

"No friggin' clue, Bridge. You got any?"

Bridget thought for a minute. "Seems too coincidental after what happened to you in the ED yesterday." She paused. "I may have been too cavalier brushing it off when you called me."

"Thanks for saying that." A pause. "I got a strange text right after I hung up on Sarah. Another restricted number. I assumed it was Sarah. Something about I should have been nicer to her '*amigo*' in the ER yesterday."

Bridget pursed her lips. "It said '*amigo*,' Spanish for friend?"

"Yeah. The guy who attacked me was Latino, used the name 'Gonzales.'"

So much for an uneventful day.

"What do you need from me, Zack?"

"Most of all, your brain. Any clue what might be happening?"

"Thinking cap on, but no clue."

His silence lasted too long for comfort.

"Anything else, Zack?"

"I don't suppose you'd have time to meet me at the MCPD headquarters? We could talk to the detectives together. Two heads and all."

Bridget sighed. "In truth, I have a slack schedule at the office, so, yeah. But I need to take a shower first. What's the address?"

Dustin came down the stairs just as Bridget, showered and dressed, was putting on her coat to go meet Zack.

"Have a good day, Mom." He stopped, tilted his head, and frowned. "You're going to your office, right?"

Bridget sighed. Busted. "I have to meet Dr. Winston. Work thing."

Dustin raised his eyebrows. "Work? For real?" He folded his arms, took a haughty stance.

Like his father used to do.

Bridget set down her coat. "What are you saying, son?"

He gave her a dismissive wave. "Nothing."

"I'm not buying 'nothing.' What?"

Dustin went into the kitchen and studied the contents of the refrigerator. Bridget followed. "What?"

He extracted a carton of milk and turned to face her. "I'm not some witness you can cross-examine, Mom."

Bridget folded her arms. "No. You are my son. As your mother, I sense something troubling you. Out with it before it grows into something bigger than it needs to be."

Dustin replaced the milk carton in the refrigerator before he turned back to Bridget.

"You and Dr. Winston had a thing while dad was still alive."

Bridget blinked. "That's not true."

"I saw you two sitting close on the couch. And that going out running together BS. In the middle of winter?"

Bridget took a deep breath. "Dustin, I swear to you, Dr. Winston and I are associates and friends, nothing more. Have you forgotten how much he helped us when dad was in the hospital?"

Dustin scoffed. "Good excuse to be around you."

Her anger flared. "That is enough. He helped us make hard decisions. I don't know where this is coming from, but it's not true. There is nothing between Zack... Dr. Winston... and me."

Doth this lady protest too much?

Bridget moved closer to her son. "Look, it's been hard for you, for both of us, since dad died. We need to move on. I swear to you that, for me, it doesn't mean taking up with Dr. Winston."

Dustin scooped up a spoonful of cereal, chewed and swallowed, then smiled. "Okay, Mom. I believe you."

"Really, or are you just trying to shut me up?"

"No, I believe you. I know you and dad weren't getting along, but I don't hold it against you, or him; and not Dr. Winston, either." Tears came to his eyes. "I just miss my dad, okay?"

Bridget hugged him. "I know. I miss him too."

More than I ever imagined I'd miss the cheating SOB.

She broke the embrace and held Dustin at arm's length. "Full disclosure. I'm meeting Dr. Winston at the Montgomery County Police Department. A follow-up from what happened in December."

"Okay."

A thought occurred to her. "Dustin, have you heard or seen anything of Tyler Rhodes lately?"

He thought for a few seconds, then shook his head. "No. Not since he disappeared after he showed up at the hospital when Annie Winston was in the ICU."

"Okay. If you hear or see anything, let me know, okay?"

"Why? Is he back?"

"Annie thinks she saw him last night. Then he called her."

Dustin scrunched his eyebrows. "Strange. Yeah, I'll let you know."

Bridget donned her coat. "I have to go now. If you don't have any plans this evening, maybe we can watch a movie together."

"I'd like that." He hugged her. "Thanks, Mom."

Bridget took her Range Rover keys from the hook by the door and entered the garage. She stopped and looked at Marshall's cherished cherry red Mercedes SL 450 convertible. It had not moved since he parked it there after coming home from his fatal tryst with Fiona Delaney in Richmond. He would have spent his first free day cleaning off the dust and road scum, then polishing it to its original showroom sheen.

If only he'd been so compulsive about preserving our marriage.

Bridget opened the door to her trusty old Range Rover squeezed into the space next to Marshall's prized vehicle. Her hand stopped just before inserting the key into the ignition.

"Screw him."

She went back into the house, hung up the Rover keys, and grabbed Marshall's Benz keys. She pushed the remote to open the garage door, got into the 450 SEL, drove it out of the garage, and went on her way to meet Zack.

When she merged onto I-395 north, she opened up the throttle and moved into the fast lane. The G-force pressing her back and rump into the bucket seat exhilarated her. Bridget chuckled.

Dustin had just become the Range Rover's primary driver.

Chapter Twenty-Three

WHEN ZACK AND BRIDGET walked into the Montgomery Police Department, the duty officer escorted them to a private conference room.

"Detective Martinez is on her way. She should be here soon." The officer gestured for them to sit. "Can I get you anything to drink?"

"Coffee would be good," Bridget said.

"You, sir?"

Zack declined. He still hoped to get some sleep later in the day before going on the night shift. Then he gave in. "Sure," he said, "I would like some coffee." It would not be the first time, nor the last, that Zack showed up unrested for a night shift. This phenomenon often happened on transition from days to nights. Even a veteran BAFERD could not command his circadian rhythm to switch gears on demand.

He and Bridget sat and sipped their coffee in uncomfortable silence. They needed to talk, but not now, not here. Martinez might come through the door at the most delicate point in their conversation. Zack sensed Bridget felt the same, or maybe she didn't feel the need. Her change of mood and attitude from the previous day had jolted him.

How do women do that?

A few minutes later, Detective Martinez entered the room. She wore casual clothes, not her usual business suit. The detective did a slight double-take when she saw Bridget, then greeted Zack first.

"Thanks for coming, Doc." She turned to Bridget. "I didn't expect you, Ms. Larsen."

"I asked her to join," Zack said. "Two heads and all."

Martinez gave him a blank look. "Sure. No problem." To Bridget, "Welcome."

The detective sat across from them and addressed Zack. "I understand you heard from Sarah O'Brien. And your daughter from Tyler Rhodes?"

"Right," Zack said. He looked at Bridget.

"My son told me he's not had any contact with Tyler since last month," she said.

Martinez held a hand toward Zack. "You brought your phone?"

"As directed." Zack handed her the phone.

She stood. "I'll be right back. I want to get the techs started on this."

Zack and Bridget drank the last of their coffees in silence while the detective was out of the room.

When Martinez re-entered the room, FBI agent Tony Mason accompanied her. He wore jeans and a sweatshirt. Bridget did a slight startle reaction, apparently recognizing him. Both Zack and Bridget stood.

Martinez said, "I believe you all know each other."

"Indeed," the agent said. "How are you, Doctor, Ms. Larsen?"

"Good, thank you," Bridget said.

"Fine," Zack said.

As Detective Martinez motioned everyone to the table, Zack gave Bridget a quizzical look.

"Mr. Mason and I met briefly in the hospital," Bridget said. "When you were in the ICU. We heard Tyler Rhodes' confession."

Zack nodded. FBI and Homeland Security agents had been present when Tyler Rhodes confessed his alternate role as "Roach," the nefarious factotum at The Good House. He had described Annie's abduction and escape, and his own flight from the perpetrators. Zack wondered why Detective Martinez had called him in.

As if she knew his thoughts, the detective spoke. "Mr. Mason was most kind in joining us. If you all don't mind, we're waiting for one other person. I'd rather not start without her, so we won't have to repeat anything."

The group engaged in small talk for about ten minutes before the door opened and a fit woman in a jogging suit entered the room. She addressed Detective Martinez. "Sorry, I was on the trail when you called."

Detective Martinez smiled. "No problem. Thank you for joining us." To Zack and Bridget, she said, "This is special agent Hannah Bloom from the Homeland Security Center for Combating Human Trafficking."

After greeting the newcomer, Zack turned to Detective Martinez. "What's going on?"

She gave him a solemn look. "If everyone is ready, we can get started." Nods around the table affirmed.

"I must first state that this discussion is not for repetition outside this room." Martinez looked at Zack and Bridget. "Will that be a problem for either of you?"

Zack squinted. "Are you saying we can't discuss it with each other?"

"Only in an assured private setting. To be more specific, Doctor Winston, you must not talk about this with your daughter."

Zack felt anxious, threatened. "Why not?"

"You'll understand once we get into it."

Again, Martinez looked around the table. "Those of us with security clearances must not divulge any classified material in here, since neither Dr. Winston nor Ms. Larsen hold clearances."

She looked at Zack and Bridget. "That's correct, right?"

Both Zack and Bridget nodded. "Please," Zack said. "What's going on here?"

Detective Martinez turned to the DHS agent. "Ma'am."

The woman looked around the room, then directed her words to Zack.

"Last month, the kidnapping of your daughter, the piracy of her implanted embryo, and the attempt to murder her, were part of a larger conspiracy of which Dr. Adam Good, known to you as Dr. Sebastian Barth, was only one cog. I'm happy your daughter survived, although I understand she has some residual post-traumatic effects?"

It took a second for Zack to realize she expected him to answer. "Yes, she suffers from PTSD. She's in therapy for that."

The agent nodded, then addressed the room. "At the unclassified level, we have reliable information that Miss Winston's stolen embryo was, in fact, a payment to a group of international conspirators whose goal, or target, we have yet to figure out."

She turned to Detective Martinez. "We're here now to learn about recent developments in this case and to discuss the next course of action."

"Right," the detective said. "Within less than twenty-four hours, Dr. Winston and his daughter have received contacts from two suspected low-level players in the conspiracy. Tyler Rhodes approached Annie Winston in a restaurant yesterday evening, then phoned her later that night. This morning, Sarah O'Brien called Dr. Winston from a restricted number."

She turned to Zack. "Doc, can you tell us about those incidences?"

Zack related all he knew. Except he left out Sarah's sexual jibes.

FBI special agent Tony Mason spoke up. "Notwithstanding Mr. Rhodes' eventual repentance and confession, he aided Sarah O'Brien's kidnapping of Annie Winston. His disappearance from the hospital after he confessed to Ms. Larsen doesn't exactly attest to sincerity."

The DHS agent nodded. "Agreed. We must consider him still a member of the conspiracy." She looked at Zack. "Have you or your daughter heard anything from Sarah O'Brien or Tyler Rhodes before last night and this morning?"

Zack shook his head. "Nothing from Sarah since she tricked Annie into…" His voice trailed off.

Bridget came to his rescue. She addressed the agents at the head of the table. "What do you all make of this?"

The agents looked at each other, as if deciding how much to disclose.

Zack spoke up. "Look. I get your security clearance issues. I'm a former Navy officer. I had a secret clearance. But this involves my daughter, so loosen up a bit. It's not like I'm going to sell what you tell me to the highest foreign bidder."

The DHS agent shrugged. "Okay. Fair. Dr. Winston, you helped set up Sarah O'Brien's sister, Fiona Delaney, as a confidential informant about The Good House conspiracy."

Zack allowed himself a half-smile. "I did."

"Well, her information has been less useful than we'd hoped. She's frightened. All we've learned is that The Good House conspiracy was one part of that larger multinational cabal I mentioned earlier."

Tony Mason said, "Plus, she seems to have lingering loyalty to her sister, Sarah. Afraid of what might happen to her."

Bridget scoffed. "Wait a minute. Are you all saying that Fiona is willing to spend the rest of her life in prison for murdering my husband, rather than help take down the cabal that includes her sister?"

"Remember," Mason said, "Fiona was also a member of that conspiracy. She and Sarah went by the nicknames, Nan and Flossie, aka The Bobbsey Twins. We suspect there may be a plan to, uh, 'liberate' Fiona. We've kept her in her current role as Acting US Attorney as a smoke screen, but that will stop."

The DHS agent laid a hand on Mason's wrist. Mason nodded and smiled at Zack and Bridget. "You didn't hear what I didn't just say."

Zack looked at his watch, then addressed Detective Martinez. "I'm sorry, but I have a night shift in the ED. Are we going to wrap up soon, or do I need to get someone to cover for me?" Not something Zack would want to foist on any of his colleagues on short notice.

Detective Martinez reassured him. "That won't be necessary. We can cut to the chase now." She gave Zack an intense look. "As we said, the reappearance of Tyler Rhodes and

Sarah O'Brien within the last day seems beyond coincidence." She paused, choosing her words with care. "If we can draw them out and get our hands on them, we might get valuable information."

Bridget stiffened beside Zack. "You want to use Zack and Annie as bait?"

"Well, not in so many words," the detective said.

A flame erupted in Zack's gut. He stood. "Never, not Annie." He touched Bridget's shoulder. "Come on, Bridget. We're done here."

He turned and left the room. Bridget hurried after him.

Chapter Twenty-Four

Bridget pulled the Mercedes into the parking spot next to Zack's Lexus in front of the Tastee Diner in Bethesda. When she entered the restaurant, he beckoned her from a booth near the back.

"Thanks for coming, Bridge."

"Of course."

He stood as she sat, then resumed his seat across from her. "I don't have much time. Still have to get home, maybe get in a quick nap, then shower and change for work."

She looked him in the eye. "How much sleep have you had?"

Zack scoffed. "None since this morning." He let out a long breath and half-smiled. "I'll be okay. I'm used to it, especially the first night after a string of day shifts."

Bridget shook her head. "I don't know how you do it."

He ruminated for a few seconds. "I don't either. I'm starting to believe what I've heard at specialty meetings. Emergency medicine is a young man's field."

She laughed. "Well, that has to include you, Zack Winston."

Zack gave her a curious look.

"Because if you're an, uh, older man, that makes me an older woman. You know, the ones who become invisible after forty?"

"You are not invisible, Bridge. You sure weren't in that meeting. That FBI guy couldn't keep his eyes off your chest."

"You noticed that?"

"Duh." He opened the menu. "We need to order."

They made small talk until their meals arrived. Zack dug into his cheeseburger while Bridget spooned droplets of vinaigrette into her salad. Once he'd swallowed a few bites, she put down her fork and looked at him. "Well?"

"Well, what?"

"The topic we're both avoiding."

He cast her a wondering look, then shook his head. "Now's not the time for relationship talk."

Bridget scoffed. "Not that topic, Zack. I meant the meeting we just walked out on."

Zack raised his eyebrows. "What's to talk about? No way will I put Annie in danger again."

"Of course you won't. I was referring to you drawing Sarah out."

The cheeseburger halfway to Zack's mouth came to an abrupt halt. "Why would you think that's a good idea?"

"Read between the lines, Zack. They've gotten nothing actionable from Fiona. Their investigation is floundering."

Zack chewed on his burger, then took a swig of coke. "Hey, would I ask those dicks to help me resuscitate someone in hemorrhagic shock? Investigation and crime-solving is their job, not mine." He finished the burger, followed by another swig of coke. "They can break Fiona if they want to. Took little effort from me to get her off her game."

"By threatening to kill her with a syringe-full of saline that you portrayed as Fentanyl. I don't think law enforcement can use such coercive tactics."

Zack's face turned red. He looked into Bridget's eyes. "The last person on earth I want to see right now is Sarah. After what she did to Annie, I would relish choking every last breath out of her."

"What she did to Annie. And to you."

He waved her off. "Whatever. I can't promise I won't kill the whore if I ever see her again."

Bridget let his anger pass. "So, you won't help the investigators? No way?"

He shook his head. "None."

"Not even if it involves national security?"

"Huh?"

As a lawyer, Bridget had learned to read a room better than Zack had. "Come on, Zack. Who calls in the FBI and DHS for a crank phone call?"

The server brought their bill. Bridget reached for her purse, but Zack stopped her. "No. It's on me. Least I can do for the good company. And the cogent advice."

Bridget winked at him. "They don't call lawyers 'counselor' for nothing." She stopped herself from going further.

Flirting, Bridge? Get a grip.

Zack stood. "I need to hustle to get to work." He paused. "I'll, uh, think about what you said." Then his eyes hardened. "But no way will I put Annie at risk. Now or ever."

"Of course not." Bridget followed him toward the exit. At the door, he stood back and opened it for her. "Thanks again."

He seemed to struggle with his thoughts. "About that other topic..."

"Too soon, Zack."

He nodded. "Okay." He walked with her to the Mercedes. She unlocked it with the remote. He opened the door for her. "Nice ride," he said. "Maybe give me a spin someday?"

"Sure."

He closed the door and turned toward his Lexus. Bridget let out a long breath.

I would love to give you the ride of your life, Dr. Zack Winston. Someday.

Chapter Twenty-Five

Annie didn't tell the other girls that this was her first sleepover. Ever. Her mother wouldn't allow it, least of all with her few friends in La Jolla. So what if they smoked pot? Annie had tried it a few times. No big. Just made her thirsty.

No one at the Durans smoked pot. No alcohol either. Girls talking about boys and not much else. Annie figured it would be the same even without Mrs. Duran's watchful but welcoming eye.

Have I just become an effing nerd?

Maybe the psychological damage she'd suffered, or some brain damage from the near-drowning, had altered her personality. Annie shrugged, sipped from her soft drink, and helped herself to another Buffalo wing. She couldn't remember when she'd had a better time in her life. She was making friends. Real friends. Girl friends. So much better than the horny immature boys she thought she preferred in California.

Annie lost interest after midnight. Mrs. Duran had gone to bed after admonishing the girls to stay in the house and not venture outside. The group of eight girls lounged around the family room watching their second YA movie of the night. It seemed silly to Annie. Nothing like real life.

She jumped when her phone buzzed.

Please, not Dad checking up on me.

Annie looked at her phone. A text. Not her dad. A random number. Annie didn't recognize the area code, so she almost ignored it.

Tyler, maybe? She opened the text.

hey bitch

Nonplussed, Annie punched in a reply.

who u

A quick reply:

y u not dead slut

Icy fingers squeezed Annie's head. She let out a slight cry.

Rocky turned to her. "You okay, Annie?"

"Uh, weird text."

"Lemme see." Before Annie could react, Rocky grabbed the phone and looked at it. She shot Annie an angry look. "Whoa. You know this creep?"

Annie stifled a sob and shook her head. She reached out for her phone.

"We'll fix this," Rocky said. She typed into the text, pushed send, then handed the phone to Annie.

Annie gasped at what Raquel had written.

fuck off asshole

Rocky smiled. "Only one way to deal with a bully. You out-bully them. Trust me on that."

Annie's phone buzzed with a text reply.

u dead ass bitch (devil emoji)

Fingers shaking, Annie closed the text box. She glanced at Rocky. "It worked. Thanks."

No way that was Tyler.

Annie closed her eyes and took deep breaths to ward off an impending panic attack. The other girls didn't notice because they were engrossed in a silly teen flirtation scene.

What to do?

She considered calling her dad, but she didn't want to interrupt him at work. What if he was saving someone's life? A crank call couldn't disrupt him now. What could he do about it, anyway? She would show him the text tomorrow.

Annie returned the phone to her pocket. Rocky turned and eyed her with concern. "You okay, Annie? You look like you just met the devil."

Annie forced a smile. "I'm fine. Just weirded out by that text."

Rocky snorted. "Forget about it. We all get them. Creepy boys." She turned back to the TV.

Annie stared at the TV screen. Her mind spinning, she paid no attention to the movie.

Chapter Twenty-Six

BY MIDNIGHT OF BATTLING through the overflow crowd of patients in the ED, had to admit the truth of what he'd told Bridget earlier. Emergency medicine seemed more and more a younger man's game. Fatigue had invaded both his body and mind.

He had inherited a full department when he walked in at 6:00 PM. In the ensuing six hours, he'd not seen a bed empty for longer than it took the staff to change the sheets. He'd taken to examining patients with minor complaints in the ED waiting room or in the hallway outside the treatment area. Patients with non-serious injured extremities or small, non-suturable lacerations he could "meet and street" without them taking up precious bed space.

One such patient took umbrage.

"I twisted my ankle, Doc. Need an x-ray."

Zack did a thorough exam, then asked the patient if he could walk four steps.

"What? On a broken ankle?"

"Could you just try it, sir?"

The man cast Zack an ominous look, but then stood and walked four steps. He put weight on the injured ankle with minor discomfort, then sat back down.

Zack made entries on the ED tablet record, then smiled at the patient. "Good news, sir. You don't need an x-ray."

"What? You gonna put a cast on it without doing an x-ray?"

"No, we're going to put an ACE wrap on it and let you be on your way. We use an algorithm called the Ottawa Ankle Rules, which gives us almost a hundred percent reliability in predicting whether an injured ankle needs an x-ray or is almost certainly a sprain. Based on my exam and your weight-bearing ability, your ankle falls well into the sprain range."

Zack smiled. "So, congratulations. Your ankle isn't broken."

The man glared at Zack. "That's a crock. Look, Doc. I came here for an x-ray, and I'm not leaving without one."

Zack gave him his warmest smile. "Sure thing, if that's what you want."

He placed the order through the tablet for a full ankle x-ray series, then spoke to the patient. "I'm sorry, but the ER is jammed with seriously ill or injured people tonight. It may be a few hours before the x-ray folks can get to you. You're welcome to stay here in the waiting room. At least the TV can keep you entertained." He motioned to a wall-mounted TV that showed old black and white Western movies.

The man huffed and crossed his arms.

"I'll review the x-rays whenever they're done," Zack said. "Meanwhile, enjoy the movie."

He walked away, then turned back. "Oh, by the way, I can't guarantee your insurance carrier will cover those x-rays, given the lack of physical indications and the Ottawa Ankle Rules."

He turned back toward the treatment area.

"Hey, Doc." The man's voice stopped Zack at the door to the treatment area.

"Yes?"

"I'll take the damned ACE wrap."

Zack smiled. "Sure. I'll send the tech right out to do that for you."

When Zack returned to the main treatment area, the charge nurse approached him. "Full code inbound. Sixty-six-year-old white male, a guest at the Bethesda Marriott Hotel. Collapsed and stopped breathing while having sex. Medics report asystole on the monitor."

Zack shook his head. Not the first time he'd heard that story, always on night shifts. The deep shift had its unique moments. Plus, the asystole augured a disastrous outcome. He'd seldom seen a patient recover in the ED after they had gone flat-line and stopped breathing in the pre-hospital setting.

When the patient arrived five minutes later, one look convinced Zack he would not survive. The obese man, still naked save for a towel covering his privates, had that blue-purple cyanotic skin color of the recently dead. The paramedics had intubated and ventilated him, but rivulets of pinkish white froth dripped down his chin. Quick assessment revealed no pulse, no spontaneous breathing.

No life.

Zack called off the code ten minutes after the victim arrived.

"The companion's in the quiet room," the charge nurse said.

"On my way." He cast her a weary smile. "Try to keep the chaos down to a roar while I'm gone."

Zack entered the quiet room to find a young, attractive woman dressed in sweats and flip-flops sitting alone on the couch, head supported between her two hands. He guessed her age at mid- to late-thirties. "Mrs., uh,.."

She looked up. Zack noticed the absence of a wedding ring.

"I'm not . . ."

"Are you related?"

She shook her head, embarrassed. "No. We are... We were friends."

Zack took a breath. "I see. Do you, uh, have contact information for his family?"

The woman reached into her purse, extracted a phone, and punched at it. She showed Zack the screen. "That's his wife."

Zack copied the number onto the tablet he was carrying. "Thanks," he said. "I'll send someone in to—"

She raised a hand. "Won't be necessary. I suppose you need me to stay around?"

I don't, but the police might.

"If you could."

She stared at the carpet. "Okay."

"Thanks."

Zack left the room and returned to the workstation to call the dead man's wife. The area code indicated a Chicago suburb. The woman who answered sounded half asleep.

Zack told her that her husband had suffered a fatal heart attack, from which there had been no chance of recovery. He offered his condolences and was about to pass the phone to the charge nurse to make further arrangements when the wife's suddenly alert voice stopped him.

"Wait a minute. Did you say you were calling from Bethesda, Maryland?"

"That's right."

"Then you've made a big mistake. My husband's in Boston, not Maryland."

Zack pursed his lips, then read the dead man's social security number to the wife.

She broke into sobs.

"Again, I'm sorry, ma'am."

Zack handed the phone to the charge nurse. He whispered. "Good luck."

He picked up the tablet and went on to the next patient.

Some things that happen on night shifts shouldn't happen at any time.

By 3:00 AM, the department had finally settled down. Only a few patients remained, some awaiting test results, others waiting for overworked medical residents to admit them to the hospital.

Zack absconded to The Bunker for a quick break. As he sipped his home-brewed smoothie health drink, he thought about Annie. He had intended to call to see how she was doing, but it was too late now—even for a teenager on a sleepover. She might not have appreciated a call in the middle of her sleepover, no matter the time.

How do you give space to your teenage daughter whom you're just now getting to know? After she almost died and may still be in danger?

Maybe Bridget could help with that. Zack frowned. He did not know where her head was these days, either.

The intercom buzzed. "Dr. Winston, we have a new patient. Another one from the Marriott. Headache."

That place must be hopping tonight.

Zack finished his smoothie, went to the bathroom, spruced up, and headed back to the treatment area.

The staff had put his new patient in the isolation room, a more remote, quieter venue than the hectic main treatment area with its multiple cubicles and general milling about of staff. This setting was more conducive to treatment of patients with headaches. Or potentially communicable infectious diseases.

A short and fit Latina woman regarded Zack through squinted eyes. An arm covered her forehead. The ED record identified her as Soledad Ruiz, age thirty-five. Zack thought she looked older; a bit hardened. The only address on the record was the same Bethesda Marriott Hotel where the philandering older man had suffered his cardiac arrest.

Unrelated, Zack figured.

He approached the bed, glanced again at the tablet. "Ms. Ruiz, can you tell me about your headache? When it started? How it feels?"

She half-opened her eyes. Spoke in accented English. "Is migraine. I have history. Right side. Started few hours ago."

"Is it your typical migraine? Anything different about it?"

She groaned. "Worse than usual."

"On a scale of one to ten?"

"Eight."

"Nausea?"

"Yes."

"Light bothers you? Makes it worse?"

"Oh, yes." As if to demonstrate, she looked at him with eyes shielded by her hand.

"What do you usually take for it?"

The thousand-dollar question.

"My doctor in Mexico gives me drug that start with a *D*. Demo something."

"Demerol?"

"Yes. That's it."

"Where in Mexico?"

"Ciudad Juárez. Next to Texas."

Zack sighed, looked at his watch. 3:30 AM. With any luck, he could get this woman treated and released before his relief showed up at 6:00 AM. He tried his most supportive, reassuring voice.

"We can definitely help you, Ms., uh, Ruiz. But, we don't use Demerol for migraines in the US anymore. Not for anything, really. We have other medications that are more effective than opioids."

She looked skeptical. "Better than Demerol? Or morphine?"

"For sure. Plus, I see you're dehydrated. Have you traveled lately?"

"On airplanes all day yesterday."

Zack smiled. "That probably precipitated the headache. You got dehydrated, and that started the cycle." He gave her a reassuring nod. "We can help you."

She shrugged. "Okay, Doctor."

He turned to leave. "I'll send the nurse in to start an IV and give you fluids. Then we'll start some medication through the IV. Hopefully have you feeling better in time for breakfast."

She forced a smile. "*Gracias*, Doctor."

Back in the workstation, Zack ordered a liter of normal saline IV fluid and his favorite "Migraine Cocktail" composed of prochlorperazine (a drug for nausea), diphenhydramine (an antihistamine), ketorolac (a non-steroidal anti-inflammatory medication), and dexamethasone (a steroid). Zack could not remember when he'd last given a patient with a true migraine any narcotic medications.

Could this woman be a user looking for a fix? Zack trusted his intuition. She had shown none of the typical signs, nor did she seem desperate for the narcotic. Just someone improperly treated in the past. It happened. As much in the US as anywhere else.

A glance around the workstation showed no other patients to see. With any luck, Zack could get a brief rest before discharging the migraine woman and then heading home for a few hours of sleep before he had to pick up Annie at the Durans.

Asleep on top of the bed in The Bunker, Zack startled awake at the invading blare of the intercom. An excited voice followed.

"MVA in five. Single victim. Bad."

Crap!

As if on cue, an announcement thundered from the overhead speaker. "Trauma Alert, Trauma Alert. Five minutes." Zack looked at his watch. 5:10 AM. A serious vehicular accident victim would occupy him past the scheduled end of his shift.

So much for getting rest before I pick up Annie.

An ambulance siren approached, distant at first but louder by the second. Zack rolled off the bed, rubbed his eyes, and ran his fingers through his hair. He hurried from The Bunker.

After donning a surgical gown, hair covering, mask, and face shield, Zack entered the resuscitation room. The trauma team had started their well-practiced choreography to prepare for an incoming victim of multi-system trauma. As the emergency physician on the team, Zack stepped to the head of the narrow bed and prepared to manage the victim's airway.

A minute later, he nodded to Dr. Autry Robertson when the portly trauma surgeon entered the room dressed in similar attire as Zack. He looked sleepier than Zack felt. Not one of Zack's favorite physicians. Few surgeons were.

Robertson growled like a mongrel dog awakened by an intruder. "Whatta we got?"

The lead nurse on the trauma team responded. "Single vehicle, head-on, single occupant, fortyish female, tachy and hypotensive on scene, respiratory compromised. Head trauma and probable compound femur fracture."

The surgeon growled again, crossed his arms in a judgmental stance. "Injuries above and below the diaphragm." He glanced at the clock on the wall, then turned to the lead nurse. "Is there an open OR?"

"Yes, sir."

Robertson looked at Zack. "You know the drill. We don't waste time here in the ER. We get her to the OR for an ex-lap."

Zack's eyes narrowed over the top of his surgical mask. "First, we do the ABCDE drill, Autry, same for all trauma cases. Of course, we'll expedite, but we won't cut corners." He tilted his head. "Do you have some place else to be this morning? Early breakfast meeting?"

Robertson glared at Zack. "We both know she needs her abdomen opened soonest. That's called definitive care."

Despite his annoyance at the diatribe, Zack recognized the bluster as Robertson's way to fend off his pre-resuscitation jitters.

Just then, paramedics wheeled the patient head first on a gurney through the wide entrance to the resuscitation room. A familiar shock of curly red hair stifled Zack's retort to Robertson. He gasped.

Sarah?

On closer look, not Sarah. This woman brought a harsher reality, but Zack had no time to process it. She had stopped breathing.

"She's apneic," he said. "Intubating now." Within seconds, Zack performed rapid endotracheal intubation without difficulty. He connected the endotracheal tube to a ventilator.

Lifesaving procedure complete, Zack took a deep breath and looked at Robertson. "I know this woman. Fiona Delaney, acting US Attorney for Southeastern Virginia." He grimaced under his mask. How much could he reveal? Not much. Nothing.

"I don't care if she's the fucking president," Robertson said. "Her abdomen's distended. I need her in the OR now." He turned to the nurses. "Let's move, folks."

"Stop." Zack spoke in a stern, commanding voice. "Distended neck veins. We need an echo first."

He didn't wait for Robertson to respond, but moved next to the patient's chest, edging the surgeon out of the way. He spoke to the nurses. "Get me the ultrasound. Now."

In less than a minute, Zack had ultrasound evidence of what he had suspected. "Pericardial tamponade. Set up for pericardiocentesis."

He turned on Robertson. "We'll get her to the OR as soon as we drain the pericardial blood that's squeezing her heart to death."

Zack spoke to the lead nurse. "Contact the thoracic surgeon on call. Tell them to meet Dr. Robertson in the OR." He turned back to the surgeon. "You'll do simultaneous chest and abdominal procedures, right?"

Robertson nodded, eyes wide and angry.

Zack addressed the nurse. "After thoracic surgery, please contact Detective Tina Martinez at Montgomery County PD. You'll find her business card in my wallet in my civilian clothes in the Bunker. Just tell her we have 'Fiona' in the OR."

He turned back to the patient. "Now let's do this life-saving procedure so Dr. Robertson can have his turn."

Zack inserted a long needle attached to a fifty cc syringe into the space between the tip of Fiona's breastbone and lower rib, then used the real-time ultrasound image to help him guide the tip of the needle into the pericardial sac around her heart. Dark red blood filled the syringe. Fiona's vital signs immediately improved.

Zack stepped back and spoke to the nurse. "We need blood, urine, and hair samples for toxicology and drug screens."

"Already done, sir."

"Hair too?"

The nurse frowned. "Yes, of course."

Zack smiled. "Of course, of course. Cleared for transfer to the OR." He looked at his watch. 6:05 AM. Not as late as he'd expected.

When Zack returned to the main treatment room for turnover with his day-shift relief, Dr. Paula Cho, patients occupied every bed. Paula had already seen some patients.

Zack found her in a cubicle. "Paula, I'll clear the patients who were here before the Trauma Alert." No way would he leave his unfinished patients for Paula to complete. First, it would violate his own ethics. Second, it would be dangerous. Medical errors, especially in the ED, often happened at changes of shift, when continuity of care got interrupted from one physician to the next.

He was halfway through his patient dispositions and charting when Wayne Snodgrass, the ER secretary, approached him.

"Dr. Winston, there's a Detective Martinez on the line for you."

"Thanks, Wayne. Ask if I can call her back in about fifteen minutes. I need to finish these two patients."

Patients always come first.

Zack returned to the isolation room to check on his migraine patient. He came to an abrupt stop just inside the door. The empty bed mocked him. Zack's eyes followed the plastic tubing from the almost full IV bag hanging by the bedside all the way to the empty bed. The ripped adhesive tape that had held the cannula in the patient's vein lay across the bed—a drop of diluted blood at the tip.

He had erred about the patient being an opioid seeker. Or had he? Something felt out of kilter in the scene before him. Had she left the ED undetected? Unlikely. Maybe during the chaotic resuscitation of Fiona Delaney. Still. . .

Back at the workstation, Zack reported the patient's escape to the charge nurse. "Maybe call that hotel, see if she returned there."

The nurse offered a skeptical shrug. "Sure."

"Something doesn't fit," he said. "That woman showed no signs of being a drug user."

The nurse shrugged again and picked up the phone.

Zack called Detective Martinez to report the near-demise of Fiona Delaney.

"I'll come to you," she said. "Can you wait there for me?"

There goes the morning.

"Sure."

"I'll contact our FBI and DHS friends," Martinez said.

"Right."

When Zack hung up, the nurse spoke to him. "Bethesda Marriott has no one registered under the name Soledad Ruiz. Or any other Ruiz." She smirked. "You got scammed, Doc."

Zack shook his head. "She got no opioids from me."

Chapter Twenty-Seven

ZACK CARRIED A MUG of fresh black coffee into the ED conference room. After almost twenty-four hours of no sleep and the night shift he'd just endured, he doubted the caffeine would help his fading senses.

Detective Martinez, FBI special agent Mason, and DHS agent Hannah Bloom arose in unison to greet him. Martinez cast him a wary eye.

"Rough night, eh, Doc?"

"You get used to it." Zack hoped he sounded more convincing to her than he did to himself.

Agent Bloom cleared her throat to speak. She wore a leather jacket over a fitted button-down light blue blouse and khaki pants. Her coiffed blond hair just touched her shoulders. Had she dressed for this meeting, or was she on her way home from a date when she got the call? She had worn a working uniform of dark gray cargo pants and navy-blue tee shirt when Zack met her the day before.

She gave Zack a sly look, as if she'd noticed him observe her attire. "What can you tell us about Fiona Delaney, sir?"

Zack spread his hands. "She sustained a head-on collision on the Beltway. I don't have many details, but hers was the only car involved."

The agents all exchanged glances.

Zack furrowed his brow. "Anything you all can tell me?"

Detective Martinez responded. "Did you do a toxicology screen?"

"Of course. Preliminary results should be available by the time we break from this meeting."

Again, the agents exchanged glances.

Zack splayed out his hands. "I can help more if you level with me and quit trading furtive glances like my daughter and her high school friends do."

Agent Tony Mason shifted in his chair, leaned toward Zack. "Okay, Doc. After our meeting yesterday, where you mentioned the sudden emergence of her sister, Sarah, we determined Fiona was in immediate danger. US Marshals planned to meet her early this morning for transfer to witness protection. We assigned a protective detail from MCPD to her residence for the interim."

He glanced at Detective Martinez, shook his head. "When the federal marshals arrived a few hours ago, Fiona and her car were gone. No protective detail on the premises. No sign they'd ever arrived there."

Zack narrowed his eyebrows. "Was that an interagency snafu, or...?"

Mason shook his head. "No clue."

Zack turned to Martinez. "So the interest in a tox screen?"

"To find out if someone drugged her, or controlled her in some other manner."

Zack fought off the weariness infusing his body. "Other than the tox screen, how can I help?"

"Besides keeping her alive," Agent Bloom said, "any clues from her injuries?"

"High speed unrestrained blunt trauma. External injuries are consistent with a head-on impact. We might get more information once she's out of the OR and the surgeon can report his findings."

"Unrestrained, as in no seat belt?" Mason asked.

"Right."

Detective Martinez spoke. "No skid marks on scene. No signs of braking."

"Then she may have been unconscious prior to impact," Zack said. "I'll go look for those tox results."

He excused himself, left the conference room, and returned to the main ED. He stopped on the way to refill his already empty coffee mug.

Zack found the department in full warble, every bed occupied. Paula Cho hustled to keep up with the flow. It was an unusual sight so early on a Saturday morning, when most potential ER patients were having family time or sleeping off an alcohol-infused Friday night.

He sat at the only available computer station and called up the results on Fiona Delaney's toxicology screen. Just then, the ED secretary approached and handed him a phone.

Autry Robertsons's tired voice resonated in Zack's more tired brain. "We got Delaney to the ICU, but not looking good."

Zack looked at the toxicology report. No surprise there.

"Autry, can you meet the law enforcement folks and me in the ED conference room? That way, you only have to do the brief once before you can get out of here."

"Coming right down. As soon as I find some coffee."

"Plenty here. Fresh brewed. Dark roast and strong."

"See you in a minute. Or less."

Zack returned to the conference room and resumed his seat next to Detective Martinez. He passed her a printed copy of the toxicology results. "The tox screen is positive for a sedative, Rohypnol, and an unknown opiate." He looked at the others in the room. "We saw the same combination in our pediatrician who nearly drowned in the Potomac, a victim of The Good House conspirators. We also found it in an emergency physician who died on-duty in a rural ED, probably also courtesy of The Good House gang."

"Damn," agent Mason said.

"Something doesn't fit," Agent Bloom said. "How did this woman OD on those drugs, then get into her car and drive on the Beltway? Where was she going?"

Detective Martinez punched numbers into her phone. "Any word from the protective detail assigned to Fiona Delaney?" Her chin dropped. "Stay on it. I want regular reports." She clicked off the call and spoke in a thick, defeated voice. "No word from or sign of the detail since they left the precinct. Hours ago." She stared at her hands folded on the table.

"Let me guess," Agent Mason said. "Delaney's house was in pristine condition. Nothing out of place. No fingerprints."

Martinez offered a sad smile. "Correct. Our investigators are still there, but so far, nothing. Hopefully—"

Agent Bloom interrupted. "They won't find anything. That includes the bodies of your protective detail officers. I should say, body parts." She eyed the others in the room. "We're dealing with a highly sophisticated operation here. Way more than your so-called 'Good House conspirators.'"

The door to the conference room opened to admit Dr. Autry Robertson. The conversation stopped.

Holding a giant mug of coffee, Autry took the seat next to Agent Bloom. His disheveled scrub suit and facial stubble made a sharp contrast to her appearance that resembled a seasoned politician running for high office.

As if on puppet strings, the entire group turned to the rumpled trauma surgeon. He took a deep quaff of coffee, then put down the mug. "Multiple internal injuries, massive blood loss, closed head injury, myocardial contusion. Should I go on?"

"Can you give us more detail?" Agent Bloom asked.

"Sure. Dr. Winston here reversed the immediate life-threatening injury when the patient was still in the ED. A pericardial tamponade. That's blood filling the sac around the heart and squeezing it to death. The underlying injury was a myocardial contusion or bruised heart. Result of her chest hitting the steering wheel."

Noting the puzzled looks, Zack explained. "When the car came to a sudden stop, Fiona's body accelerated forward until the steering wheel stopped it."

"You treated that injury in the ED?" Mason asked.

"We withdrew the blood from around her heart," Zack said. "But the underlying bruise to the heart is as bad as a major heart attack."

"Got it," Mason said. He turned to Robertson. "The other injuries?"

"Ruptured spleen, torn liver, contused kidney. Plus a compound femur fracture. Major blood loss from all those injuries."

"Will she survive?" Detective Martinez asked.

Autry nodded. "Probably. She's out of immediate danger, and we have superior critical care capabilities here. We'll keep her alive."

"What about brain function?" Agent Bloom asked. "Will she become lucid again?"

"Too early to tell," Autry said. "She might." He tilted his head. "Or might not."

Detective Martinez looked at Autry. "We'll post a twenty-four-hour protective detail on her." She took out a phone and called for the detail.

Hopefully, less vulnerable than the one assigned to her house, Zack thought.

Chapter Twenty-Eight

THE FLY'S JOINTS HAD stiffened during the two hours she squatted on the lid of the commode inside the narrow stall in the restroom in the hospital's basement. As expected, only a few women had come and gone during that time. The non-essential maintenance and supply staff would be off early on Saturday morning. No one had noticed The Fly. She'd taken to doing stretch breaks inside the stall whenever the restroom seemed unoccupied.

Earlier, from her observation post in the ED's isolation room, she'd overheard the urgent announcements and hyperactivity that accompanied their target's arrival, still alive. When they had taken the woman to surgery, The Fly had reported to *El Fuego*, who was directing the operation from an 'undisclosed' location. Undisclosed to The Fly, but not others. A blunt hint that she had not achieved full membership in the inner circle of *Los Hermanos*. She would have to deal with that later.

She had texted *El Fuego*.

target lives

The expected reply had come at once.

plan b

In less than a minute, The Fly had extricated herself from the clumsy IV and taken advantage of the chaos to escape the ER without detection. She had hurried to the basement to take up her new position in the restroom while other accomplices monitored the ongoing situation.

The Fly hated idle time, no matter how pertinent to the mission. She disliked being alone with her thoughts and memories. Worse when fatigued, as she was now. Just as she'd reached the limit of her endurance, her phone buzzed with a cryptic message.

ICU

The Fly edged out of the cubicle and opened the small supply closet where she'd hidden her change of clothing. A calculated risk, but a safe enough early on a Saturday morning.

Every mission carried risks, not all of which she could eliminate. Just had to manage and mitigate it.

She donned the one-piece coverall she'd stolen earlier from a maintenance staff locker, then opened her purse, lifted the false bottom, extracted the syringe full of clear liquid, and placed it in the left front pocket of the coverall. Then she took out the Smith & Wesson pistol and put in the right pocket, where she could grab it quickly if needed.

The Fly would not shoot the victim. She had strict orders to immolate herself should the plan go awry. Death over capture and coerced confession or disclosure. Such was the solemn code of *Los Hermanos de Guadalajara*. She'd had enough second thoughts about her current status that the pistol seemed reasonable.

The Fly looped the lanyard with the phony hospital ID around her neck and left the restroom. In the supply room, she grabbed a linen cart and headed into the hallway to the service elevator. She got off the elevator on the correct floor and pushed the cart toward the ICU. Passing the waiting room, she glanced at Diego, an accomplice, sitting in a chair while he scrolled on his phone. He glanced up as she passed. The two exchanged slight nods.

At the ICU entrance, The Fly showed her fake ID to the police officer standing guard. The woman stepped aside and allowed The Fly to enter the unit. Once inside, she pushed the cart down the center aisle between patient cubicles. As expected, the nursing staff went about their duties without so much as glancing at her.

Menial staff, always invisible.

The Fly pushed the cart past each pair of beds. She saw no patient with red hair. Had she entered the wrong unit? Then she noted a private room at the end of the row. A uniformed police officer stood guard at the closed door.

Shit. The target must be in that room.

A sudden commotion near the ICU entrance attracted both The Fly's attention and that of the police officer.

Diego burst through the ICU doors with the policewoman guard in pursuit. Diego shouted in Spanish, "I must see my wife! You can't stop me." He started down the aisle between the cubicles.

The policewoman tried to restrain him, but he turned and swatted at her. The male officer at the door of the private room rushed past The Fly to help his colleague.

With only seconds to accomplish her task, The Fly moved like lightning. She rushed into the unguarded room, verified the patient with red hair, took the syringe from her pocket, and plunged the contents directly into the IV line. It took only ten seconds for her to accomplish the task. She stole from the room to her cart and pushed it toward the front of the ICU.

Diego quit struggling with the police, who cuffed him and removed him from the unit.

The Fly waited three seconds, then followed them through the door. The police officers had Diego restrained against the wall in the hallway. One spoke into the radio on his shoulder.

Diego had become docile. The officers shouted at him in English, but he responded in Spanish. "*No hablo inglés.*"

The Fly approached them. "Excuse me, officers. I can help. I speak Spanish."

The female officer regarded her with a suspicious eye. "No need, ma'am. We've called for backup to take him to headquarters. We have interpreters there."

The Fly backed away. "Okay. Just trying to help. He looks so scared."

The other officer instructed The Fly to tell the man he was under arrest and to cooperate. She carried on a whispered, terse Spanish conversation with her accomplice, then turned to the police officers.

"He says he's sorry. Didn't want to cause trouble. He thought his wife was a patient in that unit, but he didn't see her there. He's made a terrible mistake, and hopes you will forgive him and let him go. He just wants to find his wife."

The two officers exchanged glances. "We need to get back to our duty," the woman said.

"Fine," the other officer said. He took the cuffs off their prisoner, who dropped to his knees and offered profuse thanks through his tears.

"Tell him to get the hell out of here before we change our minds," the officer said. He spoke into his radio to cancel the backup call.

The Fly whispered to Diego in Spanish. "Get out now." The man got off his knees, offered thanks in Spanish, then hurried down the hall.

"Thank you, officers," The Fly said. She turned and hurried in the opposite direction from her colleague.

Back in the basement, she abandoned the linen cart and entered to the restroom. She returned the pistol to the hidden compartment in her purse. As she changed back into street clothes, an overhead announcement caught her attention.

"Dr. Robertson to ICU stat. Dr. Robertson to ICU stat."

Mission accomplished.

She must hurry. Grabbing her purse, she left the coveralls on the floor of the restroom and rushed to the loading dock.

Chapter Twenty-Nine

"Dr. Robertson to ICU stat. Dr. Robertson to ICU stat."

Everyone in the conference room startled at the sudden overhead announcement. Autry Robertson stood and started toward the door. Zack followed him.

Detective Martinez barked into her phone. "Get that detail here now!"

As Zack and Autry hurried to the elevator, another urgent overhead announcement pierced the air. "Code Blue, ICU. Code Blue, ICU."

The two doctors didn't articulate what they both knew. Fiona Delaney's heart had stopped.

Zack rushed past the elevator and charged up the stairs two flights to the ICU. Puffing hard, Robertson trailed after him. Zack arrived at Fiona's bedside first. The ICU staff had begun CPR. The nurses gave looks of futility to Zack and Autry.

"What the hell?" Autry barked.

"She went into asystole," a nurse said. "No warning."

A chill ran up Zack's spine. "Any changes at all before that? Any warning?"

"None," the nurse said. "She was stable. Good vitals. She'd started cycling the vent on her own."

Zack looked at Autry. "That makes no sense."

Even with CPR in progress, Autry did a quick abdominal exam. "Soft. Not distended. Just like I left it." He spoke to the nurse. "No change in BP or pulse before she arrested?"

"Within normal limits," the nurse said.

Autry looked at Zack. "I doubt bleeding as a cause."

"Agreed," Zack said. He stepped back to assess the overall gestalt as the CPR continued. Nothing out of the ordinary, except Fiona Delaney had just died from no apparent cause. He turned to the nurse. "How long have you been doing CPR?"

"Eleven minutes, by the clock."

"Let's do an echo," Zack said. "Maybe recurrent tamponade."

A nurse brought the echocardiogram machine to the bedside. When all was ready, Zack said, "Stop CPR." He performed a rapid scan over Fiona's chest. "No fluid around the heart. Resume CPR."

"Scan her abdomen too," Autry said.

Another brief interruption of CPR while Zack did a "FAST" ultrasound exam of Fiona's abdomen. "No fluid. No free air. Resume CPR."

"CPR time now seventeen minutes," a nurse said.

"Continue," Zack said. He turned to Autry. "Any other ideas?"

The surgeon shook his head. The two men regarded each other with resigned looks. Their combined decades of medical training and experience offered no clues why Fiona Delaney had crashed, or what else they could do.

"Stop CPR," Zack said. He did a quick assessment. Fiona showed no signs of life. No pulse. No respirations. The EKG monitor showed only a wavy line. Asystole. No cardiac activity. Zack nodded to the nurses to re-start CPR, stepped back, and spoke to Autry.

"Your patient, your call."

Autry threw up his hands. "We're done." He looked at the clock. "Time of death, 9:23 AM."

Zack spoke to the charge nurse. "I want full lab work. Everything, especially electrolytes, metabolic panel, tox screen." He thought for a moment. "Take hair samples as well."

A nurse approached. "Dr. Winston, Dr. Robertson, there's a massive law enforcement presence just outside the doors. What should I tell them?"

Zack looked at Robertson. "I'll go talk to them." A thought hit him as he stepped away. He turned back to where the nurses had begun their usual routine of cleaning up after a patient died.

"Stop," he said. "Everyone step away and leave everything as is."

Robertson gave him a curious look. "What are you doing?"

"This is a crime scene, Autry."

Five minutes later, Zack sat with Detective Martinez and Agents Bloom and Mason in the ICU conference room. Autry Robertson joined them.

Zack started the discussion. "Dr. Robertson will concur that we could find no cause for Fiona's death related to her injuries, surgery, or post-surgical state." He looked at Autry.

"Concur," the surgeon said.

Detective Martinez asked, "What are you saying?"

"Something new happened. Not a consequence of the prior trauma or treatment."

"Such as?"

Zack shook his head. "I don't know. I hate to be trite at a time like this, but I suspect foul play."

Tony Mason huffed. "Really, Doc? Watched too many murder dramas?"

"Given the chain of recent events and Fiona's importance to the investigation, the thought isn't far-fetched."

Agent Bloom said, "It's a consideration, Tony."

Mason nodded. "Yeah. But who? How?"

"To be blunt," Autry said in his characteristic bombast, "Your security presence for our patient has been less than stellar."

Detective Martinez spread her arms. "I can't argue with you on that, Doc."

A knock on the conference room door interrupted. An ICU nurse entered the room with a one-page printout in her hand. She handed it to Zack. "First labs on Delaney."

Zack thanked her and took the paper. One glance clarified the nagging feeling he'd had since stopping the resuscitation attempt on Fiona.

He handed the paper to Autry, then spoke to the others. "Fiona's blood potassium level came back at 9.5 milliequivalents per liter. That's almost twice normal. It caused irreversible cardiac arrest."

The detectives looked puzzled. Bloom asked for all of them. "How does that happen?"

"By injection," Zack said. "Straight into the IV." He looked at Autry Robertson. "We need to get in touch with Eric Wolfe."

Autry nodded. "Yeah. I'll call him."

"Ask him to expedite," Zack said.

"What are you two saying?" Agent Mason asked. "Did someone murder Fiona Delaney?"

Zack bit his lip and shook his head. "Not exactly. Someone executed her. Right under our collective noses."

Chapter Thirty

THE FLY BURST THROUGH the double doors to the loading dock just as a nondescript, faded gray cargo van backed into an open space. A bearded young man, whom she now knew as Roach, jumped out of the driver's side and tried to open the back doors of the van. The edge of the dock came up a third of the way above the floor of the van and blocked the doors from opening.

"I'll have to pull the van up," the youth said.

"Hurry," The Fly said.

An announcement blared over the hospital loudspeakers. "Code Orange, Code Orange. The hospital is on lockdown. All personnel remain in place. Repeat. The hospital is on lockdown. All personnel remain in place until further notice."

Roach pulled the van forward. The Fly jumped off the dock, yanked open the rear door, and rolled into the van's cargo area. She yelled at the driver. "*Ándale. Ándale.* Get us the hell out of here."

She reached back and closed the rear door just as the youth slammed his foot on the accelerator. The van lurched from the space, throwing The Fly backwards against the door she'd just shut. She got herself up and crawled toward the front passenger seat. She made a sudden stop when she saw her small duffel bag stored behind the driver's seat. Someone else already sat in the passenger seat.

El Fuego looked back and gave her a wicked smile. "Well done, my little fly."

The van sped around a corner. The centrifugal force threw The Fly against the sidewall.

"Hold on," *El Fuego* said to her in Spanish. "We are in a hurry."

The Fly grabbed onto the side door handle, righted herself, and sat with her back against the door.

Sirens approached from the distance, growing louder by the second. Roach pulled the van to the curb and stopped until the speeding police vehicles passed them and headed toward the hospital.

The Fly had completed her mission and escaped detection. But now what? And where was Diego, her accomplice from the hospital? He, too, should have come to the loading dock for extraction.

As the van started moving again, she glared at *El Fuego*. "Why is my stuff in the van?"

He cast her a wicked smile. "You're not going back to the hotel."

"What? Where?"

"You will see."

"I'm sure as hell not going anywhere with you." She eyed her purse on the floor where it had skidded after she boarded the van. Could she get to the Smith and Wesson before *El Fuego* could react?

El Fuego turned around and raised his hand over the seat back. The Fly stared at the barrel of a pistol identical to hers, pointed at her forehead.

He spat out the words. "You are not in charge here, *chingada*. You never were. Now hand me that purse, then sit your ass down and shut up."

Her eyes afire, The Fly stared him down.

El Fuego brandished the pistol.

This pendejo is stupid enough to shoot me. She did as told.

He removed her pistol from the purse, emptied the other contents onto the floor of the van, then tore open the lining. He pulled out the garrote wire she'd concealed there.

"How stupid do you think I am?" he asked with a sneer. "Sorry about your woman products there. Bleed to death for all I care." He tossed the ruined purse out the window.

The Fly gave him a condescending smile. *You are as stupid as always, cabrón.*

Roach headed the van north, drove less than a mile, and then merged onto a highway entrance ramp. The Fly glanced at the green sign as the van sped past.

I-270 North Frederick

Fear raged inside her mind. They were on the same route she'd taken months earlier to Montgomery County Airpark. Where she killed Dr. Good and retrieved the metal case that contained the stolen embryo. The prize she had thought would cement her relationship with *Los Hermanos*.

Chapter Thirty-One

BRIDGET'S SON ENTERED HER bedroom and shook her awake. "Mom, Dr. Winston on the landline phone. Says it's urgent and you're not answering your cell phone."

She rolled over, rubbed the sleep from her eyes, and looked at her clock. 6 AM. Because she'd had trouble sleeping, Bridget had taken to silencing her cell phone at night when she went to bed.

What isn't urgent to Zack these days?

She'd also silenced the ringer on her bedside phone. She picked up the receiver. "What's up, Zack?"

"Fiona's dead."

Bridget's eyes came wide open.

OK. Some things are urgent.

"How? Where?"

"Here. In the hospital."

"How?"

"She came in as a trauma alert early this morning. Ran her car across the median on the Beltway into a head-on collision. We suspect altered mental status from Rohypnol."

"She died of trauma?"

"No. We resuscitated her and got her through surgery."

Bridget squeezed her eyes. "How did Fiona die, Zack? Did you say 'Rohypnol'?"

"No, she didn't die from Rohypnol. Someone drugged her. I don't know how or why she was driving on the Beltway."

Bridget's mind had cleared from the early morning drowsiness, just as her impatience had risen. "Zack, please just tell me how Fiona died?"

He blew into the phone. "Overdose of potassium chloride in the ICU. Someone killed her under all our noses. Like a death sentence execution."

Bridget sucked in a breath. "How does that happen in a hospital?"

"A woman got into the ICU posing as a housekeeper. Few people pay attention to custodial staff in the clinical spaces, especially the critical care units." He paused. "By the time we figured out what happened, the woman was long gone."

"Any clues to her identity?"

"A Latina woman, maybe in her thirties."

Bridget rubbed her forehead, contemplating. "What do you need from me, Zack?"

He huffed. "This is a shot across our bow, Bridge. We're dealing with a sophisticated team of criminals. We should have already realized that. I'm not paranoid when I say we're all in danger. You, Annie and me."

Bridget pursed her lips. *He could be right.* "What do we do about it?"

Zack paused for longer than she'd expected.

"Say it, Zack."

His voice sounded bone weary. "After my shift, I'm going to pick up Annie from a sleepover." A pause. "Could you come to our apartment? The three of us need a serious talk."

"Is that wise, Zack? Doesn't Annie have enough to deal with right now?"

He said nothing, but she heard his heavy breaths. Bridget did not insert herself.

When Zack spoke, his voice seemed distant, monotone.

Resolved?

"I get that, Bridge." A longer pause. "To be boldly honest, I'm asking for your help. I don't know how to deal with Annie right now."

"You think I do?"

"Well, you are a—"

"Please, don't say 'woman.'"

"I was going to say 'mother.'"

"Annie has a mother, Zack."

"Who will yank her back to California in a heartbeat if she thinks her daughter's in danger. Again." He sighed. "I'm not asking you to mother Annie. I'm asking for your advice as a mother."

Bridget tried to be gentle with her response. "Maybe the California option would be best for Annie."

Zack exploded. "No way. If these people are as evil and sophisticated as we believe, Annie won't be safe in California or anywhere else."

"Why would these, whatever, go after Annie?"

Zack huffed, impatient. "Annie saw them after the operation that took her embryo. She can identify them. They need to eliminate her. Like they did Fiona."

"And she'll be safer with you? How will you protect her?"

His voice raged. "Dang it, Bridge, I'm floundering here. I need your help. I don't know how to protect my daughter, let alone counsel her. You are the one person in this world that I trust to advise me. Please."

Bridget stared into the middle distance. "What time should I get to your apartment, Zack?"

He cleared his throat. "I, uh, have another favor to ask."

She grimaced. "Out with it."

"I have to work another night shift tonight. I'm worried about leaving Annie alone in the apartment. Could she stay overnight with you and Dustin?"

Bridget smiled for the first time in the conversation. "Of course she can. That goes without saying, Zack."

Zack let out a huge breath. "Thanks, Bridge. You know I appreciate it."

"No problem. You would do the same for me."

"Hopefully, you'll never be in this same situation."

Bridget thought for a minute. "Do you have more night shifts ahead?"

"Not until the following week. I'm off Monday, and then I go back on day shifts Tuesday through Friday. I have the next weekend off." He snorted. "Under, uh, normal circumstances, I would ask if you all wanted to do something next weekend."

Bridget smiled. "Under normal circumstances, we would enjoy that."

Another pause. "Well, here's hoping circumstances get back to normal. Soon."

"Not seeing that in the immediate future, Zack."

Heavy sigh. "Yeah, me neither."

They remained silent for several seconds before Bridget spoke. "Again, what time do you want me?"

"Well, I need to get some rest before my next shift. I should be out of here by 7:30. Annie will be awake at the Durans for me to pick her up. They live close to our apartment, so we should be home by 8:30. Does that work okay for you? I'll fix breakfast."

"Clearly, you've never had a teenage daughter at a sleepover. They won't be up before ten at the earliest."

"Well, she'll have to be up. I can't just go into a holding pattern waiting. I'll call Olivia Duran before I leave here to make sure she gets Annie up."

Bridget chuckled. "Sure thing, 'dad.' Dustin is spending the day with friends. I'll head in your direction when he leaves around 8:30. I'll pick up breakfast. After we eat and talk, I'll take Annie and you can get some sleep."

"Thanks, Bridge. I owe you big time."

"Shut the fark up, Zack. You don't owe me anything. It's what friends do."

Bridget hung up the phone and sat for a few minutes, contemplating.

Friends?

Chapter Thirty-Two

Roach drove the van through an open gate onto the tarmac at Montgomery County Airpark. He turned the vehicle away from the terminal building and drove past multiple rows of parked aircraft to a remote spot where the familiar Learjet stood with engines off and the boarding door lowered. The van stopped with its side door, against which The Fly sat, positioned a few feet from the lower steps of the jet's boarding door. Roach left the engine running as he got out of the driver's side and stepped around to open the side door.

El Fuego pointed his gun at her head. "Get out and walk up those steps into the jet." He glanced in Roach's direction. "He also has a weapon. Neither of us will hesitate to shoot you if you don't do exactly as you are told."

The Fly hesitated.

I may be dead already.

Roach opened the door with his left hand. In his right hand, he pointed a Glock at her chest.

She raised her hands. "Okay. I'm coming." She reached for the handle of her small duffel bag behind the driver's seat.

"Leave it," *El Fuego* said. "You won't need it."

The Fly glared at him.

El Fuego waved his pistol. "Go. Now."

With a toss of her head, she disembarked the van and walked straight to the jet's boarding door and climbed the steps. Roach followed close behind her, the muzzle of the gun poking at her back.

Inside the airplane, the pilot stood in the doorway to the cockpit and nodded toward the cabin. The same bodyguard who had accompanied their earlier flight to Puerto Vallarta sat in an aisle seat holding an AR-15 assault rifle. He pointed the muzzle at the seat directly across the aisle from him.

The Fly remained standing in the aisle.

El Fuego boarded the aircraft. He looked at Roach and gestured toward the door. "I'll be right out."

"Yes, sir." Roach exited the plane.

El Fuego approached The Fly and leered into her face, his pistol stabbing at her chest. "You thought you were so clever. Thought you could beat me. You never had a chance. Now you will pay. *El Vengador* will take care of that in Guadalajara." Without warning, he put his other hand behind her head and pulled her face to his. "We could have been a team." He mashed his lips onto hers and thrust his tongue into her mouth.

The Fly wanted to bite it off, but he pulled back before her thought could turn to action. "You disgust me," he said. Then he shoved her into her seat. Without another word, he turned and left the aircraft.

The pilot raised the boarding door. The guard pointed his weapon at The Fly. "Buckle up. Or not. I don't care."

With a gentle hand, she nudged the weapon's muzzle away. "Please, I have to use the restroom."

The man snorted. "No."

She glanced toward the pilot who was securing the boarding door, then cast a seductive look at the bodyguard. "It's a long flight to Guadalajara. Just the two of us back here. Perhaps we can become close friends by the time the plane lands."

The guard uttered a gruff laugh. "If I want you, I will take you."

The Fly offered a winsome smile. "Perhaps. More fun with a willing partner, right?"

The man huffed. He gestured with the weapon toward the rear of the cabin. "Make it quick."

The Fly hurried down the aisle. The man followed her. At the restroom door, she turned to him. "Really? You going in with me?"

He shrugged. "I have my orders."

She eyed his body. "No room in there for both of us. Even if we want to be close."

He leered. "I will wait here. No funny business, or…" He made a slicing gesture across his throat.

"Such a shame that would be," she said in a cooing voice. "Then we would not become friends."

The guard glanced forward down the aisle. The pilot stood in the cockpit doorway with arms folded. "Just get on with it."

The Fly slid into the narrow restroom and locked the door. She pulled down her pants, sat on the toilet, and retrieved the Glock 42 ultra compact semi-automatic pistol strapped just below her right knee.

El Fuego and that little boy never thought to pat her down. *Estúpidos.*

Now she must get off the jet before it could leave the ground. Certain death, preceded by brutal torture at the hands of *El Vengador*, awaited her in Guadalajara. She considered how to get the advantage over her guard. Seductive feminine wiles would not work any more than they already had.

The guard rapped on the door. "Enough time. Come out now or I will come in and get you."

"No problem, sir. I'm coming."

Straight in, no waiting.

The Fly flushed the toilet and ran water in the sink. She figured the guard to be about six inches taller than she was. She held the Glock at a slight upward angle, opened the door, and fired.

The bullet struck him in mid-chest. He collapsed like a sack of fish. The AR-15 clattered onto the deck.

The Fly grabbed the rifle and retreated into the bathroom. Rapid footsteps announced the pilot rushing down the aisle.

She crouched low as the footsteps came nearer. When they slowed, she wheeled around the door and fired circular bursts down the aisle. The pilot went down without raising his weapon.

The Fly stood in the bathroom's doorway, leaned out, looked and listened. Nothing there except the moans of the wounded guard. She silenced him with a single shot from the Glock to mid-forehead.

She stuffed the pistol into her waistband, hefted the AR-15, stepped over the two bodies, and hustled down the aisle.

At the aircraft boarding door, she peered out the small circular window. Nothing. She activated the door, held the AR-15 in a ready-to-fire position, and sprang down the steps.

The gray cargo van had left. The Fly turned in a circle to see if anyone had responded to the bursts of gunfire inside the airplane. She saw no one. The aircraft's noise abating structure had contained the sound within the cabin.

Where to go? She couldn't stroll around the airpark carrying an assault weapon. Nor did she want to let go of it.

Seeing no other recourse, The Fly ran in a combat crouch to the closest parked aircraft, a high wing single-engine Cessna Caravan about fifteen yards away from the Learjet. She tried the side cargo door, relieved that it opened; more relieved that the aircraft served as a cargo plane with a flat deck and no seats other than the pilot's and co-pilot's. She climbed inside, pulled the door closed, and hunkered down on the deck.

The Fly would wait until nightfall, then get away to plan her next move. And the rest of her life.

Chapter Thirty-Three

Annie Winston slept only in spurts. After the other girls at the sleepover had finally settled down, Annie's hypervigilant mind refused to let go of the disturbing text she had received.

What danger stalked her now? Who could have sent it? Surely not Tyler. If not him, who?

Somewhere in the recesses of her mind, a shadowy image emerged. Tyler, but not Tyler. Someone who looked like Tyler.

Who?

She wished she could be with Maria Santos, in her safe place, so she could recapture the memories storming the wall between her conscious and subconscious minds. In the room's darkness, as the other girls slept, Annie tried to picture herself in Maria's office. Her safe place.

Annie recalled she had lied to her dad and sister so she could meet Sarah at a Starbucks. A different time from the one she remembered. Later. After Christmas?

Yes! The day after Christmas. Bridget's husband had died on Christmas. Annie and Jenn had spent Christmas day with their dad and Bridget and her two boys. She shuddered at the memory. Dad had been so...caring toward Bridget. So clueless about...

What?

Annie had planned to meet Sarah for... a shopping trip? The memory became more clear. Dad had felt so guilty about them all spending Christmas in the hospital that he agreed to let Annie go shopping with Sarah while he and Jenn visited Bridget.

But, they didn't go shopping. They never planned to go shopping.

What did we do?

Annie remembered meeting Sarah at the Starbucks. Sarah had gotten her a soy latte. They sat, then...

She struggled to remember. It was all a fog.

Tyler. She saw Tyler's face, heard his voice. Kind. Then...?

Something in the coffee?

A nurse. She remembered a kind nurse. Did they meet when Annie was a patient in the Bethesda Metro ICU?

The nurse's name was Emily. Probably her dad knew her. Annie would ask him. Maybe she could meet up with her. She had been so gentle...

Exhausted, Annie dozed off.

She awoke in a fright, remembering the wicked text message. It couldn't have been Tyler. He never used profanity around her. He was always the perfect gentleman. One reason she liked him so much.

A frightening image flitted across her consciousness. Tyler pointed a gun at... Who? No, not Tyler with a gun. A Tyler lookalike. The image faded, but Annie thought he had pointed the gun at the kind nurse, Emily.

In the Bethesda Metro ICU? No. Somewhere else.

Annie trembled. "What the hell happened to me?" Tears filled her eyes, and she felt a powerful urge to be with her mother. She loved her dad, and she had wanted to get to know him better by living with him after she got out of the hospital. But her life had been so much easier in California. Normal. Maybe she should go back.

The lights went on in the room, followed by Mrs. Duran's voice. "Nine o'clock, ladies. Rise and shine. Some of you have parents on the way to pick you up. Be ready in fifteen minutes."

Mrs. Duran came up to Annie. "Your dad just called. He's on the way."

Annie looked forward to talking to her dad about the text. And the memories. He would know what to do.

She could trust her dad.

Chapter Thirty-Four

More exhausted than he'd ever felt, Zack turned over the ED to Louise Ritchie, excused himself from the law enforcement people, and headed to the Bunker to change clothes and drive to the Durans to pick up Annie.

He called Olivia Duran before leaving the physician's parking garage. "On my way. This place was hell last night. How did Annie do at the sleepover? She was pretty nervous about it, I think."

"Annie's fine. Eager to see you."

As soon as Zack saw Annie, he knew something was wrong. The cheerful face she put on when she said goodbye to her friends and got into the car looked like a mask. He detected a slight tremolo in her voice when she greeted him.

"Hi, Dad."

He offered her a paternal smile. "Did you have fun?"

She looked away, spoke in a subdued voice. "Yeah."

Zack glanced aside at Olivia Duran, who shrugged. Then he said goodbye, promised to have Olivia and her children over for dinner sometime, and pulled away from the curb.

After driving two blocks, he looked at Annie. "Okay, let's have it. What's wrong?"

"Nothing." She turned away and stared out the window.

Zack rounded a few corners until he was sure no one from the sleepover would drive by and recognize them, then pulled his car to the curb and stopped. He turned in his seat to face his daughter.

"Annie, do you remember our last conversation? The one where we talked about trusting each other and always being honest?"

She hung her head. "Yeah."

"This is one of those times. I don't care about what you're not telling me." He waved a hand as if to erase a chalkboard. "I mean, I won't judge you. Of course I care."

She smirked. "I get it, dad."

"I don't know if you do, or you would've told me by now. Let me remind you again. Whatever you've done, we will make it right."

Annie laughed and cried as only teenage girls seemed capable of doing simultaneously. "Oh, dad. I didn't do anything." She pulled out her phone, punched it, and held it out for him to see.

Reading the vile text, he felt as if someone had punched him in the gut. A flame ignited inside him. "Who sent you this?"

She shook her head and answered in a small voice. "I don't know." She took the phone back.

"Why did you respond with that obscenity?"

"I didn't. Rocky took my phone and texted that."

Zack pulled away from the curb. He wanted to get home to include Bridget in this conversation. "Did Raquel know who sent it?"

"No, but she said she and the other girls sometimes get texts like that."

Zack drove on in silence, at a complete loss for what to say. After they'd gone another couple of blocks, Annie turned to him. "Dad, do you know a nurse named Emily?"

He slammed on the brakes, then pulled to the curb again. "Why do you ask?"

Annie told him about her random memories, about Tyler and Emily.

Zack's heart ached. How much to tell her? Where was Maria Santos when they needed her?

We can't always rely on Maria. This is our issue. Annie's issue. We need to figure out how we deal with it.

He looked at Annie. "I know Emily, but not from Bethesda. She was the nurse at the place where Sarah and Tyler took you. Where something bad happened that you don't remember."

"What?"

He shook his head. "I'm not supposed to tell you until you feel safe knowing it. I don't think that's now. Or here." He swallowed. "And your mom should be part of it." A pause. "Maybe Bridget too. She's meeting us at the apartment to talk about things."

"What things?"

"I'll tell you when we're with Bridget." He eased the car back into traffic and headed to the apartment.

Annie sat beside him, glum and silent. As he turned the car onto their street, she looked at him with moist, sorrowful eyes. Her voice trembled. "I'm scared, Daddy."

He placed a hand on her knee. "I know. I'm scared too."

Chapter Thirty-Five

Zack sat in his favorite chair in his apartment, sipping green tea. Across from him on the couch sat two of the three most important living women in his life.

The third, older daughter Jennifer, had avoided this drama when she returned to Stanford Medical School once Annie had survived her near drowning. Although Zack communicated with her several times a week since their aborted Christmas holiday, he had neither contacted nor heard from her in the last several days. He should call her. He could trust her not to share the current crisis with her mother.

Zack feared Natalie would try to take over; perhaps renew her effort to get Annie back to California. He reminded himself that only Annie had the right to share any of the current events with her mother. Maria Santos had made that clear. He also understood that Annie had no obligation to share those communications with him, and vice versa regarding her interactions with her father.

Annie's voice interrupted his thoughts. "Earth to Dad. You called this meeting, right?"

Bridget smiled and patted Annie's knee. "Sometimes your dad appears to be lost inside his own head, but he's processing the facts and trying to reach a resolution. It's how the male mind operates. Well, some male minds."

Annie didn't buy it. "Dad, what's going on?"

Zack's mind returned to the present. "Sorry." He leaned forward in his chair. "We should approach this like we do a difficult medical case."

Bridget harrumphed and cast Annie a "told you so" look.

Undaunted, Zack continued. "We consider the subjective and objective data, then work through a 'differential diagnosis' to arrive at an assessment and plan."

Bridget folded her arms. "Okay, Doc. How about a different approach? Let's pretend we're in the ER with a critical case. We don't have time for detailed analysis or introspection." She smiled. "A lawyer's approach would be similarly linear, moving from fact to conclusion, but without diving down rabbit holes."

Zack narrowed his eyes. Then he shrugged. "Fine. What do we know?"

Annie spoke. "What's the subjective part?"

"Well, in evaluating an ER patient, it's the information the patient gives you from their perspective in terms of how they feel or what's bothering them."

"I feel scared," Annie said. "I don't remember what happened after I met Sarah at the Starbucks. A humongous missing chunk of memory. Blank spaces I need to fill."

"Over time, Dr. Maria Santos will help you fill them," Zack said. "In a safe way." In his mind, Zack worried they didn't have time for the Maria method.

Bridget spoke. "I wonder why both Tyler Rhodes and Sarah O'Brien resurfaced and communicated with you two just before someone killed Sarah's sister."

"Might not be connected," Zack said. He did not convince himself.

"Strange coincidence if not," Bridget said.

"What about that awful text message I got?" Annie said. "Whoever sent it knew my phone number. Only you, mom, Jenn, and some of my friends at school..." Her voice trailed off and her expressions turned glum. "I used my old number for the new phone."

Bridget put a hand on Annie's shoulder. "Do you remember Tyler Rhodes being there with Sarah at the Starbucks?"

Zack interrupted. "Bridge..."

Annie's mouth fell open. "I didn't know that he was."

Bridget avoided Zack's stare. "He was."

"Why?" Annie asked. "And why don't I remember?"

"Okay," Zack said. "Since Bridget opened that door, yes, he helped Sarah do...whatever she did."

His daughter's body sagged as she stared into the distance, eyes vacant, mouth turned down, face slackened. As if her spirit had left her body. Zack regarded Bridget through narrowed eyes, gave her a slight shake of his head.

The room went silent.

After several minutes, Annie blinked and looked at Zack. "Please, just tell me what happened." She looked at Bridget, then back at Zack. "I feel safe here with you two."

Zack glanced at Bridget. She nodded. "Okay," Zack said. "I'll give you the Cliff Notes."

Annie listened with wide eyes and focused attention as Zack described how Sarah had promised her an abortion, how she must have drugged Annie at the Starbucks, and how Tyler had helped Sarah take Annie to The Good House.

"I can't tell you details about what happened in that place, Annie. I didn't see it. Later, Tyler and a nurse, Emily, described it. Bad stuff. You may not be ready for details, and I don't want to intrude between you and Dr. Santos. For now, you just need to know that Tyler is an enigma. He seems to care about you, but he's also controlled by an evil conspiracy. We don't know if he's friend or foe at this point."

Annie looked puzzled. "I had a memory of someone like him holding a gun."

"Roach," Zack said. "Tyler's alter ego, so to speak. The name he used at The Good House."

Annie grimaced. Then her eyes brightened. "That nurse, Emily. I remembered her. She was kind to me."

Zack looked to Bridget for help.

She reached out and touched Annie's hand. "Hold on to the pleasant memories, Annie. You are alive and safe with people who love you." She glanced at Zack. "That includes your mom."

Zack nodded. "It does. We all love you, Annie, and we want to help Maria help you deal with the unpleasant memories."

A slow smile grew on Annie's face. "Okay," she said. "The other memories can wait. For now, I'm relieved Tyler wasn't all bad, and that Emily is real."

The three sat in silence for a while, savoring the bond between them.

Zack spoke first. "Back to the immediate matter at hand. What do we do now?" He paused. The two women nodded their agreement. "Tyler may have returned to the conspirators," Zack said. "Either voluntarily or by force."

"Tyler, as Roach, might have sent Annie the threatening text," Bridget said.

"How does any of it relate to the murder of Fiona Delaney?" Zack asked. "More to the point, how does that threaten anyone in this room?"

Bridget tented her fingers under her chin. "The conspirators won't know about Annie's amnesia. They will assume that she can identify them."

Zack frowned. "Right. Except we already know who they are. Tyler gave us that information when he came to the hospital looking for help."

Bridget nodded toward Annie. "That text directly threatened Annie."

Again, the room fell silent. Zack stood and went to the kitchen to refill his water bottle. "Can I get anybody anything?"

Bridget looked at her watch. "Shouldn't you get some rest before your night shift? I wouldn't want to be the patient who has to trust your mental acuity when you're stressed, sleep deprived, and functioning on caffeine."

"I should get some rest." He returned to his seat. "But I won't sleep unless we come up with a plan."

"Well," Bridget said. "Maybe for now, Annie comes home with me. She, Dustin, and I spend the evening watching television or playing mindless board games."

Annie raised her hand as if in class. "I, uh, was going to go to church with Rocky and her family tomorrow. How will I get to the Durans from Bridget's?"

Zack bit his lip. Olivia had not mentioned taking Annie to church. "You'll have to cancel. Not safe for you in any public place. You can reschedule once this is all over."

"Dad, I can't just go into hiding. I have friends. Rocky..."

Zack stopped her. "Got it, and I will be the last one to yank you away and put you in a cocoon. But you will have to miss tomorrow. We'll see about your going back to school on Monday."

Annie scowled.

"I'll call Mrs. Duran. We'll work it out, Annie. But not for tomorrow."

Annie pouted. "Why can't I stay over at the Durans?" She made a quick gesture of apology to Bridget. "Not that I wouldn't..."

Zack interrupted. "No. We don't know the Durans well enough, and they have their own lives. I can't be sure you're safe there, and I don't want to impose..."

Annie fired back, "But you'll impose on Bridget and Dustin? What if you don't let me go back to school? What do I do while Bridget's at work and Dustin's at his school?"

Bridget touched her hand. "We have nothing planned for tomorrow, so you won't be imposing. We'll do something fun. As for Monday, I can work from home, or the next day. All week if I must." She pointed to her throat. "Since I no longer can speak in court, I have the option of working from anywhere."

Zack folded his arms. "Perfect solution. Thanks, Bridge."

Annie scowled but said nothing.

Bridget turned to face her. "The danger will be over soon. It won't take all week."

She looked at Zack, then back at Annie. "After which, we can all get back to our 'normal' lives, whatever 'normal' is."

Annie looked at her. "Promise?"

"Never ask an attorney to promise anything," Bridget said. She smiled. "But I'm telling you what I believe is true."

"And I believe it too," Zack said.

Annie let out a groan. "Fine." She looked at Zack. "But you have to make it right with Mrs. Duran. And I have to tell Rocky myself."

Zack glanced at Bridget, then smiled at Annie. "Okay."

"Okay," Annie said.

"Now you need to get some rest," Bridget said to Zack.

He stood, then got another idea. He spoke to Bridget. "Can we see or talk to Emily? Maybe she knows something that would help."

"She's in pretrial confinement up in Baltimore," Bridget said. "Awaiting trial for her role in The Good House. I can check, maybe get in to see her on the pretense that I'm working with her defense attorney."

"Do it," Zack said.

Bridget startled at the vehemence in his voice.

He quickly recovered. "Please, counselor?"

"Okay," Bridget said. "I'll call her defense attorney, Norman Jones, whom you've met, and get him to arrange for at least me to see her. It might be more difficult to get you or Annie in there."

"That works," Zack said.

"Good," Bridget said. "Now, Annie and I will get out of here so you can rest." It was a command, not a suggestion.

Zack saluted her. "Aye, aye, ma'am."

Chapter Thirty-Six

ZACK RETIRED TO HIS bedroom while Bridget helped Annie pack her things for what they all hoped would be a brief stay at Bridget's townhome across the National Capital Area in Alexandria, Virginia.

He changed clothes, then sat on the edge of the bed and retrieved his journal from the bedside table. Had less than a week passed since his last letter to Noelle?

A tap on the door, then Annie's voice. "We're leaving now, Dad."

He opened the door and hugged his daughter. "I love you."

Annie hugged him back. "I love you, too, Dad."

He glanced past her to where Bridget stood holding Annie's carry-on bag. The one his daughter had slung over her shoulder when she and Jenn had arrived in December.

Not even a month ago.

Annie turned to leave. Zack moved to Bridget. "Thanks," he said. He reached out to hug her, but she stepped back.

"What friends do," she said. "Be safe, Zack. And get some danged rest."

"Will do."

He watched them leave, then locked the apartment door, returned to his bedroom, and wrote in his journal.

Dearest Noelle,

I just reread my last letter, so full of joy and hope. Not even a week has passed, and my life has turned to shit.

I fear for my daughter's life, for Bridget's, for everyone's close to me. Yes, for mine too. Which I would sacrifice in a heartbeat for the ones I love.

All the more, I fear for Annie's sanity. How can she ever recover from the trauma those evildoers wrought in her? Will she ever be whole again?

If you were here, you'd say something like, "Trust the process."

Bullshit.
I swear to you, if I ever see Sarah again...
No, I'm not going there. I must think of Annie and hope, not Sarah and vengeance.
Did you just put that thought into my head? Damn you, Noelle. I miss you so much.

Zack put down the journal and pen, relived in his mind some of his joyful times with Noelle. The time a Japanese gentleman had gotten a Tokyo restaurant full of people to toast their engagement. Their prior trip to Miyajima Island, where he had proposed. Watching her F/A-18 Hornet launch from the carrier deck...

...Noelle's broken body in the ship's OR, dead from a fatal crash.

He picked up the journal and wrote.

Your body died in that crash, but not your spirit. I love that I still have that.

He paused to wipe a tear from his eye and stare into the distance. Then he wrote,

I wish I could see you again. I love you.
Always,
Zack

Chapter Thirty-Seven

THE FLY AWAKENED TO the sound of nearby voices. Familiar voices.

She took time to orient herself and remembered she was laying in a Cessna Caravan cargo plane. Her entire body ached. She rolled onto her hands and knees, winced as her bony joints pressed against the steel deck. She crawled to the Plexiglas side window of the Caravan and raised her head to peer outside.

Night had fallen. Darkness bathed the tarmac, and the aircraft parked on it. Two circles of light meandered back and forth in the near distance.

El Fuego and Roach. Theirs had been the voices she'd heard. They were searching each parked airplane. Why had they come back? Did they find the bodies on the Learjet?

"Caramba!" El Fuego's voice bristled with rage. "I will kill that whore with my own hands."

"Where could she have gone?" Roach's voice.

"We find her, or we both die." *El Fuego*, now more anxious than angry.

"Bodies inside the jet." Roach sounded terrified. "But no weapons."

"She took the weapons, idiot." A pause. "Forget the bodies. Our people will clean up the mess and dispose of them."

El Fuego spoke Spanish in a subdued voice, as if on a phone. Then he spoke in a normal voice in English, apparently to Roach. "They will send a pilot and crew to fly the jet away, then dump the bodies into the ocean. Not our problem. We must find The Fly quick, or our bodies will also be on that plane."

The pain in her joints caused The Fly to shift position. A light swung in her direction. She ducked.

"There," Roach said. "In that airplane. I saw movement."

Shit!

Rapid footsteps approached. The Fly slung the AR-15 over her shoulder and held the Glock ultra compact in her right hand.

She waited until the footsteps stopped beside the aircraft, and Roach said, "There's a side door here."

The Fly slammed the door open, knocking young Roach to the ground. Before she could jump out of the aircraft, *El Fuego* loomed over her and grabbed her left arm. He hesitated. He could have killed her then, but he seemed intent on seizing her instead.

The Fly did not hesitate. She fired a shot from the Glock into *El Fuego*'s chest. He gasped and fell backwards to the tarmac.

"You grabbed the wrong arm, *pendejo*." She jumped from the airplane, but didn't wait to make sure *El Fuego* was dead. She turned on Roach, who had just gotten to his feet. His shaky hand pointed a pistol at her.

She aimed her weapon at him. "You won't do it, *chico*. You are no killer. I am. Get your butt out of here or I will leave your corpse next to his."

Roach balked just long enough for her to overtake him, wrestle him to the ground, and disarm him. She hauled him up.

An approaching siren filled the air.

"Get a real life while you still can, *bebé*." She pushed him away. "Run now. *Ándale!*"

The youth ducked his head and scampered away into the darkness.

The Fly looked in the opposite direction from the approaching siren. Dense foliage lay just past the chain-link fence on the perimeter of the airfield. She crouched and ran toward it. When she reached the fence, she tossed the AR-15 over it and thrust the Glock into her waistband. She scaled the fence with ease and somersaulted over the top. She landed on her feet, facing the tarmac, then reached down to retrieve the AR-15.

A shot rang out. Searing pain bored into her left groin. She looked up. *El Fuego* lay prone on the tarmac, his right hand clutching the pistol he'd just fired. A last shot.

The Fly raised the AR-15 to return fire, but a security vehicle with flashing lights rolled up fast. El Fuego's head dropped onto the asphalt.

The Fly slung the automatic weapon over her shoulder and held the Glock in her right hand. Her left fist applied pressure to the groin wound. She limped away and crawled into the darkness of the underbrush.

Had the security guard seen her? Even if not, *El Fuego* would rat on her. If he lived.

Chapter Thirty-Eight

THE FLY HUNKERED DOWN in the thick woods. The gnashing pain in her left groin intensified while icy numbness spread down her left thigh. Sharp stabbing pains penetrated her pelvis—worse than her most difficult menstrual cramps. She had stanched the bleeding in her groin with pressure, or at least slowed it down.

But now?

A serious injury. Fatal?

Without medical help soon, she might die in these woods. She looked at the Glock in her right hand. Better to shoot herself in the head right here and now.

Never!

A cacophony of sirens approached from different directions. The security guard had alerted law enforcement. How many? From where?

They would search the woods. Had Roach eluded the security guard and escaped? Or did he surrender? No matter. Police would find her either way.

The Fly risked taking her fist off the entrance wound in her groin. A gush of blood followed. She reapplied the pressure and tried to rise to her knees. A sensation like her brain leaving her head force her back to the ground.

Mierda! I am dead.

As if to verify the thought, a wave of crushing pain coursed through her lower abdomen, then abruptly let up as her bladder emptied itself.

The Fly gripped the Glock and held the muzzle to her temple.

End it now.

She placed her finger on the trigger.

El Fuego wins.

The Fly took her finger off the trigger.

"That double-crossing asshole must not win." The sound of her own voice speaking the words encouraged her. She lowered the pistol, squinted her eyes, and scowled. "Never!"

Sirens and reflections of flashing blue lights filled the night around and across her hiding place deep in the brush.

A sudden, delightful thought motivated The Fly to move. Despite the pain and dizziness, she crawled out of her hiding place, dragging the now weak leg behind her. Using the AR-15 like a crutch, she half-limped, half-crawled toward the chain-link fence.

When she got close to the fence, The Fly dropped the Glock and the AR-15 to the ground. Then she inched closer to the fence, stopped, positioned the weak leg beneath her, and rose to her knees. She put her hands on her head and shouted.

"Over here. I surrender."

A bright searchlight swung in her direction. She tried to stay erect, hands still on her head, but the dizziness overcame her and she fell forward to the ground.

Voices shouted, footsteps ran toward the fence, then the rattling of chain links as people climbed over it. Strong hands gripped her arms and legs and rolled her onto her back. A bright light shone into her face, the shadow of a figure behind it.

"She's alive. Call for EMS."

The Fly whispered toward the light. "I am Nilda Flores, from Guadalajara, Mexico. Do not let me die. I will help you bring *Los Hermanos de Guadalajara* to the justice they deserve."

Chapter Thirty-Nine

Although she still felt hungry, Annie let Dustin Hilliard take the coveted last piece of pizza. She had witnessed Bridget's son losing his father only a few months ago, and she felt sorry for him. The affinity stopped there. As much as Annie liked Bridget Larsen, she could not warm up to Dustin. Too nerdy for Annie's taste. Too immature compared to Tyler's worldliness.

She settled for a hunk of dry cheese bread, then followed Dustin into the family room. Bridget fumbled with the remote control to the sixty-five-inch Samsung TV mounted on the wall.

Bridget offered Annie a chagrined smile. "I always let Marshall do the technical stuff."

"I got it, Mom." Dustin took the remote and pushed buttons at a staccato pace.

There are places in this world for nerdy geeks, Annie thought.

The trio sat spaced out on the L-shaped theater couch while Dustin started the movie.

Annie's phone buzzed with a new text message. She glanced at the screen.

Tyler?

Curious, she leaned away from Dustin and opened the text.

where u

Wow. Not even a hello?

Annie texted back. where u

need to see u

What? Annie scowled and glanced at Dustin and Bridget. Their attention stayed on the movie.

what up

can't say

sounds weird

bad shit

A shiver of worry ran up Annie's spine.

Cannot trust him.

Not after what she had learned about him from her dad and Bridget.

Better to be straight with him.

can't see u

y not

u roach

The long pause had Annie thinking maybe he had hung up. She hovered her finger over the "End" button, but then he replied.

u know

yeah fuck off roach

wait not like u think

u judas me

saved u

Annie harrumphed, which got Bridget's attention.

"You okay, Annie?" She glanced at Annie's iPhone. "Who's that?"

Dustin looked at her too, curious.

"Just Raquel from school. Homework stuff."

"Should we pause the movie?"

"No. I'll be off in a second."

Bridget and Dustin turned their attention back to the screen. Annie looked at her phone. Tyler had added a text.

gotta see u and make it right

no

u not at your place

He's at the apartment?

go away

please I can help you

Annie scrunched her face. She didn't need his help. Not anymore. She had to end this scam. Now.

goodbye forever

She ended the text string, then shut off her phone. A tear came to her eye as she turned back to the movie and forced a smile.

"All done."

Bridget regarded her with worried eyes.

Chapter Forty

Less than an hour into his night shift, the charge nurse interrupted Zack's examination of a child with an earache.

"I'm sorry to interrupt, Dr. Winston. We have a trauma inbound."

Zack gave her a curious look. "Okay, you know what to do. Trauma Alert and such."

The nurse continued. "Heavy law enforcement. Suspected terrorist."

"Got it," Zack said. He finished his exam, reassured the child's mother, and ordered a prescription.

The Trauma Alert blared on the overhead speakers.

When Zack entered the trauma resuscitation room, he detected a higher than usual level of frenzy among the staff as they prepared to receive their patient.

"What have we got?" he asked.

"Female, GSW to the groin. Suspected terrorist."

"What have we got?"

Zack turned to the voice from behind that had echoed his question—pleased to see Dr. Beth Jaklic, the trauma surgeon for the day. Opposite personality from Dr. Autry Robertson of the previous night's shift. Where Robertson was bombastic, frenetic, and overbearing, Beth exuded quiet confidence, professionalism, and collegiality. She was also the most competent trauma surgeon on the staff, a fact she didn't need to wear on her sleeve.

Zack briefed her. "Don't know much. Female. GSW to the groin. The word 'terrorist' has come up. Heavy law enforcement on scene."

"Great," Beth said with a weary smile. "A fun way to end my twenty-four-hour shift." She turned to the charge nurse. "Just in case, who's the vascular surgeon on call?"

"That would be Dr. Shelton," the nurse said.

Beth looked at her watch. "Put him on alert. He's a night owl, so should still be up." She scoffed. "Hopefully sober."

Inbound sirens had stopped outside the ER, but no activity from the ambulance entrance. No onrush of paramedics with a patient. Zack stepped out of the trauma room and almost collided with Detective Tina Martinez.

"What are you doing here?" He said to her.

The detective wiped tired eyes. "Waiting to see who this 'terrorist' is." She gave him an earnest look. "You're about to be overrun with law enforcement. FBI and DHS already alerted."

Great, Zack thought.

The ambulance entrance doors whooshed open and paramedics rushed through with their patient on a gurney. They wheeled past Zack with a female patient who looked familiar to him. He followed the entourage into the trauma room.

A paramedic gave a report. "Thirtyish Hispanic female, GSW to the left groin, hypotensive on our arrival, responding to fluids. We've kept pressure on the wound. Stable during transport."

Another medic added, "Fortyish Hispanic male dead at the scene from a GSW to the chest. Two more dead males on board a nearby Learjet with Mexican tail number. Livor and rigor mortis indicated they'd been dead for hours. FBI and Homeland Security on scene as we departed."

Zack recognized the patient as the Latina woman whom he'd seen the previous night. A Ms. Ruiz. He'd treated for a migraine headache, but she'd disappeared from the ER. His thoughts flew to the "execution" of Fiona Delaney by an unidentified Latina woman posing as a housekeeper. The loose pieces of the scenario fell into place like Scrabble tiles on a triple word score.

"You going to join me here, Zack?" Beth Jaklic's voice interrupted his reverie.

"Sorry." He took his place at the head of the gurney. "I saw this woman yesterday. She faked a migraine. I think she killed another patient in the ICU."

"Doesn't matter right now," Beth said. "Unless you want her to die, too."

Zack assessed the woman's airway while Beth turned her attention to the groin and abdomen.

The paramedics had placed an oxygen mask over the victim's nose and mouth. Although her respirations were rapid and shallow, her skin color appeared only somewhat pallid. Likely from blood loss and not airway or breathing compromise. He listened over her chest and heard adequate breath sounds, equal on both sides.

"Airway and breathing okay," he said to the room. He looked at the monitor. The woman's blood pressure had dropped and her pulse sped up. Ongoing blood loss?

"Get another IV going," he said. "Run the fluids wide open. Get O-Negative blood now."

A slight grunt from the patient got his attention. The woman looked at Zack with entreating eyes. She tried to speak.

Zack bent over, placed an ear close to her mouth, and lifted the oxygen mask.

"Please." The woman spoke in quick gasps. "Don't...let me...die. I know... to help... you."

Zack replaced the oxygen mask and talked into her ear. "You won't die. Just stay calm."

Beth Jaklic's voice diverted Zack's attention. She spoke to the nurse. "Please call Dr. Shelton. Tell him we have a probable laceration of the femoral artery. He can meet me in the OR."

She continued her exam, then looked at Zack. "Blood in the rectum."

A nurse inserted a urinary catheter. "Bloody urine."

Beth announced to no one in particular. "We've got femoral artery, bladder, and rectal trauma. At least."

"OR is ready," a nurse reported.

Beth looked at Zack. "Cleared for transport, Zack?"

"Yep. Good luck. Let me know what you find."

Beth looked at him like an older sister. "Of course."

In less than a minute, Beth and a large entourage of staff had whisked the patient away, leaving Zack alone in the trauma room.

He took a deep breath, then went to find Detective Martinez.

Chapter Forty-One

At around 10 PM, the sudden ring of Bridget's front doorbell startled the trio watching the second movie of the evening.

An unwelcome sense of dread struck Annie. She wanted to run and hide somewhere.

"I'll get it," Dustin said.

Bridget paused the movie.

The front door opened, followed by Dustin's jarred voice. "Tyler? What the hell?"

As if tethered to each other, Bridget and Annie both rose in unison from the couch and headed into the living room. Annie gasped when she saw Tyler Rhodes, dressed in dungarees with red streaks across the chest.

Blood?

Annie hoped so, a surprising reaction. She wanted to attack him, rip his throat out.

Bridget stepped forward. "Tyler?"

Tyler cast a desperate look at both Annie and Bridget. "I'm in trouble. Nowhere else to go."

Bridget folded her arms. "Home, perhaps?"

Tyler's eyes pleaded. "Can't. No one else there." His anxious eyes darted around, as if expecting a snake to strike at him. "First place they will look for me."

"They?" Bridget asked, skeptical. "Who are 'they'?"

Beads of sweat appeared on Tyler's forehead. He cringed. "The men who want to kill me."

Annie fumed, spat out her words. "Kill you, or Roach?" She wheeled on Bridget. "Get him out of here. Please."

Bridget put a hand on Annie's shoulder. "Chill. I got this." She turned to Tyler, who stood just inside the front door that Dustin was still holding open. "You'd better come in." To Dustin, "Close the door."

Tyler stepped into the room. Dustin locked the door.

Annie backed away toward the kitchen. She couldn't bear to be close to Tyler, but she also didn't want to miss anything.

Bridget pointed to the couch and spoke to Tyler. "Sit."

Tyler slunk to the couch and sat.

Bridget beckoned Annie over and pointed to a chair. "Sit."

She pointed to another chair. "You too, Dustin."

Annie inched forward, sat in the chair, and turned her body away from Tyler. She thought she might throw up.

Bridget stood in front of Tyler, as if about to cross-examine a hostile witness. "Explain," she said in a commanding, albeit hoarse, voice. "Who wants to kill you?" She paused a beat. "Roach." She stepped closer. "And why do you have blood on your shirt?"

Tyler looked from Bridget to Annie and back with wide eyes. His voice trembled when he spoke. "The cartel. They killed..." He looked at his feet, struggling to hold back tears. "The Fly shot *El Fuego*." He buried his head in his hands.

What fly? Annie wondered.

When he looked up seconds later, Tyler's cheeks glistened with tears. "They will think I helped her. I can't let them find me."

Her? What her? Annie thought.

Tyler pleaded in a pathetic voice. "Please. Hide me."

A wave of rage flared in Annie. "You make no sense, moron."

Bridget turned on her and spoke in a sharp voice. "Hush. I told you I have this."

Annie slunk back in the chair, her rage now divided between Tyler and Bridget.

Bridget stepped away from her overbearing position on Tyler and took a seat next to him on the couch, shifting from a cross-examining lawyer to a mother.

"You need to slow down, Tyler. Who is *El Fuego*? Who, or what, is The Fly?"

Tyler looked at her, genuine terror in his eyes. "I am in such deep shit, I can't..."

Bridget touched his hand. "Start at the beginning. Tell us everything. Leave nothing out."

When Tyler finished his story, Bridget pulled out her phone and called Zack.

Chapter Forty-Two

Zack found himself in all too familiar scenario. He sat at the ER conference room table with Detective Martinez and the agents from FBI and Homeland Security. The tense mood was like a thick fog around him. Auras of urgency emanated from the law enforcement people.

Straight in, no waiting, Zack thought.

"Our trauma patient is the woman who killed Fiona Delaney."

The others exchanged looks. Special Agent in Charge Tony Mason spoke. "Yep."

"And she offered to help us," Zack said. "She said so to me in the trauma room."

"Did that in the field, too," Detective Martinez said. "Identified herself as one Nilda Flores. We don't know if that's her real name or an alias. We haven't found it in any of our databases."

"First time I saw her," Zack said, "she called herself Soledad Ruiz."

"We know," Mason said. "No data on that name, either."

Agent Bloom from DHS picked up the narrative. "We've identified one of the dead men at the airpark as Damáso Mendez, aka *El Fuego,* or 'The Fire,' one of the three brothers who lead the Guadalajara drug cartel known as *Los Hermanos de Guadalajara.* He's the youngest of the three. Known to be a real hothead. The oldest brother, Wilfredo, runs the business. Goes by the nickname, *El Víbora,* The Serpent. Very cool customer. Seldom gets upset. The third, and most dangerous, is a half-brother, Enrique Mendez, *El Vengador.* Full handle is *El Vengador de la Sangre,* Avenger of Blood. Thought to be the primary assassin in that cartel. No one knows his actual body count."

She paused. "The Learjet has a Mexican registration, and the other dead men were the pilot and a bodyguard."

Detective Martinez spoke next. "We're running ballistics on the bullet that killed Mendez, but we expect it will match the Glock surrendered at the scene by your patient."

"Which suggests..." Zack didn't finish the sentence.

"Yep," Tony Mason said. "She's a cartel *sicario*, an assassin."

Zack looked from one to the others. "Why would a *sicario* kill Fiona?"

"Connect the dots, Doc," Martinez said.

Zack thought for a moment before speaking. "Fiona had turned confidential informant on The Good House." He scoffed. "Except not so 'confidential' after all. Does her murder imply that The Good House conspirators are involved in the drug trade?"

A sudden thought hit him. "The phony police officer who killed Dr. Good at the airpark was a Latina, right? You never found her."

"Until tonight," Mason said.

The blood drained from Zack's head. He took a few breaths before he could speak. "Annie's stolen embryo…"

"Possibly barter for something associated with the international drug trade," Agent Mason said. "Except frozen embryos don't command high prices. Why would a cartel be interested?"

Zack swallowed hard. "The value was not in that embryo itself, but in the process that retrieved it." He pursed his lips. "We understand that The Good House contained a fully equipped OR and tissue preservation lab. Dr. Good, a local obstetrician we knew as Sebastian Barth, stole Annie's embryo from her uterus, froze it, and transported it to the airpark. It was proof of concept, direct embryo transfer from uterus-to-uterus, bypassing the in-vitro fertilization process, IVF."

Agent Bloom scratched her head. "Why would the cartel be interested in that?"

"Yeah. How would that be any better than *in vitro* fertilization?" Detective Martinez asked.

"Cheaper and simpler than IVF, but worth bazillions to whoever owned the new process. To my knowledge, it's never been done. Just need a willing donor." Zack winced. "Or, as in Annie's case, an unwilling but incapacitated donor." He stifled a tear.

After a pause, Agent Bloom spoke in a quiet, empathic voice. "Can you go on, Doctor?"

Zack took a deep breath and nodded. "The Good House began as a baby-trafficking enterprise. They lured wayward, unattached, late-term pregnant women under the pretext of getting rid of their babies after birth. They promised the women a return to life, unencumbered. Instead, after they delivered, they abandoned them in a remote location." He paused. "Or killed them and disposed of their bodies."

Agent Mason frowned. "That changed?"

"Yes," Zack said. "Annie became their trial case. Their first victim in very early pregnancy. They kidnapped her, did the operation to steal her embryo, then tried to drown her in the Potomac and make it look like suicide."

Bloom shook her head. "That's...diabolical."

Zack continued. "Barth, aka Good, was on his way to that Learjet. He shot and wounded the nurse who was with him, Emily Morgan, when she refused to board the jet. We thought an MCPD officer shot Good, but apparently it was this *sicario* posing as an officer. She disappeared with the transfer case containing the embryo. She must have boarded that jet and flown to..."

"Mexico," Agent Bloom said.

Agent Martinez stroked her chin. "So this female assassin eliminated Dr. Good, took the embryo, and absconded to Mexico." She thought for a moment. "It still doesn't compute. Why would the cartel be interested in that new procedure? I can't picture them getting into that business."

"To sell," Agent Bloom said. "Maybe to the highest bidder."

"Not buying that," Agent Mason said. "They're rolling in dough from their drug trade."

"Maybe it's not money they want," Zack said.

All three agents looked at him, curious.

Zack tried to wrap his mind around a germinal thought, but he couldn't bring it to full consciousness. "Something else. Something they need for... I don't know, something."

Mason scoffed. "That's good, Doc. Very helpful."

Detective Martinez said, "Chew on that thought some more, Doc. Let us know when you have something more concrete."

Zack deflated. Then another thought hit him. "The woman knows things about the cartel she's willing to divulge."

Mason shook his head. "Yeah, right. We've got her for at least the murder of that *El Fuego* guy and probably the other two morts at the airpark. If you're right, Doc, also for Fiona Delaney and Dr. Sebastian Barth aka Dr. Good." He shook his head. "She'll need to come up with more than 'things' to work any kind of deal with us."

Detective Martinez looked at him. "No harm in pursuing it, right?"

"We need her alive first," Agent Bloom said.

"Let me see if we have anything on that," Zack said. He picked up the phone and called the OR. "How's Dr. Jaklic's case going?"

He listened for a minute, then hung up and turned to the agents. "Still in the OR, but she will live. Won't be able to communicate for some time. Extensive pelvic trauma plus a damaged femoral artery. It's questionable whether her left leg will survive after going so long without adequate blood supply. She'll be in the ICU on a ventilator for at least twenty-four hours, maybe longer."

"Same place where she killed Fiona Delaney," Agent Mason said. "Assuming the doc is right."

"I am right," Zack said. "Which means the cartel might send someone for her as well."

"Okay," Mason said. "Let's go with that. Maximum protection and security. No one gets close to that woman except verified medical staff, and then only under close observation." He cast a pointed look at Detective Martinez. "No housekeepers, janitors, or laundry folks. Medical staff only."

"Got it," Martinez said. She rose to leave the room. "I'll get on it."

Before she reached the door, it opened. A nurse looked at Zack. "Dr. Winston, there's a Bridget Larsen on the phone for you. Says it's urgent."

What?

Zack looked at his cell phone. Dead battery. "I'll be right there." He followed the nurse and Detective Martinez out of the room.

Chapter Forty-Three

Bridget heaved a grateful sigh to hear Zack's voice on the phone.

"What's up, Bridge? Is Annie okay?"

"We're all okay, Zack. Tyler Rhodes showed up at my door. He's telling quite the story."

Silence on the other end.

"You still there, Zack?"

"Get him out of there. You know who Tyler is."

"He came looking for help." She summarized Tyler's story.

"Not good," Zack said. "He's put you all in danger." He told her about the trauma patient he'd received, the suspected cartel assassin, no doubt from the same scene that Tyler had escaped at the airpark.

Bridget's heart raced. "Seriously, Zack?"

Dustin interrupted before she could say more. "Mom, there's an SUV parked in front of the house."

Bridget walked to the window and looked out. A dark blue SUV, similar to the one that had followed her from her office parking garage, sat on the cul-de-sac in front of her house. Engine running.

"Zack, there's an SUV parked in front of our house."

An identical SUV pulled up behind the first one.

"Make that two SUVs."

"Hang on," Zack said.

Bridget heard him talking to someone in the room. Then his voice came back on the line, anxious. "Police on the way. You and the others get to a safe place. Now. Stay on the line if you can. I've got you on speaker with Detective Martinez."

"Got it." Bridget went to the kitchen to alert the others. Where to go? She thought about upstairs. No, they would be trapped if someone invaded the house. They needed to leave the house.

"To the garage. Now. Turn off all the lights on the way."

Dustin led Annie and Tyler through the kitchen door into the attached garage. Bridget checked the lock and deadbolt on the front, turned off the lights, and followed them. A sudden thought stopped her.

Marshall's gun.

She had forgotten about her earlier resolution to get rid of the thing. As her thoughts raced, car doors opened and closed on the street. An electric shock pierced her heart, and she drew in a quick breath.

Move it, Bridge.

She rushed up the stairs to the bedroom, opened the drawer on the bedside stand, and filled her hand with her late husband's Smith and Wesson.

Marshall had kept it unloaded. Bridget fumbled through the drawer to find the box of ammunition stuffed in the back. With trembling fingers, she loaded the pistol, held it in her right hand, and headed back to the stairs.

The sudden crash of the front door collapsing stopped her. Multiple sets of footsteps clomped into the house, followed by voices shouting in Spanish.

Bridget chambered a round in the pistol.

Zack's voice came through the phone. "Bridge? Are you all still there?"

"*Arriba*," a gruff voice said from downstairs.

Bridget knew enough Spanish to understand the word meant "up." She pocketed the phone, still on, and inched back into the bedroom.

Another voice from below terrified her. "*El garaje.*" The garage!

She closed the bedroom door, hurried to the opposite side of the bed, and hunkered down behind it.

Footsteps pounded up the stairs.

Chapter Forty-Four

Annie, Dustin, and Tyler huddled between the Range Rover and Mercedes in the attached garage.

The door between the kitchen and garage stood open. "Where's Bridget?" Annie asked.

Dustin's eyes widened. "Maybe she went upstairs to get dad's gun."

Annie glared at Tyler. "If we get out of this..."

The crashing sound of the front door collapsing inside the house startled them. Rapid voices yelled in Spanish.

"*Arriba,*" one said.

"*El garaje,*" said another.

Dustin turned to Annie and Tyler. "They're coming. We need to get out of here." He looked around, desperate. "Get in the Range Rover. Keys should be in it. I'll drive."

As they piled into the vehicle, two gunshots erupted from over their heads inside the house.

"The master bedroom," Dustin said. "Mom..."

The door from the kitchen burst open and the garage light flipped on. Two men dressed in black dungarees charged into the garage. Both carried semi-automatic weapons that they pointed at the three youths. One man appeared to be middle age, angry and dangerous. A hideous gray/red cross stood out on his forehead. The other invader, a youth, looked to be similar in age to Tyler or Dustin.

"Hands up," the older man said in accented English. "Move away from the cars."

The younger man pointed his weapon at Annie and Dustin and forced them to move back. The other man struck Tyler across the face with the butt of his weapon.

Tyler fell to the ground. The assailant zip-tied his hands behind, yanked him up, and pushed him hard toward the door into the house. He leered at Annie and Dustin, then spoke in a deep growl to the young man guarding them.

"*Mátalos.*"

Annie cringed. In her Spanish class, she had recently learned the word *matar,* meaning "to kill."

Sirens approached from the distance, at first faint, then growing louder.

The older man shoved Tyler into the kitchen and called toward the stairs. "*Vámonos! Ya viene la policía.*" In the doorway, he turned back to the youth and shouted. *Apúrate!* Then he disappeared into the kitchen.

Their young captor moved closer to Annie and Dustin. His voice trembled. "Turn around. On your knees."

Annie and Dustin turned and dropped to the floor. Annie's heart raced and her head pounded. Dustin sobbed next to her.

Their assassin moved closer.

Annie sensed the weapon's muzzle inches from the back of her head.

"Bridge?" Her dad's voice, muffled and distant, as if in a dream. The last sound she heard before the gunshot explosion caused a ripping sensation inside her head.

Her would-be killer slumped forward, knocking Annie to the floor of the garage and landing on top of her. She took a deep breath.

Not dead.

In the next instant, someone lifted the man's body off her.

Bridget's voice. "You're okay. You're both okay."

Annie turned toward the voice and sat up. Bridget stood near her, her left arm around Dustin. Her right hand clutched a pistol.

Sirens wailed outside the house, then stopped.

Bridget let go of Dustin, stooped, put the weapon on the floor, and extracted a cell phone from her pocket. She raised the phone to her lips.

"I have them, Zack. Both safe."

All at once, she slumped. Dustin helped his mother to the floor. A stream of blood spread from her left shoulder and ran down her arm.

Chapter Forty-Five

TWO LITERS OF NORMAL saline plus a blood transfusion had corrected Bridget's hypovolemic shock and restored her consciousness. Zack touched her right hand and looked into her eyes as she came awake.

She startled, then looked at him with narrowed eyes. "Zack?" she asked in an uncertain tone.

"We can't keep meeting like this," he said.

She tried to look at him, but winced with pain. Her head turned toward the bandage over her upper left arm and shoulder. She looked back at Zack, mystified. "Where am I?"

"The trauma resuscitation room at my hospital," Zack said. "Given the, uh, circumstances, we thought it best to transport you here. It meant bypassing several other hospitals, but you seemed stable enough for it."

"Stable?"

"Someone shot you. The bullet shattered your left proximal humerus, the bone in your upper arm. It nicked your axillary artery. You arrived in shock from blood loss." He glanced at the bandage and tried to give her a reassuring smile. "At least you're right-handed. That left arm may not be useful for a while."

A pained expression came to Bridget's face. "Someone? Shot me?"

"Yeah," Zack said. "The guy who meant to kill you."

She blinked in successive movements. "I remember. They came to the house. I went to the bedroom for Marshall's gun..." Her face twisted, and her right hand cupped her mouth. "I, I shot a man."

"Two men, Bridge. Both dead. You would be dead if you hadn't done that. So would Annie and Dustin."

Her breath quickened, nostrils flared, chin quivered. "Dustin? Annie?" She looked at Zack with wide eyes.

"Dustin and Annie are safe, shaken, but not injured. They're in the quiet room with police protection until we figure everything out."

Bridget's brow furrowed. "Tyler was there. What about Tyler?"

"Gone," Zack said. "Before the cops arrived. We think the cartel got him."

"Cartel?"

Two surgical techs rolled a stretcher into the room. Zack smiled at Bridget, squeezed her right hand. "There's a lot I want to tell you, but for right now, our best orthopedic and vascular surgeons need to fix your shoulder."

She gripped his hand. "They won't put me under, will they?"

"Afraid so."

She released her grip, shook her head. "No."

"I get it," Zack said. "You hate to lose control. But it's safe, and the only option. We'll all be here when you return." He nodded to a nurse who approached the bedside.

The nurse administered a pre-anesthetic sedative through Bridget's IV line.

"Dustin..."

Zack leaned over and kissed her forehead. "I'll look after him. You won't be out long."

Bridget had lapsed into unconsciousness. Zack couldn't tell if she'd felt his kiss. He looked at the clock. Despite all that had happened since he came on duty, he still had five hours left in his night shift.

What else might go wrong?

Zack followed the gurney bearing Bridget out of the trauma room. As her entourage headed toward the elevators to the OR, Zack turned in the opposite direction back to the ER workstation.

Louise Ritchie and Jerry Hartman met Zack on his arrival in the treatment area.

"I've got the rest of your shift," Louise said.

"We've locked down the hospital," Jerry said. "Police mandate."

Zack looked around, noticing for the first time a multi-agency law enforcement presence. His ER looked more like a war zone than a haven for the sick and injured.

He thanked Louise and Jerry, then headed to the quiet room to check on Annie and Dustin.

Chapter Forty-Six

THE FLY STARTLED AWAKE. She gagged against a hard object protruding through her nose and down her throat. She tried to reach for it, to pull the object out, but struggled against restraints that tied her arms to...? A bed?

A noisy machine next to her made rhythmic pumping sounds that matched streams of air forced into her lungs. She lifted and turned her head toward the sound, which made the object shift in her throat and cause more gagging. Her head fell back onto a pillow and the gagging stopped. The streams of pumped air continued. Opening her eyes wide, she turned her head just a little to take in her surroundings.

A mechanical ventilator connected to the object in her nose and throat. A breathing tube!

She opened her eyes wide, looked past the ventilator, and recognized the intensive care unit in which she had murdered Fiona Delaney.

The Fly panicked. Would anyone here recognize her?

Must get out of here. Now.

She thrashed against the restraints, desperate to remove the breathing tube and make her escape. A high-pitched alarm sounded over her head.

A team of nurses appeared at her side.

"She's awake," one said.

"Fighting the vent," another said.

"Sedation," a male voice said.

A fourth person came up to the other side of the bed. The Fly watched in helpless surrender as the person injected something into a tube coming out of her forearm. Just like she had injected potassium chloride into Fiona Delaney's IV.

They mean to kill me.

She struggled harder. Then, oblivion.

***

"Are you awake, ma'am?" A kind voice. Female. A soft touch to her arm.

The Fly opened her eyes and squinted. A woman wearing surgical scrubs and a hair net smiled at her.

"There you are," the woman said. Another soft touch, but firmer. The woman bent close to The Fly's face.

"I'm Dr. Jaklic. I took care of you last night. You suffered a nasty gunshot wound to your groin." She looked into The Fly's eyes, as if searching for signs of memory.

The Fly squinted to clear her vision. She tried to raise her head, but the tube irritated her throat and she gagged, and feared she might vomit.

"We can take that tube out of your throat now, ma'am," the doctor said. "Just follow my directions." She looked across the bed and nodded.

The Fly followed her gaze to a young man standing on the opposite side of the bed. "Hi," he said. "I'm Jacob, your nurse. We're going to extubate you now. It will be a little uncomfortable, but then you won't have that tube in your throat anymore."

"Deflate the balloon," the doctor said.

The Fly watched as the man named Jacob did something with a syringe in front of her face, but too close for her to see clearly.

"Okay," the doctor said. "Now take a deep breath, then exhale."

The Fly shook her head, as if she didn't understand.

"It's okay," the doctor said. "We've got it."

Without warning, she grabbed the tube and pulled it out through The Fly's nose. Uncontrollable spitting and coughing followed a moment of excruciating discomfort.

"Here's some O-2 for you," the young man said. He placed a plastic mask over The Fly's nose and mouth and secured it with a strap around her head. A pleasant flow of what felt like clean air entered her throat. She drew a long puff and tried to hold it in her lungs like smoke from a joint. Then she blew it out and took eager breaths in rapid sequence.

The doctor and the young man looked over her head. Now that her head had cleared, she figured they were scanning a monitor.

"O-2 sats are good," the doctor said. She looked at The Fly. "We'll keep the tube out, but you'll need to inhale the oxygen for a while. I'll be back to talk to you in a few minutes."

While the young man fussed around her, cleaning up the debris and straightening the bed, The Fly closed her eyes and relished full breaths without the annoyance of the tube. As she did so, she assessed her situation. Based on what she had done earlier, she was not safe in this hospital, not even in this intensive care unit. *Los Hermanos* would come for her soon. Squinting through partly opened eyes, she evaluated her immediate surroundings. Two uniformed, armed police officers guarded her. She imagined there would be others in the area. Unlike the unfortunate redhead The Fly had killed, her presence here had attracted heavy attention.

How would she play it?

She thought of *El Fuego*. Dead. Or not. Others? She shuddered at the thought of *El Vengador* coming after her. What had become of the mission? Had they aborted it? Had the youth, Roach, turned on them? No matter. *Los Hermanos* would never give up.

Did the hospital people and the cops know her identity? She frowned as she remembered calling herself Nilda Flores when she surrendered to the police. Yet, she carried no identification. Had anyone here said that name? That ER doctor she'd fooled might still think she was Soledad Ruiz.

The Fly smiled. She could be whoever she wanted to be, until she got the right moment, the right protection, to exact revenge on *Los Hermanos pendejos*.

While The Fly ruminated, the doctor returned.

What was her name? Jack something.

Dr. Jack-Something sat next to the bed by The Fly's head. "We need to get some information from you, then I can tell you about your condition and recovery." She smiled.

The Fly gave her a blank look.

"Let's start with your name," the doctor said.

The Fly looked baffled. She took a few seconds to find her voice. "*No hablo inglés*."

The doctor beckoned to the nurse. "Help me out here, Jacob."

The nurse came up to the other side of the bed. "*Cómo se llama?*"

The Fly blinked hard, put on a distraught expression, then stared into space.

The young man repeated the question. "*Cómo se llama. Cúal es su nombre?*"

The Fly forced tears into her eyes and shook her head. She looked at the doctor and the young man as if panic-stricken.

"*No recuerdo,*" she said.

The young man frowned, took a breath, and looked at the doctor. "She doesn't remember her name."

Chapter Forty-Seven

ANNIE WINSTON DIDN'T STOP shaking until she returned from the restroom to the ED conference room at Bethesda Metro Hospital. She had done her best to rinse the blood, bits of bone and muscle, and stuff that looked like raspberry custard out of her hair and off her neck and face. She still felt like death clung to her, and she ached to take a long shower and shampoo her hair.

What is Dad doing now?

Annie understood that, as the emergency physician on duty, her dad needed to take care of Bridget. But Annie needed him here. With her. To hold her and tell her it would all be okay.

Will it be? What if those men...?

She tried to put the scary thought out of her head as she resumed her seat next to Dustin at the conference table.

Detective Martinez, whom she'd met what seemed like months ago, nodded to her. "Feel better, Annie?"

Annie frowned. "No, ma'am."

"Understood," the detective said. "And it's Tina, not 'ma'am,' remember?"

"Okay," Annie said.

Tina looked at the notes she'd taken during the time she and the fat FBI guy, whose name Annie didn't remember, had interviewed Dustin and her. While the rest of them sat at the conference table, the FBI guy paced the room like he was late for an important meeting.

Tina frowned at the man, and he stopped pacing. Then she looked at Annie and Dustin with kind eyes. "Anything else either of you can remember?"

Annie and Dustin shook their heads.

The burly FBI guy spoke. "You can't give us better physical descriptions of the men who broke into your home, the men who assaulted you in the garage? Anything besides a cross on the one guy's forehead?"

"Too scared," Annie said. "We thought they would kill us, so…"

"Yeah," Dustin said. "We weren't taking notes on their appearances."

Annie gasped as a fuzzy picture in her mind cleared. "One of them had like a cross on his forehead. Ugly."

Detective Martinez sighed, nodded her head, glanced at the FBI guy, then closed her notepad. She looked at Annie. "You said they spoke English to you, but Spanish to each other, right?"

Annie nodded.

"Do either of you know Spanish? Any clue what they said to each other?"

Annie sucked air through her teeth. "Yes. I recognized the word *mátalos*. 'Kill them.' From *matar*, the verb 'to kill.'" She buried her head in her hands. "I thought we were both dead."

The agent looked at Tina. "Not much help."

She shrugged. "Maybe later, it might be."

Later? Annie shivered.

The detective noticed Annie's discomfort and offered a reassuring smile. "I meant in case we catch them; it might help identify them if you remember what they said or how they said it, or even their voices."

The FBI guy scoffed. "*If* we catch them."

Fear recaptured Annie's body. "Please," she said. "Can we be done here?" She looked at Dustin, whose pallid face had not changed since they looked at each other in the garage. After his mother shot…

"We need to be done," she said in a more forceful voice. "You can talk to us later, right?"

"Of course," Tina said. "We'll leave you now. You're safe here. We have two officers guarding the door."

Annie wondered if she would ever feel safe again. "Thank you," she said.

As soon as the detective and FBI guy left the room, Annie pulled out her phone. She had already started crying when her mother answered.

"Mom," she said in a sobbing, tearful voice. "Mom, something awful happened. I need you."

Chapter Forty-Eight

An hour and a half later, Zack led Maria Santos into the ICU. Beth Jaklic joined them. Zack introduced them to each other.

"Dr. Santos, Maria, is a clinical psychologist. But she's also done forensic psychology for various law enforcement agencies. I've briefed her on the history with our patient here, and she's agreed to help us evaluate the extent of her amnesia."

"You say that like you don't believe the woman," Beth said.

"We'll leave that to Maria to determine." He pointed out the Latina woman's ICU bed to Maria.

"Let me talk to her alone," Maria said.

Zack stepped aside and allowed Maria to enter the cubicle and close the curtain. He and Beth stood in the open space as Zack strained to overhear the conversation.

Beth scowled at him. "Seriously, Zack? Eavesdropping? Why? You don't speak Spanish, right?"

Zack offered an embarrassed shrug. "Thought I might catch some emotional expressions."

She grabbed his arm and led him away from the cubicle. "Let's get coffee while we can."

Twenty minutes later, Maria entered the conference room, where Beth and Zack sat and sipped coffee.

She pointed to the mugs. "Got any more of that?"

"Of course," Zack said. He prepared a mug from the Keurig on a counter and handed it to her. He waited for her to take a couple of sips before he spoke. "Well?"

"For sure, she's faking the amnesia. I tripped her up in the first few minutes."

"Did she admit to why?" Beth asked.

"Terrified," Maria said.

"Of the cops?" Zack asked.

Maria shook her head. "Not quite. She's afraid of law enforcement all right, but she's terrified that her bosses will find and kill her. Even if she's in police custody."

"Bosses?" Zack and Beth asked in unison.

"The people behind what she's done. To be blunt, the ones who ordered the murders she's committed in the last few weeks."

"Specifics?" Zack asked.

Maria hesitated, glanced at Beth.

"You can be open in front of Beth. She's the patient's attending surgeon. She needs to know."

Beth raised her hands. "Maybe we should include the law enforcement folks in this discussion, too."

Maria shook her head with vigor. "No can do."

Both puzzled, Zack and Beth leaned toward her.

"I promised to share what she told me only with her doctors," Maria said. "Specifically, no police or other authorities."

"Why did you do that?" Zack asked, miffed.

"Otherwise, she would clam up and share nothing. I needed her to open up."

Zack huffed. "Okay. What did you learn?" He nodded toward Beth. "Or are we sworn to secrecy, too?"

Maria smiled. "Indeed, you are. I need you both to assure me what we discuss stays among the three of us."

Zack blew out a long breath. "How does that help any of us, especially my daughter, and Bridget?"

Maria smiled. "We'll get there, Zack. Trust me. Okay?"

"Yeah, sure," Zack gestured to Maria to continue.

"When I asked her for details," Maria said, "She mentioned some Spanish nicknames. *El Fuego*, which means the fire; *El Víbora*, for viper." She paused. "I surmised that 'The Fire, *El Fuego*,' may be out of the picture. 'The Viper, *El Víbora*,' seems to be the boss. Our patient has mixed emotions about him."

"If we don't know who these people really are, how does that help us?" Zack said.

Maria cast him a patient smile. "Stay with me a little longer here. You'll see." She lowered her voice, as if she feared being overheard. "The woman mentioned a third individual, *El Vengador*, which means the avenger. Actually, it's *El Vengador de la Sangre*, The Avenger of Blood." She paused and moved closer. "Just saying the name elicited a fight-or-flight reaction in your patient. The whole syndrome, within a few seconds of saying his name."

"So that's who terrifies her?" Beth asked.

Maria nodded. "*Por seguro.* For sure."

"Why?" Zack asked.

"From what she said, amplified by the emotional reaction I witnessed, he's a ruthless killer, a psychopath who tortures his prey without mercy before he kills them."

Maria leaned back. "To summarize, I got no sense of fear from the patient about this *El Fuego*. More about domination than anything else. As for *El Víbora*, she seemed disappointed and sad." She thought for a second. "Like a daughter whose dad turned out not to be the all-loving parent she'd put her faith in." Another pause. "But this *El Vengador* goes beyond terrifying her. She believes he's after her, to torture and kill her, and that no law enforcement agency in the world can stop him."

"That seems an exaggeration," Zack said.

"May be," Maria said. "But to this woman, it's real. And that's what counts."

The three sat in silence for a while before Zack spoke. "So, what do we do now?"

Maria looked at Beth. "What's her prognosis? How long do you intend to keep her in the ICU?"

Beth shrugged. "The next twenty-four hours will determine that. She suffered extensive damage to the neurovascular bundle in her left groin. We haven't yet tested her sensation in that leg. Too early for a definitive exam there, but I expect significant loss. The vascular damage presents a higher danger." She paused. "Worst case, she loses the leg. Best case, well, she won't run any marathons in the future."

"So her life, whatever it is, will change," Zack said.

Beth nodded. "Yep."

Maria said, "That's your connection to her. She seems to trust both of you, although I'm not sure how she would even know Zack."

"I saw her before," Zack said. "In the ER. She came in under a false name, complaining of migraine. Spoke good English, by the way. I figured her as a drug seeker. When I refused to order narcotics, she absconded. That same night, a Latina woman posing as a housekeeper killed Fiona Delaney." He shook his head. "I never saw that person, but I believe it was this same woman." He rubbed his forehead. "No one remembered seeing the woman who injected potassium chloride into Fiona's IV. To the ICU staff, housekeepers are invisible."

Maria said, "We'll have to see about the relevance of that. In my interview, I learned she's killed before, many times. I suspect she's a *sicario*. An assassin."

Zack frowned. "Hired by whom? These Mexican guys?"

Beth offered Zack a patient smile. "Hello, Zack. Can you spell c-a-r-t-e-l?"

Maria nodded. "Exactly my thinking."

A sinking feeling struck Zack's heart. If a cartel was involved, not only was their mystery patient at risk. They all were, including Annie and Bridget. And, if a cartel were involved, what was its goal?

He let out a long breath. "So, what do we do now?"

Maria stood. "Let's all three of us go talk to her. As I said, she seems to trust her doctors."

All rose, but before they could leave the room, the beeper on Beth's waist let out a screeching yowl.

"Trauma alert?" Beth said. "I thought we were on lockdown."

As if in response, a strident announcement blared over the hospital loudspeaker. "Trauma Alert. Trauma Alert."

Beth looked at Zack and Maria. "Sorry. Duty calls." She headed out the door.

Without knowing why, Zack followed her. He turned to Maria. "Our mystery patient will have to wait. Can you talk to her again? See if you can get the identities of these mysterious people?"

"I'll try," Maria said.

Chapter Forty-Nine

When Zack and Beth got off the elevator from the ICU to the emergency department, they had to maneuver through a sizeable crowd of gawkers from areas of the hospital not part of the emergency department. Zack reasoned that the unusual level of interest in a trauma alert related to the hospital being on lockdown. Many of the onlookers had nothing better to do.

But how did they receive a trauma patient while on lockdown? Emergency medical services units knew better than to transport to them under that condition.

As the two physicians traversed the crowd on their way to the trauma room, Zack heard one young man, dressed in a janitor's uniform, say, "His dick? Seriously?"

Zack turned to scowl at the man as he entered the trauma room. When he turned back, a simultaneous trio of unanticipated terrors struck him like bricks thrown at his forehead:

The partially clothed, badly beaten body on the trauma table belonged to Tyler Rhodes. Zack almost didn't recognize him because of the blood and bruising around his face, accentuated by a torn ear lobe and an entire row of missing teeth. Zack's gaze migrated past the bruises and superficial knife wounds on Tyler's chest and abdomen to his pubic area. A dark red mass of coagulating blood covered Tyler's crotch. Next to Tyler's body, a purple/maroon-hued, limp severed penis with macerated edges at the hilt lay alongside its owner.

"What the hell?" Zack looked at Louise Ritchie, who had taken her position at the patient's head to manage the airway.

"Dumped out of a speeding car in the ER parking lot," she said. "The vehicle got away before the officers could respond. They had stuffed the, uh, organ there in his mouth."

Beth Jaklic took her position as the trauma surgeon on the right side of the patient. She barked out orders. "Get that penis in saline solution. Call urology, STAT. It might be viable for reimplantation." She passed over the obvious injury in the groin region to examine Tyler's chest and abdomen.

"Compromised airway," Louise Ritchie said. "Let's intubate."

In less than a minute, she had used a fiberoptic scope to thread a plastic tube through Tyler's mouth and into his trachea. A respiratory technician ventilated him using an ambu bag while another tech set up a portable ventilator.

Meanwhile, other nurses had inserted two large bore IVs and began running fluids wide open. Others had grabbed blood for labs and type and crossmatching of blood for transfusion. Everyone involved in the resuscitation followed protocol, with no one having to give orders or any team members wondering what to do. As they followed their routine, the glaring genital injury became secondary to life-preserving interventions.

Louise listened over the patient's chest. "Bilateral breath sounds. Equal."

"Abdomen is soft, non-distended, no penetrating wounds," Beth said. "Let's turn him."

When they rolled Tyler onto his side to examine his back, they discovered a handwritten Spanish note in magic marker pinned to his back.

"Somebody translate that," Zack said.

A technician stepped up, read the message, and stared at Zack with wide-open eyes. "It's for you, Dr. Winston."

Zack reeled from what felt like a hard precordial thump to the chest over his heart. He steeled himself. "What does it say?"

The young man took a deep breath and spoke in a trembling voice. "I will do much worse to the fly, your girlfriend, and your daughter." He took a breath. "It is signed, '*El Vengador de la Sangre.*' The Avenger of Blood."

All eyes in the room stared at Zack. He took a deep breath, shook them off, then turned to Beth and Louise. "How's the patient looking?"

"Ready for the OR," Beth said. She cast a worried glance at Zack, then spoke to the charge nurse. "Any response from urology? "

"On his way," the nurse said.

"Then let's go," Beth said. As they maneuvered the gurney with Tyler out of the room, she said. "Call plastic surgery too."

Less than a minute later, Zack stood alone in the vacated trauma room. He trembled from both fear and anger. He hyperventilated. Then his eyes narrowed and his fists clenched. He stood tall and spoke in a firm voice.

"I'll give him blood. We'll see which of us is the true avenger."

As Zack left the trauma room, a sudden question hit him.

"The fly?"

Chapter Fifty

THE FLY ALMOST SMILED when the friendly psychologist returned to her bedside. Almost.

She needed to keep her wits about her until she could be sure who to trust, who to avoid, and whom she could use. An escape plan had begun to form in her mind. Perhaps she could use the psychologist to put some pieces in place.

"How are you feeling?" The doctor asked in Spanish.

The Fly tilted her head. "I have much pain in my left groin, and I cannot feel my left leg very well."

"I understand from the doctors that the picture will become clearer in a couple of days," the psychologist said.

The Fly squeezed her eyes and pursed her lips. "Even with the police, I do not feel safe in this place." She threw the doctor an icy stare. "I know how easy it can be to kill someone here, even in this ICU."

"What do you mean by that?" The doctor sat next to her, as if they were engaged in casual conversation about the weather.

The Fly paused before speaking. "I have certain information that some people might find useful."

The doctor did not respond, but simply looked at her with dispassionate eyes.

The psychologists' trick of using the discomfort of silence to make patients talk too much.

The Fly could play that game too. She remained silent. It became a contest who would speak first.

After a few minutes, she realized her disadvantage. The Fly was the only one who had anything to lose in this situation. The psychologist was just doing her job.

So The Fly spoke. "I would put myself at grave risk if I told what I know to the police."

"You can tell me," the doctor said. "I may not share it with anyone else without your permission."

The Fly remained silent, thinking. Then she gave the doctor a challenging look. "Nor could you help me get out of this predicament."

"Then you will need to decide what works best for you."

The FLy stared at the ceiling for quite some time. How to play this? She like to plan several steps ahead, knowing that in the last resort she could run and hide. But now this damned left leg...

The doctor spoke. "Perhaps consider what other lives might be in danger if you remain silent. Innocent lives. A physician. A woman. A sixteen-year-old girl." She looked The Fly in the eye. "Would your life be different, better, if someone had spoken up when you were sixteen?"

The Fly's breathing quickened as she remembered how *El Fuego* had taken her away from her home, her parents, the nun who tried to warn her. She stared into space. Then she decided.

"I will tell these things only to Dr. Winston."

The psychologist nodded. "I understand. As soon as Dr. Winston is available, we will come back to talk to you."

"Okay," The Fly said.

The doctor rose to leave. "In the meantime, get as much rest as you can. You will need it."

If I live that long.

Chapter Fifty-One

BRIDGET STRUGGLED TO SIT up against a heavy body that pressed her chest and abdomen into the bed. She tried to roll to her left to get out from under the weight, but the immediate excruciating pain in her left shoulder stopped her. Powerful hands pulled on her right shoulder and pressed it down. Her right hand searched in vain for Marshall's pistol.

A voice clamored in her ear. "You're okay MS Larsen. Surgery over. You're in recovery. Quit struggling or you'll hurt yourself."

Through the post-anesthetic fog in her brain, Bridget understood. She quit struggling, opened her eyes, and encountered friendly but alarmed looks from a man and woman dressed in green surgical scrubs. The realization that she was in a hospital setting did nothing to relieve the deep pain in her left shoulder. More distressing, when she tried to find a more comfortable position, she had no sensation below her left elbow.

Bridget looked at the young man. "My left shoulder is killing me."

The man placed a pushbutton apparatus into her right hand and guided her thumb to the button. "You have PCA, patient-controlled analgesia. When the pain gets bad, you push this button. The apparatus will inject a dose of morphine into your bloodstream."

Bridget punched the button. In seconds, a soothing warmth filled her body. She pushed the button again.

The nurse offered an empathetic smile. "But if you try to administer more than your doctor has ordered, it won't work."

Bridget sighed. "I understand now, thank you." She jammed her thumb on the button.

The two nurses fluffed her pillow and rearranged the bedding on top of an uncomfortable semi-hard pallet.

Another warm glow infused Bridget's body. The pain in her left shoulder subsided, but did not go away. She leaned her head back onto the pillow and tried to relax.

Snippets of the prior night's events invaded her memory.

Marshall's pistol. How much she had hated that thing. How she did not hesitate to use it.

Twice.

The explosions. The smell.

The blood. The sinew. The brain matter.

Dustin and Annie, alive.

Two young men, dead.

Dead by Bridget's hand.

Tears flowed down her cheeks as she suffered unrelenting remorse. She pushed the button and waited for the glow.

Nothing.

Too soon.

Those young men had mothers. Fathers. Brothers? Sisters? Women they loved?

Bridget tried to reassure herself she'd done the right thing. Dustin and Annie would be dead now if she hadn't...

Killed.

Two young men.

Had there been a better way? A way not irreversible? A way of not taking the lives of others?

Bridget's breathing became heavy.

What did I do?

I saved the lives of my son and Zack's daughter.

Did I?

Bridget squeezed her eyes against the tears. The pain in her left shoulder intensified. She pushed the button.

No effect.

What if those men did not intend to kill? What if they just meant to scare, to intimidate? Maybe they felt the same fear as Dustin and Annie. Did they need to die? Was there no other way?

Dustin and Annie, alive. Two young men, dead.

Bridget Larsen...?

She pushed the button.

A merciful somnolence assuaged her physical and emotional misery.

Chapter Fifty-Two

As Zack left the vacated trauma room, a nurse came up to him.

"Dr. Winston, Detective Martinez needs you in the conference room right away."

What now?

He needed to look after Annie. And Dustin, as he'd promised Bridget. Instead, he headed toward the conference room.

An intense murmur of frenzied activity greeted Zack when he walked into the conference room. While he had been engaged in the resuscitation of Tyler Rhodes, the conference room had become a makeshift but fully equipped law enforcement control center. Agents and officers either talked into cell phones, hunched over laptops, or conferred over tactical maps or other documents.

Zack became alarmed. Did all these people have clearances? Were they all really police? What if someone snuck...

"Dr. Winston." Across the conference table, Detective Martinez beckoned him.

He went up to her. "Not sure I want to know whatever you're going to tell me."

"Not want, but for sure need to know," the detective said. Her brow furrowed and her lips pursed. "You remember Emily Morgan?"

A jolt of alarm pierced Zack's mind. He fought it off. "Of course, I do. The nurse at The Good House who tried to help Annie. She later confessed to her role in the conspiracy." His eyes narrowed. "She's in pretrial confinement."

Martinez took a breath. "She was, at the Pretrial Detention Facility in Baltimore. Someone there attacked her with a shiv. She's now a patient at Baltimore Shock Trauma. Critical."

Zack sat and buried his head in his hands. "How critical?"

"We were hoping you could find out. Shock Trauma won't release any information to us."

"Of course." Zack pulled out his phone and placed a call to the emergency department at the Baltimore Shock Trauma hospital, where a former residency colleague was the medical director.

"Hopefully Dr. Baraff is on duty."

Ten minutes later, Zack hung up from his call. Detective Martinez got the attention of everyone in the room, then nodded to Zack.

"Emily Morgan sustained multiple knife wounds to chest and abdomen. Major blood loss and hypovolemic shock, plus a collapsed lung and internal organ damage. They've given her massive blood transfusions, re-expanded her lung, repaired the damage to her liver, and removed a lacerated spleen. She's not out of the woods, but the prognosis is hopeful given her younger age and otherwise good health. The next twenty-four hours will tell."

The agents returned to their tasks.

"Has to be related," Martinez said to Zack.

He glowered at her. "How the hell did they...?"

Martinez winced. "Happens more often than you want to know, Doc."

Sudden panic seized Zack. "Where's my daughter?"

"Under guard in that room in the ED you call The Bunker."

"Under guard? Like Emily Morgan was under guard?"

He turned and rushed from the room.

Chapter Fifty-Three

Zack walked through the ED main treatment area, acknowledging no one who looked at or tried to speak to him. At the back of the department, he showed his hospital ID to the police officer guarding the door to The Bunker.

"Has anyone been in there?" Zack asked.

"Just nurses looking after your daughter," the officer said.

Zack fumed. "Not anymore."

The officer tried to respond, but Zack stayed him with a raised hand. "No one enters that room but me or Dr. Jaklic. No one. I don't care what kind of 'ID' they flash at you."

"Sir, our orders . . ."

"Screw your orders. I'm giving you *my* orders. No one but Dr. Jaklic or me, understood?"

"I'll have to confirm with Detective..."

Zack got up in the officer's face. "Let me be perfectly clear, Officer..." He looked at the man's name tag. "Officer Engel, this is my ER, and I give the orders here."

He moved so close that the officer reached toward the cuffs on his belt.

A voice from behind Zack interrupted the altercation. Detective Martinez.

"You can stand down, officer," she said. "I was coming to give you the same direction."

The officer stood back. "Yes, ma'am." He stood aside to allow Zack into the bunker, glaring as Zack passed.

Inside the bunker, Annie lay on the bed while Dustin Hilliard sat at the desk. Annie got up and held her phone toward Zack.

"You need to call mom."

Zack was taken aback. "You called your mom?"

Annie gave him a "duh" expression. "Couple hours ago. She's either had time to calm down, or to let her anger grow into total rage. You never know with her."

Zack responded in a meek voice. "I wish you'd asked me before you called her."

Annie's voice hardened. "If I'd known where you were or when you might come back..."

Zack broke eye contact and blinked. "Got it. And, sorry. Lots going on, none of it good."

"Call her." Annie handed the phone to Zack.

Zack had hoped for the calm-down alternative, but Natalie answered his call in full-blown fury.

"What the hell, Zack? Annie called me hours ago. Terrified. She didn't know where you were. Where have you been?"

"Trying to save lives," he said in a huff. "She's in no danger here. Police protection and all."

"You are such a dildo," Natalie said. "She may be physically safe, but she's an emotional wreck." She blew into the phone. "I'm coming out there. Early flight."

The words hit Zack like a sledgehammer. He took a few seconds to recover. "You can't."

"The hell, I can't." She huffed again. "Don't worry, Zack. I won't be there long. I'm bringing Annie home with me."

Again, Zack could only say, "You can't."

"Not up to you, Zack. My daughter needs me, and she's not safe with you."

Zack took a few seconds to settle himself. He glanced at Annie, who listened to his side of the conversation. Dustin stared at his phone, hands covering his ears.

"I meant," he said to Natalie, "it's not safe for you to come here. Not safe for Annie."

Natalie spoke in a measured voice. "Explain."

Zack summarized the events of the last several hours, including the attack on Emily Morgan. He looked at Annie.

Not how I wanted to inform her, but...

To Natalie he said, "The people behind this, conspiracy or whatever, are dangerous and relentless. Looks like they are out to eliminate anyone with knowledge of that Good House thing, including Annie. She's under constant police guard, in a safe place that no one can get to without attracting attention. You take her out of here, to an airport or whatever, you will put her in danger. You'll put yourself in danger too. As her mother, you would become a prime target to smoke her out."

Silence.

Zack heaved a sigh. "You need to trust me on this one, Nat."

Silence.

He took another deep breath. "When this is over, and it's safe again, we can talk about what happens next." He glanced at his daughter. "Annie will have a major say in that conversation."

At last Natalie spoke. "Describe for me, in detail, why you think she's safer there than with me."

Zack shook his head. He remembered the threatening calls Annie had received on the same phone he was using now. "I can't."

"Goddamn it, Zack."

"Okay," he said. He spoke as if to the conspirators instead of Natalie. "She's in a safe place, here with me, where no one can find her or get to her without going through a phalanx of police." He emphasized his next words. "And me. I will kill anyone who comes after her, then spit on their dead bodies."

Natalie blew into the phone. "You've always had such a flair for melodrama, Zack."

"Best I can do at the present," he said.

Another long pause before Natalie spoke. "Okay. We'll do it your way. For now. You have twenty-four hours, then I'm coming out there and bringing my daughter home to a normal life."

She hung up without waiting for his response.

***

Annie's dad handed the phone back to her.

"Sorry you had to hear all that."

Annie was still processing what she'd overheard. "You talked about the nurse, Emily."

"I did."

"Someone attacked her?"

Dad nodded. "Yes. In the pre-trial detention center in Baltimore."

Annie's chest ached. "Will she live?"

"We think so."

Annie shivered. "I'd like to see her again. She was so kind to me."

Dad shrugged. "Might happen. We don't know at this point." He paused. "Do you remember anything more about her?"

Annie squeezed her eyes, as if that would help her remember.

"I...was on a bed, but not a bed. Too narrow. Not a bedroom. A living room." The memory lingered on the edge of consciousness. Then part of it burst into her mind.

"Sarah." Her eyes made rapid blinks. "Sarah was there, and...Emily. She said her name, and that she was my nurse."

Dad looked at her with kind eyes.

"I had cramps. Emily said that was normal after my, uh, 'procedure'?" Annie closed her eyes and tried to remember more by mentally putting herself in Maria's safe place.

"Sarah and Emily helped me up some stairs." Then a flash. "Tyler was there. He had a wheelchair."

"A wheelchair?"

"Yes, and he wanted me to sit in it. But Emily said, 'I won't let you take her, Roach.' I wondered why she called Tyler by that other name."

The memory opened like a floodgate. "Sarah came up behind her, said something like she couldn't stop it." Annie's words came in rapid staccato as the memory gates burst open. "Then Emily hit Sarah with her elbow. Then she tried to tackle Tyler, but he shoved her aside. She yelled at me to run away as fast as I could. I only made it a step or two before Tyler grabbed me. He held a gun to my head, said he would have to kill me if I caused any more trouble."

As the fog in Annie's mind cleared, she fought back tears. "Then Sarah said they should kill both Emily and me." She trembled as the memory continued. "Someone with a big voice stopped them. They called him Dr. Good."

Dad touched her arm in gentle strokes. "What then?"

"Dr. Good told Sarah to put me in a room, then he took Emily downstairs with him." I never saw her again. She looked at her dad with pleading eyes. "Emily saved my life. She has to live."

Neither spoke through the ensuing silence. Finally, Annie voiced the thought she'd held inside since she overheard her dad's conversation with her mother.

"They want us all dead," Annie said.

"They do," Dad said.

Another long pause.

"Would I be safer in California?"

"I don't know." He looked her in the eye. "I can't promise you would be. If they got to Emily..."

Annie pursed her lips. "I don't want Mom to come."

"I know."

"This is our fight, Dad."

He looked surprised by that, stared into space before he replied. "I know."

"So, what are we going to do?"

"We're keeping you out of sight and out of reach. We're keeping you safe."

She bristled. "Safe? Out of sight? Dad…"

He raised a hand. "You heard what I told your mother."

Annie shook her head. "Dad, I've had a gun to my head twice now. I'm not a little girl anymore."

He looked at her through pained eyes. "Safe. Out of sight."

"I can help. I need to help."

"No."

Her anger flashed. "I'm the victim here, Dad. Not you. Not Bridget. Not Tyler." She thumped her chest. "Me."

"Not up for discussion," Dad said.

Annie folded her arms and glared at her father. "You got that right."

Chapter Fifty-Four

AFTER THE STANDOFF WITH his daughter, Zack returned to the ED conference room to see about any further developments.

Detective Martinez approached him.

"Two things, Doc. First, the psychologist, Dr., uh, Santos, had to leave. She asked us to pass along that the Latina woman in the ICU wishes to speak to you." She frowned. "Only you."

Zack raised his eyebrows. "The second thing?"

"Bridget Larsen is doing well. They are moving her from the recovery room to the ICU."

"Is that wise?" Zack asked with a scowl. "Putting her near a known assassin?"

"Who remains under heavy guard. Plus, that groin injury should keep her in bed. Not like she's going to jump out and attack Ms. Larsen. Who will have her own protective detail."

"It's the most logical and safe solution, Zack," said a voice behind him. He turned. Beth Jaklic gave him a reassuring smile. "How about you concentrate on being the dad and, whatever you are to Larsen, and let we who are less emotionally involved handle the medical care and logistics?"

Zack couldn't argue with her logic, or her tone.

"Fine," he said. "I'll look in on Bridget first, then see what our *sicario* wants."

They had moved Bridget to a private room in the ICU and stationed two armed police officers at the door. Zack showed his ID. The officers, only one of whom he recognized, allowed him to enter the room.

Bridget lay on her back, eyes closed, surrounded by the usual IV bags and other accouterments of intensive care.

Zack pulled up a chair to the side of the bed, took hold of Bridget's right hand, and squeezed. The hand remained limp. Remembering that she had suffered damage from her shoulder wound to the nerves supplying her arm and hand, Zack wondered if he had touched the wrong limb. The bandages around Bridget's left shoulder, opposite the side from where he sat, attested that he had. Maybe she just didn't feel him touch her. He squeezed her hand a little tighter.

Bridget flinched, and her eyes opened. She cocked her head toward him. "Zack? Why are you here?"

Zack blinked, puzzled. "To make sure you're okay."

"Oh, didn't Dr. Jaklic tell you?"

"She did," Zack said. "As far as the physical perspective." He sucked his lower lip. "I'm concerned about your emotional wellbeing after all that happened."

Bridget waved him off with her good hand. Her usual hoarse voice sounded strained. "I'll deal with that later. After the law enforcement folks clear out all this mess."

"That's my concern," Zack said. "I'm not so satisfied with their efforts thus far."

Bridget's eyes narrowed. "What more do you expect from them?"

"Catch and prosecute the villains who are behind all this," he said with a vengeance.

Bridget cast him a concerned look. "With or without your help?"

Zack pursed his lips, then said, "I was thinking more like with *our* help. As we've done before."

Bridget scoffed. She glanced to her left. "Seriously, Zack?" She pointed at her left shoulder with her right hand. "I not only have this, uh, postoperative wound healing situation. I also can't feel my left forearm or hand." She cast Zack a withering look. "That's not to mention the severe pain in my shoulder, for which I continue to max out the PCA."

All at once, Zack felt like a complete idiot. He tried again to squeeze Bridget's good hand, but she moved it away from him.

Silence enveloped the room. "I was way out of line. Sorry. I, we, all of us, just want you to get better. Forget about all of this other stuff. They have you in a safe place now." He choked on his next words. "We've got this, Bridge."

Bridget cast him a blank look, shook her head, and pushed the PCA button. "If you don't mind, I need to get some rest now." She turned away from him.

Chapter Fifty-Five

His heart sagging, Zack left Bridget's room and went to the nearby cubicle occupied by the suspected *sicario*. The woman's eyes caught him as he approached the bed and stood to her right side, opposite her groin injury. She pushed the button to elevate the head of the bed, then used her good right leg to push herself up into a semi-sitting position. Her dark, intense eyes never left Zack's.

He felt she penetrated his soul.

"How are you feeling?" Zack asked.

She blinked, then spoke in a raspy voice not that different from Bridget's.

"Bastante bien."

Zack shook his head. "Sorry. I don't speak Spanish."

The woman stared at the ceiling, as if pondering. Finally, she beckoned Zack closer. He bent and tilted his head so she could speak into his ear.

"I speak fluent English," she said in a conspiratorial whisper. "I said, 'Well enough.'"

Zack looked into her eyes. They seemed to plead. "Go on," he said in a quiet voice that he hoped sounded reassuring.

The woman took a deep breath. "Can I trust you?"

"I'm the doctor who treated you in the ER. We have a bond."

"But can I trust you? Can you trust me?"

"How about we agree to trust each other until or unless one of us betrays that trust?"

The woman looked around with furtive glances. "Is it okay that we talk like this?"

Zack noticed two nurses at the workstation desk watching his interaction with the mysterious woman. He thought for a second, then turned and closed the curtain around the cubicle. That brought rapid footsteps. Zack poked his head through the gap in the curtain just as a nurse reached out to open it and enter the cubicle.

"Just doing an exam," he said.

"I can help," the nurse said.

Zack gestured toward the woman's bandaged groin area. "She's quite shy." He smiled.. "And essentially restrained. I'll holler if I need help."

The nurse gave Zack a suspicious glare. "I'm not sure..."

He stopped her with a raised hand and a firm voice. "If you don't mind, nurse, I'm finally building some rapport with mystery woman here. Please don't blow it."

The nurse huffed, then walked away.

Zack returned to the patient's bedside. "We don't have much time. What did you want to tell me?"

The woman's breathing quickened, her body tense. An uncertain, almost panicky expression crossed her face.

Zack touched her hand. "We trust each other."

Her body relaxed, and her eyes warmed. She spoke in a softer voice. "I will tell the truth. Everything. I know many things, people, places." She sucked her lip. "But you must protect me from *Los Hermanos.*"

"Who?"

"The three brothers. The cartel. The murderers."

She shied away from Zack, her eyes wide, muscles tense, face harried.

"*Madre de Dios.* I've done it."

Zack reached out to touch her hand.

She grabbed onto his hand with a tight grip. "Please, you must protect me. If not, I am a dead woman."

Zack returned to the conference room that had become the law enforcement operations center. He beckoned Detective Martinez and Agent Mason aside.

"She wants to deal," he said.

Mason huffed. "For what? She's a terrorist looking at life without parole. That's only because Maryland has no death penalty. No way will any prosecutor worth their salt make a deal with her."

"Does the name *Los Hermanos* mean anything to you?"

Mason looked at Martinez, then rubbed his brow. "Do you mean *Los Hermanos de Guadalajara*?"

Zack shrugged. "She said only *Los Hermanos.*"

Mason huffed again.

Detective Martinez spoke to Zack. "*Los Hermanos de Guadalajara* is the most notorious drug cartel in Mexico. Three brothers." She glanced at Agent Mason. "Well, only two now. The dead guy at the airpark was one of them."

"Homeland Security is all over this," Agent Mason said. "I don't see how your patient can help us, or tell us anything we don't already know."

A wave of anger overcame Zack. "You already knew about the cartel connection?"

Martinez offered an apologetic nod.

"But no one thought it important to tell or warn the potential victims, including my daughter?"

Agent Mason raised a hand. "Need to know. You didn't have it."

Furious, Zack said, "The hell I didn't." He moved closer to Mason, threatening. "You didn't think we, I, needed to know that cartel assassins had invaded this hospital, put my daughter and Bridget in danger…?"

Mason shrugged. "Maybe we should have…"

"Damn right you should have." Zack fumed. "Yet, you don't believe this patient, whoever she is, can help us?"

"Like I said, Homeland Security is all over this." Mason folded his arms. "If they think this woman has useful information, they have ways of getting it out of her." His eyes narrowed. "Without making deals."

Zack got up in Mason's face. "That woman is a patient in this hospital, my hospital. No one, and I mean no one, talks to her without the permission of her attending physician, Dr. Jaklic, or me." He stepped back. "Is that clear, Agent Mason?"

Mason shook his head. "You don't have that authority."

"The hell we don't," Zack said. "Watch us."

He turned and left the conference room, dialing his phone as he went.

"Beth, we need to talk. Now."

Chapter Fifty-Six

NILDA FLORES CAST A wary eye at the man and woman who approached her bedside. Although they wore surgical masks and gowns, he recognized them as her doctors.

But could she trust them?

"We're moving you to isolation," Dr. Winston said.

"You have a serious, life-threatening infection," Dr. Jaklic said. Then she winked at Nilda and beckoned for two nurses to join them.

Without further discussion, the four medical personnel wheeled Nilda's bed and accouterments into a closed private room. As The Fly, she had seen Dr. Winston visit someone in an identical room next to this one.

As soon as they had her settled in the room, Dr. Winston spoke to the nurses. "No one enters this room except nursing staff, Dr. Jaklic, or me. No one."

Dr. Jaklic said, "Tell anyone who wants in that they will risk incurring a fatal infection."

The nurses looked confused, but both nodded and left the room. As soon as they did, the two doctors removed their face masks.

Dr. Winston turned to Dr. Jaklic. "Thanks, Beth. I owe you big time."

"Which I will be glad to collect at a future date," she said. Then she left the room.

Dr. Winston pulled up a chair beside Nilda's bed.

"Here's the deal," he said. "We made up the infection story to get you out of the main ICU, and in here, where we have better control of who comes and goes. Also, so we can have a private discussion about your immediate future."

Straight in, no waiting. I am committed now. No matter what.

Dr. Winston continued. "The law enforcement folks refused to make a deal with you, but I'm not giving up. The lives of my daughter and my friend mean more to me. So, even if the authorities won't deal with you, I will. Follow?"

Nilda nodded. "But what can you do the authorities can't?"

"You'll have to trust me on that." His voice became earnest. "You don't have a choice. Either you let us protect you in exchange for information, or you die. You said so earlier."

Nilda knew he spoke the truth. "Okay," she said. "What do you want to know?"

"Start with your real name, and where you are from."

Nilda let out a long breath. "I already told the authorities. My name is Nilda Flores. I was born, raised, and live in Guadalajara, Mexico."

Dr. Winston put out his hand. "I'm happy to meet you, Nilda Flores from Guadalajara. How do you say it in Spanish? *Mucho gusto?*"

Nilda nodded, smiled, and shook his hand. "*El gusto es mío.* The pleasure is mine."

"Okay," the doctor said. "Now we can talk in trust." He pointed outside the room. "Those law enforcement folks aren't interested in making a deal with you because they already know about your *Hermanos...*"

Nilda stopped him with a raised hand. "Please, they are not my brothers."

Dr. Winston did a double take. "Sorry, I assumed..."

Nilda shook her head. "Employers." She raised her eyebrows. "Former employers." She averted her eyes. "And abusers." She looked back at him. "I will spit on their rotting corpses."

The doctor's eyes hardened. "As would I, for what they did to my daughter. And my friend."

Nilda gave him an earnest look. "Then we are *conjuntos*. We are together."

"As one," he said. "We are both victims here."

She looked into his eyes for several moments, feeling the bond between them. The bond of those who thirst for justice.

"I will tell you everything about them. The truth."

"And I will do everything I can to help you." He swallowed hard. "But I cannot promise you anything." He pointed with his thumb behind him. "We will have to move ahead without those authorities." He shook his head. "So, no guaranteed outcome."

"I understand." Nilda's eyes pleaded. "You are my only hope."

"Then we have a deal."

Over the next half-hour, Nilda confided in Dr. Winston all that she knew about *Los Hermanos* and their schemes. She admitted she did not know their intended outcome, but it involved trading drugs and drug money for embryos. Those they would sell to other foreign interests.

"There was an Asian man at the meeting on the yacht on Banderas Bay. Chinese or Korean, I don't know for sure."

The doctor winced. "The *Hermanos* would sell Annie's embryo to China or North Korea?"

Nilda. "Seems so. I don't know for sure."

"For what?"

"Again, I don't know."

Dr. Winston thought for a time. "So that's how Dr. Good was involved? To harvest and sell embryos?"

"Yes. He called it 'proof of concept.'"

The doctor leaned forward.

"Anything else?"

"Yes. There were two Americans on the yacht, along with the Asian and the Cuban. They also came to a meeting at the Marriott Hotel, where I got my assignment to kill..."

"Fiona Delaney."

"Yes."

His look became almost desperate. "Do you know who those Americans were?"

"Not by name. Well, they called the man 'Spider,' not his real name. The woman had red hair, like that Fiona woman I killed."

Dr. Winston's face turned red, his muscles tensed, fists clenched, eyes widened. "Sarah O'Brien."

"I remember someone calling her 'Sarah,'" Nilda said.

The doctor moved closer, spoke in an earnest voice. "Do you know where any of those people are now?"

Nilda did not hesitate. "I don't know about *Los Hermanos,* but the red-headed woman and the man called 'Spider' went to that Good House."

Chapter Fifty-Seven

Detective Martinez met Zack as he left the ICU after his talk with Nilda Flores.

"Conference Room," she said in a commanding voice. "Now."

"I'm busy doing patient care." Zack tried to walk past her.

Hands on hips, Martinez blocked his path. "I said, 'Now,' Doctor. You can walk with me, or I can put you in custody. Your choice."

Zack glared at her. She didn't move or change her expression.

"Fine," he said. "Make it quick."

She scoffed. "That will depend on you."

When they entered the ED conference room, a man Zack had not seen before greeted him from the head of the table.

"Dr. Winston, I presume."

Zack nodded.

The man motioned him to an empty chair. Detective Martinez, Agent Mason, Agent Bloom, and other officers occupied the other seats or stood along the wall.

"I am Special Agent in Charge, SIAC for short, Maxwell Smith," the man said. "From the Department of Homeland Security."

Zack cast a quizzical look at Agent Bloom, who had represented Homeland Security up to now. She did not meet his gaze. He looked back at the head of the table and gave the man an exaggerated shrug.

Agent Smart offered no respite from his stern demeanor. "By 'in charge,' I mean in charge of this entire operation." He looked at the other DHS agent. "Thank you, Agent Bloom, for blowing the whistle on this charade." He followed with a hostile sneer at Detective Martinez.

"Now that we have established the link of this case to *Los Hermanos de Guadalajara*, it becomes a matter of national security. At the highest levels."

"Okay," Zack said. "How does that involve me? I have to look after my patients."

"Did you not just conduct an unauthorized interview with a known cartel assassin in your ICU?"

Zack scowled. "Unauthorized? She's my patient and I can see and talk to her whenever I want."

"Does that include moving her into an isolation room for a bogus diagnosis of infection?"

Zack did not back down. "I exercise my clinical judgment in the best interest of my patient."

The SIAC scoffed. "Could you please share your diagnosis with the rest of us, Doctor?" He pronounced "doctor" like one might say, "felon."

Zack stared at him. "I don't have one yet. Pending lab results and further evaluation."

Agent Smart smiled. "Of course. Any presumptive diagnosis?"

Zack reached inside his brain for a plausible answer. "We don't know where she's been before she appeared in my ED. Could be a third world country. She might have contracted a serious viral disease. Something like Ebola, or worse." He scanned the others in the room. "In the interests of everyone involved, especially law enforcement personnel, I opted for maximum caution."

He folded his arms. "I, for one, will not be responsible for the early phases of a pandemic."

The SIAC smiled, leaned back in his chair, and clapped. "Very good, Dr. Winston. Masterful extemporaneous fabrication. You should get an 'A' in drama."

Zack spread his hands. "What do you want, Agent Smith? I have patients waiting."

"How about I tell you something *you* want to know? Or need to know." He offered a "gotcha" grin. "Your 'patient' is Nilda Flores, aka '*La Mosca*,' which means 'The Fly.' She is one of the most wanted international criminals in the drug trade, a principal *sicario* for *Los Hermanos*. We don't know how many murders she's committed, but it's in double, if not triple, digits."

Zack's heart pounded, but he spoke with calm confidence. "I knew all that."

The SIAC half-rose from his chair. "How could you possibly know?"

"She told me."

Agent Smith's eyes flashed. He rolled in for the final attack. "So, tell us now, Dr. Winston, what else did you and *La Mosca* discuss? And don't try to BS me with that Ebola crap."

Zack looked past the agent. Throughout his medical career, he'd been a proponent of the "trust your instincts" practice. Sometimes those gave better guidance than hard science. Some called it the "art of medicine."

Here, Zack trusted his instincts.

"I explained her medical condition. She might lose that left leg from an inadequate blood supply. She was quite distraught about it."

Agent Smith glared at Zack. From the seat next to him, Zack thought he saw Detective Martinez smile.

"How long, Doctor," the agent said in a slow, angry voice, "before we can move her to a prison bed?"

Zack sneered. "No time in the foreseeable future. The status of that leg is too tenuous. An ambulance ride is out of the question. Not today. Not tomorrow. Maybe not next week."

"That's your professional opinion, Doctor?"

"Yes. Sir."

"You won't mind if we request a second opinion?"

Zack felt on solid ground. He'd spoken the truth. "Be my guest. Get anyone you want." He chuckled. "Well, preferably someone trained and licensed to practice medicine in the state of Maryland." He cast a wicked glare at Agent Smith. "For sure, not some failed practitioner whose only professional recourse to make a living is to staff a prison hospital." He shrugged. "I'd be happy to recommend…"

The SIAC interrupted him. "Thank you, Doctor. We'll take it from here."

Zack half-raised a hand. "To be clear, a second opinion doesn't remove the fact that she is still my patient, as well as Dr. Jaklic's and the other surgeons involved in her case."

Agent Smith's turn to chuckle. "Okay, Dr. Jaklic will stay in charge of the woman's clinical case. Clinical only."

Zack offered a quizzical look.

"You, Dr. Winston, are in grave danger from the cartel. As is your daughter, Annie, and Mrs. Hilliard's son, Dustin."

On reflex, Zack corrected him. "Bridget prefers her maiden name, Larsen."

The agent waved him off. "Whatever. You are all in danger, including Mrs. Larsen."

"*MS* Larsen," Zack said to correct him.

"Sure," Agent Smith said. He looked at Detective Martinez. "The detective here and her staff will remove you, your daughter, and Dustin Hilliard to a secure location away from this hospital."

Zack responded in an instant. "Never. Most of all, not without Bridget. Dustin's mother."

"*MS* Larsen can join you once she's released from the hospital."

"No."

Agent Smith leaned forward in his chair. "This is not a request, Dr. Winston."

Zack looked at Detective Martinez. She gave him an embarrassed nod. He rose from his chair. "Not happening. Now excuse me, I have work to do."

Agent Smith spoke to the detective. "Detective Martinez, take Dr. Winston into custody."

Martinez stood and approached Zack. "Turn around, please, Doctor. Place your hands behind your back."

Zack raised his hands. "Never mind. I'll do as you say."

"Thank you, Doctor," the SIAC said. "That will be all."

Chapter Fifty-Eight

When Zack and Detective Martinez left the boardroom, they found Beth Jaklic waiting for them, along with the urologist and plastic surgeon who had treated Tyler Rhodes.

"We just finished up," the urologist said. He glanced at the plastic surgeon. "It went well. We may have an excellent result, notwithstanding the, uh, nature of the injury."

"Where is he now?" Zack asked.

"Recovery room for now," the urologist said. "Then CCU, since ICU is restricted."

Zack turned to Martinez. "I need to see him."

Martinez nodded. "I'll go with you."

They found Tyler Rhodes in a recovery room bed surrounded by IV poles, monitors, and a clear plastic bag half-filled with bloody fluid. A tube from the top of the bag snaked under Tyler's hospital gown.

"Is he awake?" Zack asked the nurse.

"Barely," the nurse said. "Still under anesthetic effects, plus IV morphine."

Zack approached the bedside and gently nudged Tyler. "Tyler, it's Dr. Winston."

Tyler's eyes half-opened. "Dr. Winzon. Hi."

Zack found a chair and sat next to Tyler's head. Detective Martinez stood behind him. "Can you wake up a little, Tyler?"

Tyler's eyes opened. "Hi, Dr. Winzon." He blinked himself awake. "Annie okay?"

Zack's voice turned icy. "She's fine, Tyler."

Tyler shook his head a bit. "I zorry. I didn' mean…" He nodded off.

Zack nudged him. "Tyler, can you try to stay awake? We need to talk to you."

For the first time, Tyler noticed Detective Martinez standing beside Zack. He startled. "Am, am I in trouble?"

"No, Tyler. Not right now," Zack said. "I'm hoping you can give us some information about what happened to you."

Tyler turned away and closed his eyes.

At first, Zack thought he'd gone back to sleep. He turned to Detective Martinez. "Your presence is not helpful. Could you give us some privacy?"

Martinez cocked her head and eyed Zack. "You will need to tell me what he says. Everything he says."

"I promise," Zack said. "I've been straight with you so far, right?"

"So far. Keep it that way." She turned away. "I'll be right outside."

Zack waited until Martinez had left, then nudged Tyler. "Just you, me, and the nurse now, Tyler."

Tyler opened his eyes, grimaced. "Those men, they beat me up. Then Spider…"

"Spider?" Zack asked.

"Yeah, Spider and Flossie. Well, Sarah."

Zack leaned closer to Tyler's ear. "Just to be sure, are you saying the men who invaded Bridget's house took you somewhere that you saw Spider and Sarah?"

Tyler nodded. His face scrunched up as if in severe pain.

"The men beat you up, then you saw Spider and Sarah?"

Tyler spoke in a whisper. "Yes."

The nurse approached the bedside. "This isn't good." She glanced at Tyler's groin. "We need to keep him calm and sedated."

"Okay," Zack said. "Just a few more questions and I'll leave." He turned to Tyler. "What happened next?"

Tyler continued to speak in a whisper, as if he couldn't bear to hear himself tell it. "Spider had a gun. He called me, 'Roach,' and said I'd betrayed The House."

"The Good House?"

"Yes."

"Is that where they took you? The Good House?"

"Yes." His chin quivered.

The nurse fingered the control on the IV tubing. "I'm giving him more morphine. You need to go, Doctor."

Zack raised a hand to stop her. "Please, just a few seconds longer."

He turned back to Tyler. "What happened next, Tyler?"

Tyler arose in the bed and stared at Zack in sheer anguish. "A big guy with a cross on his forehead came up and wrapped his arm around my neck. Spider said I could either let the guy choke me to death, or…I could cut off my dick." His entire body shook. "I…They…" He broke into sobs.

"You're done," the nurse said. She opened up the IV tubing.

In a few seconds, Tyler lapsed into unconsciousness.

Zack led Detective Martinez back down to the ER bunker. He summarized his conversation with Tyler, except he left out The Good House location.

Annie and Dustin had not changed positions in the bunker since Zack left them there. He explained that the detective would take all three of them to a secure, safer location.

Dustin protested. "I want to see my mother first."

Zack turned to Detective Martinez. "That's reasonable."

Annie said, "I want to see her too."

"Also reasonable," Zack said to Martinez. "They have a relationship."

Martinez scowled. "Fine. Lead the way."

When they arrived at the ICU, Zack stopped at the entrance and turned to Martinez. "I'm afraid you can't come in, Detective."

The detective stared at him. "Why not?"

Zack spoke in an earnest voice. "Because it's a risk."

She scrunched her eyebrows. "Risk?"

"Yeah," Zack said. "Infectious disease."

"That's been debunked," Martinez said.

"No," Zack said. "I mean, you pose a risk to these patients. You haven't been screened for contagious diseases. Both patients are immunocompromised."

Martinez narrowed her eyes. "Seriously? You expect me to buy that?" She tilted her head toward Annie and Dustin. "Have you screened them?"

Zack huffed. "Please trust me here, Tina. Annie and Dustin will put on protective gear before they enter Bridget's room."

"What? You only have two sets of that gear?"

Zack sighed. "We make these decisions based on relative risk. We accept a modicum of risk with them seeing Bridget because of their relationships. You don't have a similar relationship, so I will not accept the additional risk of admitting you just because you don't trust us."

"Don't bullshit me, Dr. Winston."

"I'm not. It's the truth." It was, technically, the truth.

The detective folded her arms. "You have ten minutes, then I'm coming in with or without protective gear."

"That's all the time we need," Zack said. "Thanks."

When they entered Bridget's room in the ICU, she was asleep.

"Don't wake her," Zack said to Annie and Dustin. Then he spoke directly to Dustin. "You stay here with your mother. We'll be back."

Without waiting for an answer, he took Annie by the arm and led her out of the room. He hustled her to the rear of the ICU, to the so-called "dirty utility room."

"What are you doing, Dad?"

"Trust me," he said.

About the size of a large kitchen, the room contained a cart for collection of patient meal trays, a large hamper of used linen, and a portable hazardous waste container. A counter along one wall featured two sinks. Trash bins occupied the rear of the room.

Zack led Annie past the portable laundry cart and trash bins to a door on the back wall. He opened it and pulled her through into a narrow hallway.

"The staff uses this back corridor so as not to transport trash and dirty linen through the main ICU." He looked behind him and to either side, then led Annie down the hall.

"We have to hurry," he said.

"You're taking me with you?"

"As promised. Come on."

Zack took Annie down two flights of back stairs to the basement. They left the hospital via a loading dock, then circled around to the physician parking lot where he had left his Lexus, what seemed like a lifetime earlier. He used the remote to unlock the car, directed Annie to the passenger side, then climbed into the driver's side.

As soon as he started the car, Annie asked, "Where are we going?"

"The Good House."

Chapter Fifty-Nine

TEN MINUTES AFTER ZACK pulled out of the parking lot, he turned north onto River Road. By now, Detective Martinez would have discovered his subterfuge. Every police officer in the area would look for them.

He pulled the car off the main road and stopped on a side road and made a plan.

First, he called Beth Jaklic. "Beth, can you get hold of Eric Wolfe for me? Tell him it's not about a pathology issue or running. I need the two of you to do something for me. I'll text you the details."

Beth agreed without question.

Zack texted the details of his request to Beth and Eric.

"What's all that about, Dad?" Annie asked.

He told her. "A long shot, but I don't have a better idea."

Annie forced a smile. "You've watched too many of those medical thriller shows on TV."

Zack shrugged. He programmed his car's GPS for a route to The Good House that avoided main roads. He saw no way to avoid the road to Seneca Landing, where he'd gone to rescue Annie after her last encounter with the Good House conspirators. Where Tyler Rhodes, Sarah, and Spider had thrown her into the river.

He had found Annie then by tracing her phone. At once anxious, he turned to her. "Do you have your phone?"

"Yes."

"Turn it off. Throw it away."

She gave him a stunned look.

"Like this." He took his phone from his pocket, turned it off, rolled down the window, and pitched it out of the car. "Do it. I'll get you another one."

Eyes wide, she did as told.

"Now we get the heck out of here in case anyone tracked my call to Beth." He put the car in gear and sped down the road.

Should they worry they now had no means of communication once they got to The Good House? Zack would deal with that later.

The GPS led them to Seneca Road, the same intersection where he'd turned toward Seneca Landing only a few months ago to rescue his daughter from the river. Zack had no choice but to turn onto River Road and head north to find The Good House.

Now what?

Trust your instincts, Doc.

Noelle's voice? He couldn't be sure.

After about a mile, they came upon a side road that veered away into a secluded area. He slowed and turned onto that road. After a quarter mile, he came upon a circular drive that fronted a two-story colonial-style manse with a broad porch and four columns extending from the porch to a second-floor veranda. A side building to the right connected to the main house.

Annie gasped. "I know this place."

"You've been here before," Zack said.

Annie scrunched down into her seat, as if she could bury herself in it.

He slowed and pulled his Lexus off the access road, hoping to remain unseen. The early morning light gave them enough visibility, even in this wooded area.

A dark blue Cadillac SUV stood parked in the circular drive. They saw no other vehicles, and no activity. No sign of lights in the house. No signs of activity inside or outside the manse.

They waited a full five minutes before Zack turned to Annie. "We'll get out of the car, quietly, on your side. Crouch where the car will shield us from view from inside the house. Okay?"

She drew back. "I... I can't."

Zack squeezed her hand. "We must face this now, Annie. Together. Can you be brave? I'm with you. Always."

Annie's breath erupted in rapid, heavy spurts. Then, all at once, she calmed herself, took some slow, steady breaths, and turned to Zack. Her eyes flared. "Okay." She turned and slipped out the door on her side.

Zack executed a clumsy climb over the center console, then exited on the passenger side. He watched for activity from the house, but saw nothing. What to do next? Perhaps someone had already detected them and stood ready to react once they came into full view. Maybe no one had seen them. Maybe no one was looking. Maybe no one was there at all, despite the SUV.

What would I do if this were a complicated but obscure ER situation?

He pursed his lips. *Straight in, no waiting.*

"Come on," he said to Annie. Then he stood, took her by the hand, and strolled up to the circular drive as if they were coming from church for Sunday brunch at this fine Southern mansion.

The absence of the feared gunshots reassured him. Zack led Annie up to the front door. He was about to knock, but tried the door first. It swung open, as if an invitation.

They entered the house.

Chapter Sixty

WHEN THEY WALKED INTO the spacious foyer and living room of The Good House, Annie halted and turned to her dad. She didn't know if she could continue.

He squeezed her hand. "We can do this, Annie. Together."

"They were all here," she said. "In this room. Sarah, Tyler, the man called Spider." She blinked. "And the nurse, Emily."

Her dad's grip on her hand tightened. "Maybe those memories can help us find them now."

Annie pointed up the stairs. "They took me up those stairs." She squinted, bringing the memory into clear focus in her mind. "But I didn't start in this room."

"Let's look around," her dad said. "Maybe more memories will come. I will keep you safe."

She nodded, unconvinced but striving to overcome her fear.

"Let's go upstairs." Dad put a finger to his lips. "Quietly."

They eased up the stairs, their shoes making only soft noises on the carpeted steps. When they got to the landing, Annie stopped.

"He had a gun."

"Who did?"

"Tyler." Annie pointed. "He stood right there." She blinked rapidly. "Except they called him 'Roach.'"

"Tyler's Good House name," her dad said.

Annie looked around the landing, then pointed down the hallway. "A man came from there. They called him Dr. Good. He demanded the gun from, well, Roach."

She took a breath, squinted down the hallway. "Then he told them to put me into a room until it got dark. Then that Dr. Good took the nurse, Emily, downstairs to…"

Her mind went blank. She shook her head.

"Well," Dad said, "let's look around up here first."

They found several rooms off the central hallway. All showed signs of disruption from the police search when they had raided the house a month ago after learning of Annie's abduction to there. Of the three bedrooms, two contained beds with rumpled sheets and blankets.

"Someones slept here," Dad said.

The absence of bedding on the queen-sized bed in what appeared to be a main bedroom suggested no one had slept there.

Across the hall, they entered a room that resembled a rudimentary obstetrical delivery room. The bed was made, and a bassinet perched next to it. All the drawers in a large dresser gaped open. These housed linens and surgical instruments.

Dad walked over to that drawer and inspected its contents. He removed a surgical scalpel and a pair of long, angled scissors. He put them in his pocket.

"Never know when you might need the right instrument," he said.

Their upstairs search completed, Annie and her dad sneaked back downstairs and searched the first floor, including the kitchen and dining room. In the kitchen, they found a coffeemaker with a carafe half-full of cold coffee.

"Whoever brewed this hasn't been here for hours," Dad said.

The cupboards contained mostly dry food, and the half-empty refrigerator contained leftover chicken wings, pizza, and remnants of other fast food.

"I don't think anyone lives her permanently," Dad said. He gave Annie an empathetic look. "Ready to go down and check out the rest of this place?"

A chill ran up Annie's spine. She wanted to run away. Instead, she controlled her feet and took her dad's hand. "Yeah." Her voice did not convince herself.

Annie hyperventilated as she and her dad crossed the living room and approached a narrow hallway that led to the single-level attachment to the main house. A sense of impending doom engulfed her like a death shroud.

Her dad stopped and looked at her with grave concern. "You okay?"

"No."

"We can stop."

"No." She swallowed hard. "I need to see what's there."

They crept down the hallway, Annie's dad in front. They paused at the door, and he turned to her.

"This door has a cypher lock."

Annie blinked, shook her head. "Maybe just try it?"

"Okay," he said. "Ready?"

She sucked in her breath. "Yes."

The door opened when he pushed it. The same happened with a second inner door. When they passed through that door, both gasped at what they saw.

"Holy shit," Dad said.

Annie felt faint. Flashing lights stormed the periphery of her vision. She reeled. It took all her willpower not to flee.

Dad put an arm around her waist to steady her.

In front of them, a fully equipped operating suite featured two rooms: a pre-op area with two scrub sinks and shelves containing various surgical attire that included gowns, masks, and face shields. Beyond that, an operating room with surgical lights, a table, and an anesthesia machine. Against the wall of that room, shelves contained bags of IV fluids and a variety of surgical instruments.

As they moved through the pre-op area for a better look into the OR itself, Annie's knees buckled. She saw herself on that surgical table, legs spread with knees bent. A man sat on a stool between her legs, manipulating a metal instrument that protruded into her body.

Except it wasn't Annie on the table. It was another woman.

"Hello, Zack," said a woman's voice from behind them. "And Annie."

Both turned at once.

Sarah O'Brien wore a surgical gown and a mask. Strands of red hair peeked out from beneath her surgical head covering. Her gloved right hand held a gun pointed at Annie's dad's chest.

"I'll take those obstetrical instruments now, Zack."

Chapter Sixty-One

A GENTLE TOUCH ON her arm awakened Bridget, followed by a soft voice. "Mrs. Larsen?"

The comforting morphine fog drifted away. Bridget opened her eyes.

A young man with dark eyes smiled at her. "Mrs. Larsen?"

"It's Ms. Larsen."

The man returned a sheepish smile. "So sorry, Ms. Larsen. I am José. I will take you to your room." He took hold of her wrist and examined the patient identification bracelet. "Ms. Bridget Larsen," correct?

Bridget blinked. "Yes," she said, wary. She looked around, recognizing she was still in the ICU room. She didn't remember seeing this man earlier.

"I'm already in my room," she said.

"The, uh, situation requires a move to another room. More comfortable bed."

"I'm sorry," Bridget said. "Can you give me some ID? Something that verifies you are who you say you are?"

The young man looked askance. "No one ever asks..."

From around his neck, he removed a lanyard containing a Bethesda Metro Hospital ID badge. She recognized it as similar to the one Zack and the other staff wore, although this one was gray. Zack had mentioned how they wore color-coded IDs for different jobs or positions among the staff. Zack's was green. Nurses wore blue badges.

Bridget couldn't remember seeing a gray one before. She half-sat up in the bed. "Can you hold it closer, please?"

The man handed the card to her.

Bridget took a few seconds to focus her eyes on the object. It contained a photo of the young man in front of her, and the words, "José Santiago, Patient Transporter."

"So, I guess the gray color identifies your role as transporter?"

The man smiled. "That and other roles, yes."

"Okay, José," Bridget said. "Let's get me out of here and into a more comfortable bed."

José brought a gurney alongside Bridget's bed. With gentle but firm hands, he sat Bridget up; all the while being careful not to touch or torque on her bandaged shoulder. He transferred the IV apparatus from the bedside pole to the one attached to the gurney.

She still couldn't feel her forearm or fingers.

José positioned himself on her right side. He guided her good right arm around his shoulder, placed his arm around her waist, and helped her scoot across to the gurney. "Now you can relax," he said.

"Very good," Bridget said. "You obviously know what you're doing."

"Thank you, ma'am. I've had much practice."

As he wheeled her on the gurney toward the ICU exit, Bridget saw no one manning the nurses' desk. "Where are the nurses?"

"Gone," José said. "You were their last patient."

"But don't they need to sign me out first? Check blood pressure and all?"

"You slept through all that." He made a show of looking at the IV bag. "They must have given you some great stuff in there."

Bridget felt for the analgesic push-button, but didn't push it. "Yes. I plan to take home several quarts when I get out of here."

José laughed. He pushed the gurney out of the ICU and down the hall to the elevator. He punched the "Down" button.

She looked back at him. He seemed to cast furtive glances around them. "Isn't this the surgical floor? My room would be on this floor."

"Change of plans," he said. The elevator dinged, the doors whooshed open, and José shoved the gurney carrying Bridget into the elevator. The uneven alignment of the elevator threshold and the hallway floor caused the gurney to lurch, sending shooting pain into Bridget's shoulder.

"Hey," she said. "Easy there." She pushed the PCA button. The surge of morphine calmed her.

The elevator doors opened onto a narrow hallway. Bridget turned to her transporter. "Are we in the basement?"

He didn't answer, but wheeled her through a doorway marked with a sign, "Morgue." "What the...?"

"You must be quiet," José said. He parked the gurney next to an identical one on which lay a Latina woman. She appeared as anxious as Bridget.

"What's going on?" Bridget asked.

From across the room, a door opened.

Chapter Sixty-Two

Zack's gaze shifted from the gun in Sarah's hand to the operating room scene. *Who's doing the surgery? The so-called Dr. Good is dead.*

Sarah scoffed. "Reading your mind was always so easy, Zack."

He turned back to her. "So?"

"You do not need to know that, Dr. Winston." She blinked her eyes in a flirtatious fashion. "But, here's something I believe you should know…"

"Spare us the dramatics, Sarah." Zack's eyes flitted around, seeking but not finding an escape route.

Sarah's face hardened, and her eyes narrowed. "By now, your precious Bridget is dead." She sneered. "Along with that Mexican traitor."

Her words struck Zack like a sledgehammer.

What could have happened?

Next to him, Annie gasped. "No!"

Zack recovered. "I don't believe you." He glanced at Annie. "WE don't believe you."

Sarah shrugged. "No matter. You two are dead already, too." She motioned with the gun toward the floor. "Now sit with your backs against the wall until I tell you to move." She glanced toward the OR. "Time?"

"Almost done." The voice came from the man conducting the procedure between the woman's legs. "Just hold them there."

Zack and Annie did as directed. He thought about trying to jump Sarah, but feared that might put Annie in jeopardy. He whispered to his daughter. "Just do what she says." He glared at Sarah. "For now."

Sarah shook her head. "Such a damned optimist you are, Zack Winston. It's your fatal flaw." She shook her head. "You're done. You just refuse to accept that."

They had sat in place for about ten minutes when the man spoke again. "Finished. Hold them while I get this specimen into the freezer."

Zack watched the man withdrew the instrument from the woman's vagina, then insert the tip into a vial of fluid. He dropped the instrument onto a table and carried the vial into an adjacent room. After a few minutes, the man called out. "Okay. Bring them."

Sarah forced Zack and Annie to their feet, then directed them toward the same room. The man stepped out. He'd removed the surgical mask and hair cover. Zack immediately recognized him.

"Douglas Snyder?"

The man offered a villainous grin. "AKA Spider, among other eponyms. Good to see you again, Dr. Winston."

Zack glowered at the man. "You murdered your wife."

Snyder nodded. "I did. With your help."

Zack briefly recalled how Snyder's wife, Melody, had come into the ER suffering from anaphylactic shock, allegedly from a bee sting. She had a history of allergies to bees. Zack had later figured out she'd been poisoned with bee venom extract. When he had tried to resuscitate her in the ER, Zack had failed to establish the woman's airway and she died. He marveled at how Snyder had fooled him with a convincing performance as the grieving husband.

"You also relieved me of the burden of taking out your former colleague, Dennis King."

Zack's former colleague and friend, Dr. Dennis King, had also been a Good House conspirator.

"What?" Zack said.

"Yeah, like most of you so-called BAFERDs, Dennis got too big for himself. Delusions of grandeur. Damned near exposed the entire operation. You took care of that when you bashed him in the head with that cylinder of parathion." He issued another wicked smile. "Nice job, Doc."

Dennis had died from that blow, but the authorities ruled Zack acted in self-defense because Dennis had threatened to spray him with the lethal insecticide.

Zack glanced behind him at the OR suite. "How?"

"How did I know the procedure?" He scoffed. "Dr. Good, aka Dr. Sebastian Barth, taught it to me."

Zack shook his head. "That makes no sense."

"Not to you, maybe."

"Nope. Not at all."

"Well, I wish I had time to explain in full but, suffice to say, the 'good doctor' was never in charge of this operation. We only let him think he was. Created layers of deniability."

Zack tried a play on Snyder's ego. "To some glorious end, starring you?"

Snyder gave an evil chuckle. "Oh, yeah, like I'm going to spill it to you." He shrugged. "Well, since you're dead already..." He wrinkled his mouth and nose. "Nah. I think not."

He turned to Sarah. "Get them in there while I finish this job." Snyder returned to where the woman lay on the surgical table. He manipulated the IV control.

Sarah gestured with the gun toward the side room. "In you go, Zack and Annie. We need to keep you in there while we make certain, uh, arrangements."

Zack and Annie followed her direction and entered a small room outfitted like a clinical laboratory. A waist-level cryogenic freezer stood alongside one wall, its door padlocked. A few cabinets and shelves occupied the other wall. An industrial sink completed the setting.

"Make yourselves comfy," Sarah said. "We won't be long." She left and closed the door.

As soon as he heard the cypher lock engage behind them, Zack pulled his daughter into a warm hug. For a few seconds, she wept softly on his shoulder. Then at once she seemed to steel herself and lifted her head. "What was Snyder doing to that girl?"

Zack bit his lip. "Stealing her embryo, then killing her." He took a breath. "They plan to kill us, too."

They released from the hug, and Zack studied the double-padlocked waist-high cryogenic freezer that contained the embryo stolen from the unfortunate girl on the OR table. That same freezer had contained Annie's embryo not so long ago. He seethed with anger. "We won't let them hurt us."

"Dad, we're trapped in here. When that man or Sarah come back..."

"We'll be ready for them." Zack gestured around the small room. "This place is full of chemicals. Help me find the best one."

After a few minutes of searching, he'd almost despaired at finding anything helpful. They had found some chemical reagents, but none deadly or short-acting enough to enable a swift, effective attack on their captors.

"We need a Plan B," he said.

Annie pointed to a basket on top of the freezer. A wire container held a metal cylinder that resembled the business end of an aluminum baseball bat, except about eight inches long.

"That could be a club."

"Not much use against a Glock," Zack said. "Unless..."

His eyes scanned the small room again. He crouched down to look under the industrial sink. A plastic bottle the size of a half-gallon milk container partially hid behind the plumbing. "How did I miss that...?"

He looked around for personal protective gear. Next to a small centrifuge, he found a box of nitrile gloves. "Perfect."

Zack took the metal cylinder from atop the refrigerator and handed it to Annie. "Stand guard by the door. Be ready to bash the head of anyone who opens it."

Annie looked terrified, but complied.

Zack donned a pair of the nitrile gloves, then retrieved the plastic bottle from under the sink and placed it on the counter. He unscrewed the cap, took a sniff, and nodded. "Golden." He then rummaged through some drawers until he found a tiny blade sometimes used to dissect tissue for producing specimens to mount on slides. With extreme care, he used the instrument to cut away the fluted top of the plastic bottle. He now had a small bucket that contained a clear liquid. He set that atop the freezer, then spoke to Annie.

"Here's the plan..."

Once they were in position, Zack turned off the lights. They stood in absolute darkness, unable to see each other. Annie's rapid breathing told Zack her location.

"Above all, remember," he said. "You go low."

"Got it, Dad." Her voice sounded committed, annoyed, and scared at the same time.

"Try to stay loose," he said. "We may be in this position for a while. Don't let your knees lock up or your muscles tighten."

"Sure, Dad. Just like a quiet day on the beach."

"When we get out of this, I promise a vacay at a beach."

"I will hold you to that." The slight mirth in her voice reassured him. Annie Winston would come through when needed.

Zack didn't know how long they had waited before he heard footsteps approaching the other side of the door. He judged only one set of feet, not heavy.

He whispered to Annie. "Down."

She squatted. He held the makeshift bucket in his hand. "On my command," he whispered.

"Duh, Dad."

The beeping tones of the cypher lock code penetrated the room.

Zack took a deep breath, heard Annie do the same.

A long beep from the door signaled successful completion of the cypher lock code. The twirl of tumblers followed.

The door opened.

"Now," Zack yelled.

He caught a brief glimpse of Sarah's shocked freckled face a split second before he threw the container of hydrochloric acid at it. Sarah's scream amplified with the simultaneous crack of Annie striking her kneecaps with the heavy cylinder.

Zack barreled through the door and planted a body block into Sarah's chest just as Annie rolled through the door and tackled her legs.

Sarah went down with a loud crack.

Zack and Annie didn't wait for her reaction. Both jumped to their feet. Zack quickly scanned the room. No one else there. He turned to Annie. "You okay? Any acid...?"

"All good, Dad."

Sarah rolled around on the floor, screaming. Her hands clutched her face.

Zack spotted the Glock where she had dropped it. He picked it up and motioned to Annie.

"Let's roll."

"Wait," Annie said. She bent over Sarah and thrust her hand into a pocket, came out with a cell phone. "Okay, now let's move."

They hurried through the operating room. Both noted the vacant OR table as they rushed past it.

Gun in hand, Zack led the way through the door to the main room.

No one there.

They ran straight through the foyer and out the main door. The circular drive was empty. The dark blue SUV had gone.

Zack's Lexus was no longer down the drive where he'd parked it.

"Damn," he said. "I left the keys in the ignition in case we needed a rapid getaway."

Chapter Sixty-Three

Annie rushed after her dad through the front doors of The Good House, clutching Sarah's cell phone like a weapon. She almost ran into her dad when he came to an abrupt halt on the porch. As soon as she noticed both vehicles missing from the circular drive, she used Sarah's phone to call 911.

"Someone's coming," her dad said.

The sound of vehicles on the road approached The Good House.

"Cops wouldn't get here that fast," Dad said. "Let's take cover."

They ran off the porch into the surrounding woods and hunched low in the grass.

We're too close, Annie thought. She tapped her dad and mouthed the words, "Too close."

"Too late," he mouthed back.

Two cars came to screeching halts in the circular drive. The man they now knew as Douglas Snyder, Spider, got out of Zack's Lexus. A youth who looked no older than Annie got out from the driver's side. A rage-faced, swarthy, muscled man bounced out from the passenger side. His forehead featured a pink and gray cross that stood out in bas relief.

Annie glanced at her dad, and he confirmed with a slight nod. From where had *El Vengador de la Sangre* come?

Sarah had said that both Bridget and the Latina woman were dead. Did *El Vengador* attack them while Annie and her dad made their ill-fated attempt on The Good House?

The man slammed his door, took three long strides, and got up into Snyder's face. He spoke in a loud, angry voice that Annie had no trouble hearing.

"Stupid *pendejo*," he said. "You should have killed them on sight. Now I must do your dirty work too?"

He stepped toward the entrance to the house just as Sarah stumbled out. The right side of her face glowed an angry red from the acid. One eye had swollen shut. She screamed at Spider.

"They got away. Ran out this door. They have the gun."

In unison, everyone turned and looked into the woods. Spider and the youth drew pistols. All three men charged toward where Annie and her dad hid.

"Time to leave," Dad said.

He yanked Annie's arm. They turned and ran.

"There," someone shouted from behind them. Gunfire and the spray of errant bullets followed.

"Stop shooting." Spider's voice. "We need them alive."

"*Ándale! Ándale!*." El Vengador's voice.

Dad shouted at Annie. "Run like you've never run before."

She panted. "Duh, Dad."

They made it about twenty yards before they came to a fence that divided The Good House property from its neighbors. Dad vaulted over it, while Annie tried to wiggle under it.

She got stuck part way.

He tried to pull her through. Couldn't budge her.

Voices and footsteps approached.

"Run, Dad. Police are coming. I'll be okay."

Dad gave her a desperate look. "I love you."

"Duh, Dad. Go."

Just as Dad disappeared into the woods, two men came up to where Annie was stuck under the fence. One of them climbed over it to go after her dad.

"Stop." Spider's voice. "Just take the girl. The doc will come back for her. Then we take them both."

***

Zack didn't get far before he realized the men had Annie and did not intend to pursue him. He stopped behind a tree and listened.

Spider's voice shouted across the distance. "Might as well come back now, Doc. We have your daughter. You're both dead, anyway. You can decide how painful her death will be. We have more of that acid. I'm sure my *amigo* here can find new ways to use it." A pause. "Take her."

Annie's voice. "Stay away, Dad. I've got this."

"*Cayate,*" a gruff voice said.

The sound of a slap and Annie's wail of pain told Zack all he needed to know. He crouched and waited until the sounds of retreating footsteps, including his daughter's, died out.

How much time before the police arrived? What could those devils do to Annie in the interim? Might they take her somewhere else?

Seething with rage, Zack hurried after the others at a close but safe distance. As he worked through a plan, he reasoned tactical surprise would not be an option. He thought of the patients he'd seen in the ER, the ones who came in within a breath of death, the ones where he had to make split-second decisions to intervene, taking the risk that he stood equal chances of saving a life or hastening a death.

Right or wrong, he must take action. Now. Zack checked the magazine of Sarah's weapon. Full.

He had not fired a handgun, or any weapon, since his early Navy days when he qualified for an expert pistol marksman ribbon. His motivation then had been to add another ribbon to the solitary National Defense Ribbon on his Navy uniform. His sharpshooter expertise had come as much of a surprise to him as it had to the seasoned petty officers who supervised the firing range.

Perhaps he could get away now with threatening violence?

One of those men may have already killed Bridget and Nilda Flores, despite Zack's "mitigation" plan. They would not hesitate to kill Annie.

He whispered a quick prayer that the police would get there in time and moved toward the house in a crouch. At the edge of the clearing, he took a prone position about twenty yards from the driveway and scanned the scene in front of him.

The men were forcing Annie into the SUV.

Zack fired twice at the vehicle. The first bullet missed its intended tire. The second one shattered the windshield.

Spider pulled the young man off of Annie and pushed him toward Zack's Lexus. "Get me out of here." The engine roared to a start.

El Vengador turned to where Zack's shot had emanated. He wrapped a hefty arm around Annie's neck and squeezed. She gasped for air.

Zack didn't hesitate. "Move, Annie."

His daughter leaned her head away from her captor. Zack shot the man in the upper chest. He released his grip on Annie. She twisted away from him and ran toward Zack.

Sirens approached from the direction of the highway.

El Vengador retreated into the driveway and jumped into Zack's Lexus just as it sped away.

Annie had made it halfway to where Zack stood. He rushed to her and wrapped his arms around her.

"You okay?"

She whimpered a little, then looked at him with wide eyes. "Yes."

The sirens got louder, nearing The Good House.

Zack led Annie back toward the house.

On the porch, Sarah faced them. Her one good eye begging.

Rage consumed Zack as he glared at the woman responsible for Annie's desecration and Zack's pain. Her betrayals and evil deeds ran through his mind like a fast forwarded horror video. He hyperventilated.

Sarah took a clumsy step toward Annie and him.

"Zack, I…"

Justice!

Zack reached out, leveled the Glock, and shot Sarah in mid forehead. The back of her skull exploded in a mist of blood, muscle, bone, and brain. Her already dead body crumpled to the porch.

The sirens came up beside them and stopped. Car doors slammed.

Zack turned.

Detective Martinez crouched by a patrol car. Her weapon pointed at Zack's chest.

"On your knees now, sir. Lay down the gun and put your hands on your head."

Chapter Sixty-Four

Bridget and the Latina woman turned in unison toward the sound of a door opening in the hospital morgue. Bridget tried to sink her body into the gurney.

Is this how I die? Assassination in a hospital morgue?

Instead of the feared assassin, Dr. Beth Jaklic and Dr. Eric Wolfe entered the room from the pathologist's office. Two Montgomery County Police officers accompanied them.

Bridget's fear turned to fury. "What the hell is going on? You scared the piss out of me." True statement, not a metaphor. She pointed with her good hand to the woman on the gurney next to her. "Who is she?"

Dr. Jaklic put a finger to her lips. "Not so loud, Ms. Larsen." She looked around as the police officers positioned themselves inside the entry door. "I'm sorry to alarm you, but we needed subterfuge to get you and Ms. Flores here to safety."

Beth looked at the woman she'd call Ms. Flores. "Sorry, ma'am."

"I understand," the woman said.

"Well, I don't understand," Bridget said in her characteristic hoarse voice.

Beth Jaklic gestured toward Eric Wolfe. "Dr. Wolfe agreed his morgue would be the best place to hide both of you. What assassin will look in the one place in a hospital where the patients are already dead?" She explained the complex series of events that had led them to extricate the two women from the ICU to a safer location, based on information provided by Nilda Flores, who had turned on her former bosses.

Bridget turned to the other woman. "You're a *sicario*?"

"Was a *sicario*. Now I am woman scorned."

"I understand that role," Bridget said. She turned to Beth and Eric. "Now what?"

Eric said, "I volunteered to put you both in body bags, but the cops didn't think that was necessary."

At another time and place, Bridget would have laughed. Zack Winston's friend and running buddy Eric had a reputation for his sardonic wit. Her mind shifted. "Where is Zack?"

Beth shook her head. "No one knows. He and his daughter disappeared."

"Not?"

"No. They had gone to the ICU with your son to visit you. They left Dustin in your room and absconded. Probably used the back hallway."

"Sounds so like Zack," Bridget said. "The Lone Ranger. Straight in, no waiting."

"His car is gone," Beth said. "Police have an APB on it. They'll find him."

"Or not," Bridget said. "That man can be quite sinister when he wants to be."

Beth smiled. "They'll find him." She paused a beat. "Meanwhile, you two will be Eric's guests down here while I go back and act like the innocent trauma surgeon I am."

Even Nilda Flores laughed at that line.

***

The two women became acquainted over the next several hours. At first, they talked about the situation that had brought them together in this freakish place. Later, they exchanged limited information about their backgrounds and personal histories. Each held a tight lid on certain aspects of their distant and near-past lives.

When they ran out of things to discuss, they dozed.

Sometimes a nurse or Dr. Jaklic would come by to assess their clinical status. None had any information, at least that they could impart, about the ongoing situation or the whereabouts of Zack and Annie Winston.

At mid-day, their nurse brought them each a meal tray. Still no information about the immediate matters that concerned both of them.

About an hour after lunch, the nurse returned to add morphine to their PCA pumps. Perhaps because she was high on the opiate, Bridget said, "I never imagined I'd spend a whole day with a professional assassin, in a room for dead people."

Nilda laughed. "Nor I so close to a lawyer."

A little while later, the entrance door opened to admit Detective Tina Martinez. She appeared harassed, and a bit disheveled, unlike her usual professional self.

Bridget glanced at the wall clock. Two PM.

"News?" she asked the detective.

"It's over," Martinez said. "The nurses will soon take you both back to your rooms."

Nilda beat Bridget to the question. "What happened?"

Bridget followed up. "Are Zack and Annie okay?"

Martinez looked into the distance and pursed her lips before she spoke to Bridget. "Annie Winston is safe. She's with her mother, who arrived earlier from California."

A lightning bolt of panic impaled Bridget's mid-chest. "Zack?"

The detective shook her head and frowned. "We arrested him for the murder of Sarah O'Brien."

Chapter Sixty-Five

THE NEXT DAY, ANNIE Winston lay on the plush bed in the suite at the Ritz-Carlton Hotel in Tyson's Corner. Her mother's choice of accommodations, away from Bethesda, her dad, and her friends.

So what if mom's a "member" at this hotel chain? She just wants to keep me away from my new life.

Annie fumed. Her new life would soon become her old life. Mom had tolerated no resistance to her plan to take her daughter back to California.

"What about my therapy with Maria?" Annie had asked.

"I know several psychotherapists of equal, if not superior, skills back home," Mom had said.

"But Maria and I already have a relationship."

Mom had adopted a familiar posture. Legs spread, hands on hips, scowl on lips. "Not up for discussion, Annie. You'll build another relationship with a different therapist in La Jolla."

Annie knew from experience that this would not be the right time to press the issue. She would wait for Dad...

But Dad had landed in jail after their crisis at The Good House. Annie's mind insisted he would soon be free. Hadn't he shot Sarah in self-defense? Well... So what if the woman was half-blind and not armed? She was evil. She still could have...

Annie swallowed hard at the memory of her dad's face, florid with rage. His warrior-like posture. His absolute focus on annihilating Sarah O'Brien.

What would Annie say if ever questioned in court, which seemed likely if they charged him with murder? Would Dad insist Annie tell the truth? Even if that meant...

Mom ended her phone call in the main room and came into the bedroom. She spoke without emotion.

"We leave tomorrow, eight AM flight, direct from Dulles to San Diego."

Annie raged. "Tomorrow? That's too soon, mom. Dad..."

"You don't need to play a part in his tragic melodrama, Annie. I'm taking you home." She folded her arms. "You're lucky to be alive. I'm not risking another incident."

"I won't go."

"You will go. I'm the responsible parent and you're a minor. You don't get to choose."

Annie screwed up her face. "I hate you."

Her mom shrugged. "Okay. We can live with that. For now. At least you will live."

Annie couldn't think of a suitable retort, so she just glared at her mom.

"I'm going to take a shower now," Mom said. "Then we'll go to that apartment and get your things."

"It's not safe to go there, mom. They could still..."

Mom thought for a few seconds. "I thought they had a police guard there. If they don't, I'll hire one. Either way, we're getting your things. We'll pack what we can take on the plane, then box and ship the rest."

Annie pleaded. "Must we do that today? What about Dad?"

"This doesn't involve him."

Annie lost it. "He's in jail, for Christ's sake. Maybe you don't care what happens to him, but I sure as hell do."

Mom replied in a terse, measured voice. "You don't talk to me like that. For the last time, you don't decide these things. End of discussion." She turned away and headed to the bathroom.

When Annie heard the shower water running, she picked up her new iPhone and dialed her dad's number. Voice mail.

Why did I think he'd have a phone in jail?

He had thrown his out with hers on the way to The Good House. She had compelled her mom to let her get an immediate replacement, but dad couldn't exactly...

Stupid girl.

Annie threw the phone onto the bed. As soon as it landed, it buzzed. Dad? She had put her new phone on her previous number.

She retrieved the phone. The screen announced "Unknown." She reached to click it off, when an impulse drew her finger to the *Answer* button.

"Hello?"

"Annie?" The familiar voice sent a shiver up Annie's spine.

"Tyler?"

"Yes."

Annie was momentarily speechless, then found her voice. "What the fuck, Tyler?"

"Please don't hang up."

"Give me one reason not to."

"We need to talk."

"Why would I ever talk to you again?"

"Because..."

Through her rage and confusion, Annie thought about what the cartel had done to Tyler. She stayed on the line out of curiosity, if not for another reason.

"Are you okay?"

"I'll live. If you can call my, uh, handicap living."

"I won't discuss that."

He groaned. "Of course not."

"Why did you call me?"

A long pause. "I... I want to beg you to forgive me."

Annie squeezed her eyelids shut. "So, beg."

"Please, please, Annie. I am so very sorry for what happened, for my part in it." He gulped back what sounded like sobs. "Sometimes I think I'd be better off dead. But I want to live. Even with my... Most of all, I want to make peace with you."

From the bathroom, Annie heard the shower turn off. Mom would be out soon.

"I can't talk now, Tyler. Not here."

"Can you come see me in the hospital?"

She bit her lip and shook her head. "I don't know. Mom's like all over me." She glowered at the closed bathroom door and decided. "I'll make it happen."

A deep sigh. "Oh, please. Please."

The bathroom door opened. "I have to go now," Annie said. "I'll try to call later."

"Please, Annie. I... I love you."

She hung up just as her mother came out of the bathroom.

"Were you on the phone?" Mom asked.

Annie swallowed hard. "I, uh, called Bridget."

Her mother's eyes narrowed. "Why?"

Annie shrugged. "I just did. That's all."

Mom opened her mouth to speak, then stopped. "Okay. Your turn in the shower."

Annie took her phone with her into the bathroom.

When she came back into the bedroom, her mother sat in a side chair, a pinched expression on her face, her phone clutched in her hand.

"Hurry and get dressed," Mom said. She lifted her phone. Some lawyer just called. I have to take you to court for Zack's arraignment.

Chapter Sixty-Six

OF ALL THE UNBEARABLE memories of the previous day and night, none ravaged Zack Winston's soul more than Detective Martinez handcuffing him and pushing him into the rear seat of a police vehicle like a criminal—in full view of his hysterical daughter.

The second most terrifying memory was the vision of Sarah when the bullet Zack had fired from her own gun pierced her mid-forehead an instant before the back of her head exploded.

Sarah is dead. She will no longer torment Annie. Or me.

That thought provided little consolation now. Not after the police detective he'd known and trusted arrested him and accused him of murder.

"I might get the prosecutor to entertain a lesser charge," she'd said with apology.

Zack couldn't fathom that term, murder. He'd done what he must to rescue Annie, once and for all, from the most vile of villains in the most corrupt of conspiracies.

Regret? Only that Annie had witnessed the entire scene.

Where was Annie now? Had Natalie, her loving mother, arrived from San Diego in time to comfort her? Probably arrived. Natalie always had impeccable timing, especially for playing rescuer. No wonder she'd become a psychiatrist.

Comfort? That could be a different matter, but it was between Annie and her mother.

What of Bridget? Zack's third terror after his arrest and incarceration. Spider and Sarah had insisted Bridget had died, along with Nilda Flores.

Bridget dead?

Zack could not wrap his addled mind around that horrid thought.

She's not dead until I see her dead.

Only then did the tears come. How will Dustin live without both his parents?

How will I live without Bridget? Especially if I've lost Annie. Again.

Zack buried his face in his hands and wept. For Bridget, for Annie, for himself. Even for Sarah.

When he opened his eyes, Noelle sat on the narrow bench across from him. She wore the same naval aviator flight suit that had attracted Zack many years ago. Noelle had not visited since she encouraged Zack to find Bridget after he'd saved her life a few years ago.

"Is Bridget...?" He asked with terrified eyes.

"Not for me to tell," Noelle said.

Of course, she couldn't tell. She existed only in Zack's subconscious mind. She would have no more facts than he did.

He looked at her, quizzical. "Then why?"

"Why am I here? Now?" She smiled in that knowing way she'd had when she was alive. "Because you need a friend and confidante now, Zack." She gazed around the cell. "Looks like I'm it."

He pleaded. "What should I do?"

Her eyes turned serious. "Be honest, Zack. Be brutally honest. Especially with yourself."

The sound of approaching footsteps outside the cell interrupted. Zack looked in that direction, then back to where Noelle sat.

Gone.

"You have a visitor," a voice from outside the cell said.

Zack recognized the deputy sheriff, and he somewhat recognized the fifty-something portly man with dark hair and graying temples who stood next to him. But he couldn't place the guy.

The deputy opened the cell and ushered the man inside. "I'll be right out here. You have five minutes."

The man turned to the deputy and scoffed. "I have at least ten. More if I decide to take it."

The deputy scowled and left the cell.

His visitor turned to Zack. "You may not remember me, Dr. Winston." He put out a hand. "Norman Jones, defense attorney. Bridget Larsen sent me."

The lawyer who had defended Bridget against the phony charge of murdering her husband. Possibly the most successful defense attorney in the National Capital Region.

Zack shook the man's hand. "I'm glad you're here." He stopped. "Wait. Bridget sent you?"

"She did. As soon as she heard what happened in that place."

Zack burst into a smile. "Then she's alive."

Jones raised an eyebrow. "Very much so. Why wouldn't she be?"

Zack let out a long breath and sat. He looked to where Noelle had appeared. "Thank God, Bridget lives."

Chapter Sixty-Seven

Later that afternoon, Norman Jones returned to Zack's cell. He gave him explicit directions.

"We're going to your initial hearing, or arraignment. I have one, and only one, direction for you. Say nothing. Do not speak. At all. Anything you say at this stage of the process can only hurt you. I will speak on your behalf. Clear?"

Zack blew out a breath. "Understood."

"We always plead not guilty at the first hearing, because we don't know what the police report says, nor do we know what the prosecution intends. This just gets the ball rolling. We'll have plenty of time to plan as the process unfolds." Jones put a hand on Zack's shoulder. "Don't even think the word 'murder.' It won't come down to that. From what you told me, the worst case will be voluntary manslaughter."

Zack stared at the floor, then looked up. "Will I get to go home when this, uh, hearing is over?"

Norman sucked air through his teeth. "That will be difficult."

Zack recoiled like a wounded animal. "What?" He stared at the attorney. "I can't spend another night in this hellhole. Plus, Annie..."

Norman nodded. "Your ex-wife is in town. She has your daughter."

Zack buried his face in his hands.

"Dr. Lewis arrived last night," Norman said. "She and Annie are staying at the Ritz in Tyson's."

Zack stood and paced the cell. "Of course, she would stay there." He turned on the attorney. "You've got to get me out of here. I need to see my daughter." He blew out a breath. "I need to save my daughter."

And I need to see Bridget.

Norman Jones frowned. "I'm working an option, but it's a long shot."

Before Zack could reply, the deputy sheriff appeared and opened the cell. "They're ready in the courtroom."

Norman turned to Zack. "This deputy will escort you. I'll see you in the courtroom." He left the cell without looking back.

When the deputy sheriff escorted Zack into the courtroom, the sight of Annie and Natalie sitting in the front row of the gallery hit him like a punch in the gut.

Annie stood and gushed. "Dad!"

He lunged toward her, but Natalie pulled her back into her seat; just as the deputy squeezed Zack's arm and pivoted him toward a table facing the judge's bench. Norman Jones sat at the table, a scowl on his face. He directed Zack to a chair next to him.

"You can talk to her later," Norman said in a scolding voice one might direct at an errant teenager. He scanned the gallery, as if looking for someone, shook his head, and pursed his lips. Then he sat.

Zack looked around. Other than Annie and Natalie, he recognized only Detective Tina Martinez.

"All rise," the bailiff said. "This court is now in session. The honorable Margaret Hill presiding."

A lithe middle-aged woman wearing judicial robes entered from a side door. She mounted the bench with gusto, then sat.

"Be seated," she said.

As all sat, Norman once again scanned the gallery as if looking for someone. No one else had arrived.

The judge went through the process of obtaining documents, determining that the prosecution charged Zack with voluntary manslaughter involving a firearm in the death of Sarah O'Brien. She turned her attention to where Zack sat. "Is the defendant represented by counsel?"

Norman nudged Zack to stand, then stood beside him. "Norman Jones, your honor, counsel for the defendant." Again, he glanced around the room.

"Very well," the judge said. "How does the defendant plead?"

Zack opened his mouth to speak. Norman poked him, then addressed the judge. "The defendant pleads not guilty, Your Honor. Also, we wish to be heard on bond."

The judge harrumphed. "Bond? On a charge of murder, Mr. Jones? I'm prepared to remand him to custody pending trial."

"Your Honor, ma'am. If I may?"

The judge scowled. "Yes?"

Norman cleared his throat, glanced at the courtroom doors, then looked back at the judge. "My client has no criminal record. He is a practicing emergency physician with strong ties to the community. This was a straightforward case of self defense. We would like to call one witness, whom I do not see in the courtroom. May I please have a moment to check the hallway?"

The judge frowned. "You may."

Just then, the courtroom doors opened.

"Ah," Norman said. "Our witness has arrived."

Zack turned, along with everyone else. A wheelchair entered, bearing Bridget Larsen clad in loose trousers, a blouse and sweater. A sling supported her left arm and shoulder. Dustin Hilliard wheeled his mother up the center aisle to the railing that divided the gallery from the inner sanctum.

Bridget stared straight ahead and did not look at Zack.

The judge eyed Bridget and smiled. "Well, this is getting interesting." She turned to Norman. "Will you proceed, Mr. Jones?"

"Your honor," Jones said as he gestured toward Bridget. "Perhaps you know Ms. Bridget Larsen, a prominent attorney in the National Capital Region."

The judge smiled. "You think? We went to Harvard Law together." She looked at Bridget. "How are you doing, Bridge? You look a bit 'under the weather,' shall we say?"

Bridget spoke in her typical hoarse voice. "Under the circumstances, Your Honor, I'm just happy to be alive."

The judge cast an expectant look at Norman Jones. "You have the floor, Mr. Jones."

Norman stepped around in front of the table, where he could address both the judge and Bridget. "Your Honor, before Ms. Larsen arrived, you announced your intention to remand Dr. Winston into custody, pending trial." He swept his arm around the room, to include Zack, Annie and Natalie, and Bridget. "We understand the court's reluctance to consider bail in a case of this nature. However, this is not a typical violent crime, as we will show in trial. Dr. Winston and his daughter there are the true victims."

He moved closer to Bridget. "Ms. Larsen knows the defendant well. She will avow that he is not a flight risk, and certainly not a danger to the community. She believes in his fundamental integrity and trustworthiness." He moved next to Zack. "Ms. Larsen has volunteered to post a bond for Dr. Winston's release pending trial. She offers her personal promise to assure he attends all trial procedures."

Zack cast a surprised look at Bridget. She did not look in his direction.

The judge addressed Bridget. "Is that true, Bridge... Ms. Larsen?"

Bridget replied in a hoarse voice, without inflection. "Yes, your honor, I will post bond for fifty thousand dollars on behalf of Dr. Winston. He is neither a flight risk, nor a danger to the community, and he will appear in court whenever required."

Behind Zack, Natalie gasped. He didn't turn around.

The judge stared at Bridget, pondering.

"Very well," she said at last. "I hereby release the defendant on bond for fifty thousand dollars. Dr. Winston, you must keep in contact with your defense counsel, and you must remain within the National Capital Area until the conclusion of this matter." She wrote in a notebook. "I am scheduling a pre-trial conference for one month from today."

She rapped her gavel on the bench. "Court adjourned."

"All rise," the bailiff announced.

As soon as the judge left the courtroom, Zack turned toward Bridget, intending to thank her.

Bridget nodded to Dustin, who wheeled her around and pushed her toward the exit. At no time since her unexpected arrival had Bridget so much as glanced in Zack's direction.

Chapter Sixty-Eight

Outside the courtroom, Zack searched in vain for Bridget and Dustin. He dialed her number, but it went to voicemail.

"Bridge," he said, his voice cracking. "Thank you so much for what you did. How can I ever repay you? I hope you're okay. Can we talk? Soon? Just call me when you can." He started to end the voicemail, then paused and spoke into the mouthpiece. "I... I love you, Bridget."

He stifled a sob as he replaced the phone in his pocket.

"Dad!"

He turned to see Annie rushing up to him. Natalie followed at a short distance.

Annie hugged him. She cried. "What's going to happen, Dad? I'm so scared."

He pulled her close, glanced over her shoulder at Natalie standing a few feet away.

"I don't know, Annie. Today went as well as we could expect."

"Thanks to Bridget," she said.

"Thanks to Bridget."

Again, he glanced at Natalie. She stood with arms folded, frowning.

Zack broke the embrace and regarded Annie at arm's length. "Are you okay?"

She shook her head, broke into sobs. "I am definitely not okay." She put her head on his chest and cried.

Zack looked at Natalie. "We should go somewhere we all three can talk."

"Indeed, we should." Natalie pursed her lips, looked past Zack.

Zack said to Annie, "Let me finish up with the lawyer. Then you, mom, and I can go somewhere private."

Annie wiped away the tears. She moved away and stood with Natalie.

"Make it quick," Natalie said.

Zack glared at her, then turned to where Norman Jones stood at a respectable distance.

"What happens next, Norm?"

Norman gave him a dry smile. "You go home, relax. Tomorrow or the next day, we work on your defense." He frowned. "I won't sugarcoat it, Zack. This won't be easy."

"I know," Zack said. "For now, I need to fix things with Annie." He sighed. "And her mother." He paused.. "Natalie will want to take Annie to California with her."

Norman shrugged. "She can do that. But for sure, when you go to trial or even before, Annie must return here to testify. That includes at least a day of intense preparation."

Zack nodded. "I didn't say she was leaving. Just that's what her mother will want."

Norman grimaced. "Good luck with that." He turned away, but Zack stopped him.

"What happened with Bridget?"

Normal returned a curious look, not understanding the question. "What do you mean?"

"After she testified. Where did they go?"

"Oh, that. Back to the hospital. She's still a patient there. They allowed her out long enough to come here and support you."

Zack took a deep breath. As much as he disliked the idea or returning to the hospital, he had to go back to see Bridget.

A short while later, Zack sat with Annie and Natalie in a booth at a cafe across from the courthouse.

"It's not negotiable, Zack," Natalie said. "I've already made that crystal clear to Annie."

Zack's eyes narrowed. "You can't..."

"The hell, I can't."

Zack took a breath. Confrontation would not work in this scenario.

"Why so soon? Why tomorrow?"

"She's not safe here." Natalie leaned into Zack. "To be clear, in case you thought otherwise, she stays with me at the Ritz. But even there, she's not safe from these...terrorists."

"I can get you a police guard."

Natalie scoffed. "Yeah, that's been so effective up to now."

Zack closed his eyes, pondering. When he opened them, he tried to look and sound sincere. "I get it, Nat." He cast a helpless glance at Annie. "You won't leave here without her. I understand your reasons."

He took a deep breath.

Last shot.

"Just, please, not so soon. Give us some time to decompress together. As a psychiatrist, you should see the value of that. And let Annie transition with Dr. Santos." He put on a pained look. "Forty-eight hours. That's all I ask."

Annie protested. "Dad…"

Zack raised his hand in a reassuring gesture. "I know, Annie. I don't want you to go at all. But your mother leaves us no choice. I don't want to fight over it. Let's just roll with it for now."

Annie scowled, sat back, and folded her arms.

Natalie sighed. "Okay. I'll change our flight to Thursday instead of tomorrow."

Zack smiled. "Thanks." He meant it.

"But," Natalie said, "she stays at the Ritz with me. I don't want her near that apartment, especially at night."

"Mom…"

Zack patted Annie's arm. "Your mother's right. I don't plan to stay there either. It's dangerous."

Annie squinted. "You think those guys…"

"That *Vengador* guy got away, along with Snyder/Spider." He tried to sound reassuring. "I think it's unlikely they'll try anything now, but I'd rather be safe. I'd rather you be safer."

"Where will you stay?"

"I don't know yet. Probably a hotel." He glanced at Natalie. "Not the Ritz. Out of my budget."

Natalie huffed.

Zack turned to her. "I'd like to take Annie with me from here. We can visit Bridget in the hospital, thank her for posting bond. Then we'll have dinner somewhere, and I'll get her back to your hotel by, say, eight o'clock?"

Natalie glared at him. "You think the hospital's safe?"

"It's like a fortress with all the law enforcement there," Zack said. "If it wasn't, Bridget would be dead. So would the woman who broke the case for us."

Annie looked at her mom. "Please, Mom. I want to see Bridget before you make… Before I go back to California."

Natalie pondered. Then she looked Zack in the eye. "Fine. But no later than eight o'clock." She gathered her belongings, stood, and beckoned to Zack and Annie. "Come on. I'll drop you two off at the hospital." She sneered. "Wouldn't want you to get lost, you know."

Zack sighed. "Okay. Thanks."

He glanced at Annie and winked.

Chapter Sixty-Nine

EXHAUSTED FROM THE TRIP to the courthouse and back, Bridget slept through the afternoon.

She did not enjoy a restful sleep. Distressing dreams and aching memories of her history with Zack Winston pummeled her mind.

Their first meeting, when she'd put aside her intuition and agreed against her better judgment to defend Zack against the bogus malpractice case. Zack's withholding of critical information that almost scuttled their case. The triumph of uncovering and exposing the medical conspirators behind that phony lawsuit. Dr. Dennis King's vengeful throat-slashing attack on Bridget in her building's parking garage. Zack saving her life by performing an emergency cricothyrotomy on the parking garage floor. The subsequent loss of her full voice that took her out of her vital role as a malpractice defense attorney, permanently unable to speak above a throaty whisper.

The growing attraction between Zack and her, which reached its peak with a passionate kiss on her living room sofa—an instant before her philandering husband, Marshall, entered the room. Zack's evidence-based reasoning that cleared Bridget of suspicion of Marshall's murder by rat poison. His discovery of Fiona Delaney as the true culprit, after which he co-opted her into becoming a confidential informant.

How she raced after Zack in her car as he sped toward The Good House to rescue Annie. Their diversion to the Potomac River, where Bridget's triathlon-trained swimming skills enabled her to extricate both Zack and his daughter from the raging river.

Zack's recent clueless romantic pursuit of Bridget while she labored to adjust to becoming a single mother to her teenage son, whose father was murdered.

The most recent attack on her home and family by the cartel *sicarios*. How Bridget had killed not one, but two of them. She sagged into the bed and covered her face at the recurring visions of two young men, however guilty and dangerous, losing their lives by her hand.

The gunshot wound she'd suffered at the hands of the first assassin, leaving her with another permanent disability: a frozen shoulder and useless left arm and hand.

Those images came not in coordinated, chronological remembrances, but in a jumbled panoply of conflicting images and sounds. Including Zack's voice...

"Bridget?"

The voice was real. She opened her eyes. Zack and Annie stood by her bedside.

Who let them in here? Isn't there a guard...?

Of course. Zack worked at the hospital. A trusted emergency physician could gain access almost anywhere in the facility.

I don't want to see him now.

Bridget forced a smile, directed her gaze to Annie Winston. "How are you, Annie?"

The young woman, for such had she become through the traumas that would forever mar her adolescence, shook her head.

"Been better."

"Haven't we all?" Bridget said in her hoarse voice.

She turned to Zack. "And you, Dr. Winston?"

Zack stood with one arm holding the other at the elbow. His eyes sunken. "Much better, thanks to your generosity. I will always owe you for that."

Bridget shrugged. "Least I could do. The thought of you in prison..."

Now Zack forced a smile. "I would have risen to the challenge, but so glad I don't have to."

Bridget scoffed. "You really believe that, don't you?"

He gave her a puzzled look.

An uncomfortable silence followed, finally broken by Annie. "I'm going to step out and let you two talk." She looked at her dad, who seemed concerned. "I won't go far, Dad. Meet you in the lounge in a few."

Zack blinked, then looked at Bridget with longing.

"Okay," he said to Annie. "We won't be long here. Bridget needs rest after her heroic afternoon."

Bridget fended off a wave of nausea.

As soon as Annie left, Zack reached for and squeezed Bridget's right hand, her good hand. She didn't return the squeeze. He didn't seem to notice.

"Thanks again," he said. "I really mean it when I say I owe you." He rocked on his feet, rubbed the back of his neck.

Bridget reflected on how Zack, the dauntless, confident emergency physician, could become such a wad of putty when interacting with a woman, especially one he cared about. She closed her eyes, then opened them and looked into his. "You saved my life in that parking garage two years ago, Zack. Let's not speak of owing each other anything."

His eyes widened. Silence fell between them. Zack broke it with a question. "So, really, how are you feeling?"

She shook her head. "As you no doubt know, I've lost the use of my left arm. That won't get better. Meanwhile, the shoulder is healing fine, so they plan to discharge me tomorrow."

Zack frowned. "Seems a bit early. How will you manage? Can I help?"

She paused, wondering what to say. What was one of Zack Winston's favorite ER sayings? "Straight in, no waiting?"

Bridget took a deep breath. "You can't help, Zack."

His eyes widened. He spoke in a tense voice. "What do you mean?"

"You have your own issues to deal with right now," she said. "Annie for one. Your pending trial for another."

Zack gave her a pained stare. "We both have big issues ahead of us. We've been such a good team. I thought we could work through those issues, you know, together?"

"Are we, Zack?"

"Huh?"

"Are we such a great team?"

"Of course we are. Look what we've been through together. How we've survived."

Straight in...

"How much of what we've been through have we brought on ourselves?"

"What do you mean?"

...no waiting.

"I've had a lot of time to lie here and do nothing but think, and remember."

"I don't like where this is headed."

"Not saying I like it either, Zack."

"Out with it, Bridge. What's on your mind?"

She took a few calming breaths.

"Three years ago, you were a successful emergency physician, and I was a successful defense attorney. Look how much our lives have changed in that time."

Zack threw up his arms. "Not our own making, Bridge. If you want to blame someone, how about Janice Barnett, Dennis King, Sebastian Barth aka Dr. Good, Douglas Snyder aka Spider..."

Bridget scoffed. "Flies on carrion."

Zack's face flushed, and his voice rose. "Carrion? You saying we're dead meat?"

She shook her head. "Of course not." She used her good hand to wipe her eyes. "But we seem to attract chaos, drama, tragedy."

Zack tilted his head and looked at her through narrowed eyes. "What meds are they giving you, Bridge? I'd swear you're hallucinating here."

"Other than the antibiotics, I'm off all meds. I hate losing control, especially to opiates and other mind-altering drugs."

"Well, something's got your brain in a twist." He folded his arms. "Maybe we continue this 'talk' later."

She shook her head. "Straight in, no waiting, Zack."

"Huh?"

"We're both good people, wonderful people. To tell the truth, I love you, Zack. Very much."

He threw up his hands. "Great. Problem solved. I love you too, Bridget. Together we can overcome whatever."

She hoped her smile did not appear as condescending as it felt. "Truth is, Zack, we're not good together. No matter how much we love each other." Bridget swallowed hard. "I'm sorry about that carrion analogy, but it's close to the truth. We attract trouble, and it doesn't affect only us. Annie and Dustin have been through hell. Marshall, son of a bitch that he was, got murdered."

"You can't make us responsible for all that's happened."

A flush of rage rose within Bridget. "I hate violence. I despise guns. Yet I killed two young men. I shot them dead."

She pointed her right index finger at him. "You killed Dennis King. You shot Sarah O'Brien. You're a physician. You're supposed to save lives, yet you took two. As did I."

Zack raised his hands in a stop gesture. "Now hold on just a gosh darn minute, Bridge. You're a lawyer. The concept of self-defense should matter to you."

"Was it?"

His eyebrows tented. "Huh?"

"Was it self-defense, Zack?"

"Danged right, it was." His breathing became heavy. "Your son and my daughter would be dead if you hadn't pulled that trigger." He looked away.

"Did you kill Sarah in self-defense, Zack?"

His nostrils flared, voice exploded. "You're not making any frigging sense, Bridge. She threatened Annie and me."

Bridget looked Zack straight in the eye. "What threat was half-blind, unarmed Sarah O'Brien to Annie or you when you shot her in the forehead, Zack?"

Zack glared at her for several seconds, his breathing raspy. Bridget could almost believe he was about to attack her.

All at once, his posture relaxed and his eyes softened. He blew out a long breath.

"Message received, counselor."

He backed away from the bed. "Have a wonderful life, Bridget." He turned to leave.

"Zack."

He turned. Looked at her with expectant eyes. "What?"

"Get help. Professional help. It's the only way…"

Zack did not reply. He left the ICU without looking back.

As soon as he was gone, Bridget broke into sobs.

Chapter Seventy

Annie used her dad's name and Bridget's to talk her way past the lone security guard at the door to Tyler's room. She found Tyler asleep, his serene repose discordant with her painful memories. Could this be the same guy who wooed then betrayed her? The evil Roach?

Or was he the actual Tyler? The youth who suffered a life as conflicted as hers, with whom she'd enjoyed an immediate emotional connection? Annie had once fantasized about a future with him. Could that dream revive?

Tyler opened his eyes, blinked to adjust to his surroundings. His face lit up when he saw Annie.

"Annie. You came."

She smiled. "I did."

Uncomfortable silence descended on them.

Annie broke it first. "How are you?"

He grimaced. "Overall, I'm okay. Still pretty beat up. No permanent injuries except…" He glanced at his groin and blushed.

Annie tried to sound confident. "I've heard the doctors have high hopes."

Tyler shook his head. "One thing I've learned over the last few months, hope is not reality."

"But, without hope, we despair. We must have hope."

He cocked his head. "We?"

"I meant generic 'we.'"

His face fell. He thought for a moment, then gave her a penetrating gaze. "So, what about us? Do we have hope?"

Annie bit her lip. "Who's asking? Tyler? Or Roach?"

His eyes narrowed, and his face hardened. "Roach is dead. May he rot in hell."

"How does that work, Tyler?"

He glanced away, then gave her another earnest look. "Because I'll make it work." He stifled a sob. "I will always regret what I, what Roach, did to you, Annie."

Annie shook her head. "That doesn't work, Tyler. You can't blame some alter ego for what *you* did. Call him Tyler or Roach. *You* betrayed me. Took me to that place. You put my life at risk. Don't tell me now that you care."

"But I do. Care. I helped you at the river."

"No, Tyler. You did not. I'd be dead if my dad, if Bridget, hadn't come."

Tyler looked away. After a few seconds, he turned back, his cheeks wet with tears. "I jumped out of that car. I came back to help you. I..."

"Too late. Just like you showed up at Bridget's house too late and almost got us all killed." She stopped at once, recalling the price Tyler had paid for his change of heart.

He seemed to read her thoughts. "For which I bear a permanent scar."

Another silence. This time, Tyler broke it.

"When we first met, at that pizza joint in Georgetown, you charmed me without even trying."

She shrugged. "So? You still betrayed me."

Tyler buried his face in his hands. "I know. I wish to hell..."

Annie reached out and touched his arm. "I know, Tyler. I know."

He took a deep breath. "I wasn't the only one took you there, to The Good House. Sarah..."

Annie replied in a sharp voice. "Don't you dare try to pass the blame. You did what you did. Sarah or no Sarah."

"For which I paid the price, and she gets away with it."

He doesn't know.

"Sarah's dead."

"What?"

"My dad shot her."

Tyler's eyes widened. "On purpose?"

Annie nodded. "Yeah, but...it's complicated." She summarized the events at The Good House and her dad's current legal predicament.

Tyler's face turned ugly. "That fucking bitch. I'd kill her myself if your dad hadn't done it."

"Well, you didn't, and he did. No reason to go there now."

Another silence.

Annie broke it. "I'm going back to California with my mom."

He looked thunderstruck. "What? Why?"

"She's not giving me a choice."

"You always have a choice, Annie. She can't run your life."

Annie sighed, gazed into the distance, and finalized the decision that had been on the edge of her mind. "I know I have a choice. I'm choosing to go with Mom."

"You can't. What about your dad? What about us?"

Annie folded her arms. "There is no 'us,' Tyler. Never was, never will be. As for my dad, he'll land on his feet. He always does."

Tyler looked petulant. "I don't want to lose you, Annie."

She smirked. "You never had me, Tyler. After all that happened, you never will."

He reached for her hand. "Please, give me a chance. I'll get better. I'll make it right. I promise."

Annie took his hand, looked deep into his eyes. "I truly hope you do. But I can't give you what you want from me." She sniffed. "I'll go you one better. I give you forgiveness, Tyler Rhodes, for all you did to me and my dad." She squeezed his hand. "I forgive you, and I wish you the best for the rest of your life."

His voice choked with emotion. "Please, Annie."

She put a finger to her lips, then bent over and planted a light kiss on his cheek. "I hope you get better. For yourself, not me or anyone else."

She let go of his hand. "Goodbye, Tyler."

Then she left the room, not turning around, even as his sobs reached her ears.

Chapter Seventy-One

When Zack found Annie outside Tyler's room, she informed him she would not fight her mother's demand to take her back to California.

He had no further say in the matter. "We'll make it work, Annie."

They met up with Natalie, and the three of them negotiated terms. Zack could visit Annie and her older sister, Jennifer, any time. In California. Natalie would not agree for Annie ever to return to Bethesda.

Zack had protested.

"Norman Jones, my defense attorney, will want Annie to testify in my trial."

Natalie shrugged. "She can do that virtually by video teleconference. Doesn't need to be present in the courtroom."

"What if I need her here? For support?"

Natalie scoffed, but said nothing.

"Let it go, Dad," Annie had said. "Let time heal what time can heal. Then we'll see."

When had his teenaged daughter become such a rational adult?

The trio also agreed that Annie could keep her appointment with Dr. Maria Santos the following day to achieve closure in their relationship.

After their discussion, Natalie had booked an evening flight the next day for her and Annie from Dulles to San Diego.

Zack dropped Annie and Natalie off at their hotel, then made his way to the Hilton Garden Inn Bethesda, near the apartment he'd shared with Annie. That apartment remained sealed off as a crime scene, but for a reason other than the original threat to Zack and his daughter. Law enforcement now searched it for evidence to support the murder charge against Dr. Zack Winston.

He booked a single room on the top floor of the hotel. After a restless hour of flipping between TV channels showing basketball and hockey games, he gave up and shut it off.

After dropping off Annie and Natalie, he had stopped at a running store. With a glimmer of hope in his heart, Zack donned the cold weather gear and new ASICS running shoes, left the hotel, and made his way to the familiar trail. Wearing a runner's headlamp, he jogged the trail at a slow, deliberate pace. He concentrated on the ground in front of his feet to avoid any ice that might have accumulated after a recent light freezing rain. When he rounded a familiar bend, a presence got his attention. He looked up, brimming with expectation.

Noelle waited for him at the precise spot where he'd met her during his introspective jogs two years earlier, when faced with the malicious malpractice suit. That seemed ages ago.

She wore the same tailored flight suit.

Zack stopped running. "I hoped you'd show up."

"And therefore I have," Noelle said.

He looked away, then back at her. "God, I wish you were real."

"As real as you want me to be." Her dark eyes sparkled, like they had that first night on liberty in Hong Kong, when they had become a couple.

Zack frowned. "Not the same thing."

She shook her head. "Oh, Zack. Why must you make everything harder that it has to be?"

"What's that supposed to mean?"

Noelle regarded him with kind eyes. "Haven't you just lost the most important women in your life? Well, the most important living women?"

A wave of deep, unassuaged sadness overcame Zack. "Their choices."

"Really, Zack? Have you learned nothing over the last two years?"

The sadness gave way to anger. "How dare you accuse me..." He stopped. The sadness returned.

"I haven't learned enough, it seems." He feared he might burst into tears and collapse on the spot.

Noelle huffed to get his attention. He looked at her with expectation.

"What was the last thing Bridget said to you, Zack?"

He pursed his lips. "That I should get professional help."

She nodded. "Hmmm. Know anyone around here who does that for a living?"

"Maria Santos."

"I hear her schedule will open up after tomorrow."

Zack stared at Noelle. "You mean?"

"Duh, Zack."

He looked away, stared down the trail ahead with all its curves, bends, mud, and ice. He took a deep breath. "Okay," he said. "I will see her."

Zack turned back to Noelle, but she was no longer there.

Chapter Seventy-Two

A MONTH LATER, ZACK sat in Maria Santos' waiting room. He'd arrived twenty minutes early for his appointment after making the drive from Norman Jones' office in DC to Maria's in Rockville in record time. Except he didn't remember the drive at all. His mind had churned so much after the message Norman had delivered from the prosecutor, he might have set a record for breaking the speed limit and avoiding capture.

As he waited, Zack thought of Emily Morgan, the former Good House nurse who had helped Annie. Now recovered from the stabbing attack and back in pre-trial detention in Baltimore, Emily had taken a plea deal and awaited sentencing. She had sent a message to Norman Jones requesting Annie Winston to appear as a supporting witness. Norman was still trying to get Natalie to consent.

"She'll have more impact in person," Norman had said. Natalie had promised to think about it, but Norman held little hope.

Zack's thoughts drifted to Nilda Flores, The Fly. Now out of the hospital and also in pre-trial detention, she continued to negotiate for immunity in exchange for her insider information about *Los Hermanos*. Detective Martinez had told Norman that the negotiations seemed promising. Nilda had provided useful leads that led to the arrest and capture of minor operatives in the U.S.

"Tip of the iceberg," she'd told the federal authorities.

No one knew the whereabouts of Douglas Snyder or *El Vengador*. They had made a clean escape from The Good House the night Zack killed Sarah O'Brien.

A text message arrived, and Zack's mind shifted to a more pleasant topic. Annie had kept her promise to text or call him every day after she returned to San Diego.

new school sucks miss rocky and them

He texted back.

You will make new friends there soon enough.

Zack could not bring himself to follow the teen convention of not using proper grammar and punctuation in text messages.

miss you dad

Miss you too.

what doing

Appointment with Maria.

o wow still good

Yes.

mom calling gotta go

Okay. Be good. Love you.

love you too dad

Zack closed the chat function, then re-opened it. He made another attempt to text Bridget, which he'd done daily since her discharge from the hospital, without a reply.

Still no response. Did she get a new phone? Zack didn't think so.

"Goodbye means goodbye," he said aloud.

"Well, that sounds like a fruitful topic, Dr. Winston."

Maria Santos stood by the door to her office. She smiled and beckoned him. "Come on in."

Zack started the session by telling Maria that the prosecutor had offered him a deal. He could plead guilty to involuntary manslaughter and accept a one-year prison sentence, with the probability of parole in six months. Otherwise, the charge would be voluntary manslaughter. If convicted at trial, he faced a maximum prison sentence of ten years.

"Easy decision?" Maria said.

"Right," Zack said. "I turned it down."

The usually stoic psychologist failed to hide her surprise. "Why?"

Zack swatted at the air. "Because I'm not guilty."

Maria tilted her head.

"Sarah O'Brien deserved justice."

Maria looked at him, saying nothing.

Zack flushed. "For what she did to Annie. And to me."

Maria tented her fingers beneath her chin. "Go on."

Zack fidgeted in his chair. "It should be obvious."

"I'm sorry," Maria said. "I'm not seeing obvious. Maybe tell me what you mean by justice."

He pursed his lips and scrunched his forehead. "A person has to pay for their..."

"Sins?"

"I was going to say 'crimes,' but, yeah."

"So, retribution."

"I suppose."

Maria raised an eyebrow. "Revenge?"

Zack scowled. "Well, not exactly..." His voice trailed off.

Silence fell between them. Zack wanted to bolt from the room.

At last, Maria spoke. "Last week, you told me about one cartel brother, a man who prefers to kill by his own hand instead of a weapon."

"Yeah. He was choking Annie. I took him out."

"You wounded him, and he ran off,"

"Right."

"He had an unusual name in Spanish, as I recall."

A niggling discomfort encircled Zack. "Yeah, *El Vengador* something."

"*El Vengador de la Sangre?*"

"Yeah, that's it."

"Can you tell me what that means, Dr. Winston?"

A sudden flash seared Zack's consciousness.

"The Avenger of Blood."

"I wonder," Maria said, "if you would consider *El Vengador* an agent of justice."

Zack's heart and soul imploded. He could not find a voice to speak.

***

Forty-five minutes later, Zack entered his apartment, still shaken from his visit with Maria. He had agreed to come back the next day for a follow-on session, then increase their visit frequency to three times per week until...

Until I finally put my demons to rest.

Zack changed into running clothes and hit the trail. He almost sprinted to the spot where he often met Noelle.

She wasn't there. Zack was on his own for this one.

Panting from running and the turmoil in his own soul, Zack stopped.

Straight in...

He pulled out his phone and dialed Norman Jones. The attorney answered on the second ring.

"Norman, I'll take the deal. I choose to plead guilty to involuntary manslaughter."

THE END

FREE BOOKS and OTHER PRIZES

Sign up to receive Mike's regular newsletter that offers insights into military and emergency medicine, news about Mike's books, and a monthly contest for gift cards, novellas, free audiobook downloads, and signed paperback books. No spam ever.

Join Mike's newsletter mailing list here:
https://mikejkrentz.com/newsletter

Also by Mike Krentz

Dr. Zack Winston Medical Conspiracy Thrillers

DEAD ALREADY

A DRUG-LACED CONSPIRACY. A former Navy surgeon with a harrowing history. Will a covert frame job end his career... and his life?

WARM AND DEAD

He flourishes in the heart of a hectic ER, but the threatened loss of family becomes his greatest fear. Can an intrepid doctor protect his own from a twisted mind?

Mahoney & Squire Women's Military Adventure Fiction

HER SHOW OF FORCE

She can stand her ground with the best of them. But she'll need all her strength to keep her family and her sailors afloat...

HER PACIFIC SHOWDOWN

Enemies attacking from all sides. Can she counter the offensive long enough to claim victory?

POINTS OF ATTACK

She's flanked by enemies, inside and out. Can this dedicated officer execute a strategy to save a colleague's life before they're both MIA?

Standalone

ANGELS FALLING

The lives of an ex-seminarian turned criminal profiler, an ex-priest turned cult leader, and the former nun they both loved collide in the aftermath of a heinous, ritualistic murder. Must two die for one to live?

About the Author

MIKE KRENTZ WRITES MEDICAL suspense, psychological thrillers, and military fiction based on his experiences as an emergency physician and US Navy medical officer and flight surgeon.

Born and raised in Arizona, Mike earned a classical degree in English from the University of San Francisco, a Doctor of Medicine degree from the Medical College of Wisconsin, and a Master of Public Health Degree from The Johns Hopkins University.

Following a stellar civilian career in emergency medicine, Mike rededicated his professional life to serve the men and women of America's Navy and Marine Corps and their families. He served in both land-based clinical settings and in afloat warships. His last active-duty assignment was as Seventh Fleet Surgeon on board the flagship, USS *Blue Ridge*.

After retiring from the Navy, Mike continued his service as a consultant to the Navy and Marine Corps Public Health Center, Health Analysis Department. Upon completion of that mission, he returned to his earliest life passion as a full-time writer. DEATH AGENT is his seventh published novel. He has others in various stages of production.

Mike serves as Vice-Chairman of the Board of Directors of The Muse Writers Center, where he also teaches fiction writing and leads an advanced fiction studio.

Mike, his wife Kathryn, and miniature schnauzer Yoshi live in Norfolk, VA.

Acknowledgements

M Y WIFE, KATHRYN; SON, Matthew; older children, Jewls, Lisa, Debi, and Michael; stepchildren, Kate and James. You've endured more than a fair share of your imperfect dad's life wanderings, yet remained loving through it all. You are each special in your own way, and will always have my constant and unconditional love and gratitude.

Jayne Ann Krentz (JAK), cherished cousin-in-law, for your encouragement, support, gentle nudges, and solid counsel. Your confidence helped me to believe in myself as a writer. A special salute to Frank Krentz, who is more like a brother than a cousin to me.

My colleagues at The Muse Writers Center whose cogent commentaries and enthusiastic support elevated the quality of my writing: Kelly Sokol, the late John Cameron, Susan Paxton, Kelley McGee, John Aguiar, David Cascio, Lea Ann Douglas, Jim Hodges, and Tamako Takamatsu. You all are fabulous writers whose works deserve publication. A huge thanks to Michael Khandelwal, founder and guiding light of The Muse for establishing a world-class writers' community in our hometown, and a salute to Shawn Gervin who keeps the ship sailing north. A shout out to Muse Board colleague and defense attorney nonpareil, Steve Burgess, for helping navigate the legal conundrums facing a first-time criminal defendant.

To fellow canine enthusiasts and daily dog walking "buddies" for your encouragement and support of my writing. Thanks to Jan Smith and Dave John for your review and comments on an early draft of this novel, and special thanks to dog mom and circuit court judge, Mary Jane Hall, for teaching me legal issues and helping me craft that pivotal courtroom scene. Last but not least, to canines Arlo, Chester, Grace, Lazlo, Daisy, Maxine, Ziva, Stella, Chewie, Duke, Nalli, Carli, Millie, Bruno, Ellie, the late Damoo, and most especially to our own miniature schnauzer, Yoshi, for daily examples on how to love life no matter what.

Special appreciation to Dr. Emily Bebber, clinical psychologist, neighbor, and mom of teenagers for guiding me to the right diagnosis, symptomatology, and treatment of teenage trauma and PTSD.

A tribute to the late Cissy Hartley, founder and long-time director of Writerspace/Killer Books. Cissy's foresight and spirit created and sustained a remarkable resource for authors and readers alike. Gratitude and best wishes to the inimitable Susan Simpson on your next adventure, and to Degan Outridge, Bobbi Dumas, and the staff at Writerspace for outstanding support of your authors, every single day.

Most of all, thanks to my readers. I appreciate your investment in my novels, in both time and money. I hope you enjoyed reading this story as much as I did writing it.

If you are so inclined, I would very much appreciate a review on Amazon, Barnes and Noble, Goodreads, BookBub, and/or other retail platforms.

DEATH AGENT (A Dr. Zack Winston Medical Thriller, Book 3)

By Mike Krentz

Published by Purple Papaya

Copyright © 2024 Mike Krentz All rights reserved.

ISBN: 9781621812258 (paperback); 9781621812241 (e-Book)

This is a work of fiction. Names, places, characters, and events are fictitious. Any similarities to actual events and persons, living or dead, are purely coincidental. Any trademarks, service marks, product names, or named features are assumed to be the property of their respective owners and are used only for reference. If any of these terms are used, no endorsement is implied. Except for review purposes, the reproduction of this book, in whole or part, electronically or mechanically, constitutes a copyright violation. Address permissions and review inquiries to mjk@mkrentz.com.

Cover Design: GetCovers.com

Editor: Michael Krentz, with help from ProWritingAid and AutoCrit.

Connect with Mike Krentz online: mikejkrentz.com

First Edition

Printed in the United States of America.

Made in the USA
Coppell, TX
12 August 2024

35920699R00163